Snapped 2:
The Redemption

Tina Brooks McKinney

URBAN
Renaissance

www.urbanbooks.net

Urban Books, LLC
78 East Industry Court
Deer Park, NY 11729

ISBN 13: 978-1-60162-369-0
ISBN 10: 1-60162-369-0

First Trade Paperback Printing November 2012
Printed in the United States of America

10 9 8 7 6 5 4 3 2 1

*This is a work of fiction. Any references or similarities
to actual events, real people, living or dead, or to real
locales are intended to give the novel a sense of reality. Any similarity in other names, characters, places,
and incidents is entirely coincidental.*

Distributed by Kensington Publishing Corp.
Submit Wholesale Orders to:
Kensington Publishing Corp.
C/O Penguin Group (USA) Inc.
Attention: Order Processing
405 Murray Hill Parkway
East Rutherford, NJ 07073-2316
Phone: 1-800-526-0275
Fax: 1-800-227-9604

Snapped 2: The Redemption

Tina Brooks McKinney

DEDICATION

To my friends, readers, and family, I love you all. I received some flack about the characters in the first book because some people believed Merlin was weak and Gina was stupid. Just because this is not your reality doesn't mean it isn't someone else's. The people in this story are fictitious; the situations and circumstances are not.

Judge not, that ye be not judged. (Matthew 7:1).

ACKNOWLEDGMENTS

Normally, I have this long list of people that I like to acknowledge, but this time I'm going to keep it simple so as not to forget anyone. I must thank my family; my husband, William; my children, Shannan and Estrell; and my parents, Ivor and Judy Brooks; and my sister Theresa.

To my book club supporters, much, much love. Special shout-outs to Savvy Book Club, BAB Book Club, Between Friends Book Club, and RAWSISTAZ Literary Group. Individual shout-outs to Muriel Broomfield, Stacey, Tra Curry, Sharon Jordon, Kim Flood, Patrice Harlson, Angie Simpson, Valerie Chapman, Andrea Tanner and Verlia Williams, Marvin Meadows, Ricardo Mosby, and Detris and Candace Hamm. You folks continue to touch my heart, and I love you dearly.

Chapter One

GAVIN MILLS

I should have known things weren't going to work out the way I wanted them to. They never did. So I didn't know why I thought this time would be any different. But I guess it was all water under the bridge now. The damage had been done, and now I had to figure out a way to clean up the mess I'd created for myself. I thought I could pull a rabbit out of a hat and claim the girl of my dreams. Wrong. Now I was cuffed at the wrists and shackled at the legs and on my way to a cell that was not fit for a pet, let alone human being.

I was not necessarily worried about going to jail. Been there and done that. I just didn't want to stay; this time the stakes were higher. I was not a juvenile whose sentence would disappear with time and good behavior. I was an adult now, so if I didn't find a way out, my tiny cell would become my second furnished unit.

"Watch your head," the officer barked as he pushed me into the back of his patrol car.

I did my best to shield my face from the cameras and to ignore the rude questions being shouted to me, but it was hard. Normally, I enjoyed being the center of attention, but this time I preferred to pass.

"What are all these cameras doing here?" I was dumbfounded.

The officer ignored me as he shut the door and elbowed his way back inside the motel room. I could only imagine what was going on behind the closed door. It made me sick to my stomach thinking about it. Regardless of how things looked, it wasn't my plan to hurt Cojo. The only reason I had brought her to a motel room was so I could try to talk some sense into her. I thought I could change her mind about being with me if I got her out of her own environment.

I would have taken her to my apartment if I had invested more time in sprucing it up, but it was just a room and hardly a home. I couldn't very well expect her to leave her comfortable apartment to live in my cramped one-bedroom. That would be stupid. I wanted to show Cojo she could have a life with me if she gave me a chance. But she wasn't trying to hear anything I had to say. She kept crying and fighting with me.

The front of the motel was ablaze with lights. It seemed like every faction of the media was present and accounted for, and they were bugging to have a word or two with me. I rolled my eyes as I viewed the vultures who stalked the patrol car, waiting for me to do something. Their eyes, wild with excitement, gawked at me as they shouted questions.

"Mr. Mills, why were you holding your sister-in-law hostage?" asked one person who had been banging on the glass repeatedly.

"Is it true she is the mother of your child?" another belted out.

"Is she hurt? Is that the reason why she hasn't come out yet?" called another.

When I failed to answer these questions, the crowd turned belligerent and the lies spread quickly. For the next several minutes, the focus shifted from me to a journalist as she did a teaser for her station. Cameras blazed, and for a brief moment, the people quieted down to hear what the journalist was saying. They listened until they realized they were about to lose their chance to "break" the story themselves. Almost simultaneously other reporters cued their cameras and cited their versions of what went down. If they weren't lying about my life, it might have been comical.

"I didn't hurt her," I yelled, frustrated because I couldn't wind down the window and set the record straight. I wanted them to hear from my mouth that I had wanted only to talk with Cojo. I wanted them to understand I really loved her, but they were no longer interested in me. It also became clear they weren't interested in the truth; fiction made for a better story. They were concerned only with being the first to report something, even if it was a lie.

"Good evening. I'm Natalie Spence, reporting live outside the Baymore Motel, the scene of an intense hostage situation turned violent. The police have apprehended Gavin Mills, a family member of the victim. Mr. Mills, seen behind me, is waiting for transport. A spokesperson for the Clayton County Police Department informed us they will charge Mr. Mills with attempted murder. . . ."

My heart felt like it was trying to leap out of my chest. "Murder? Are you fucking kidding me? I didn't try to kill anybody," I shouted as I butt my head against the window, trying to get their attention. If they were going to tell my story, they should at least wait until they had their facts straight.

I kept beating my head on the window. Murder? How the hell did they come up with that? I wasn't trying to kill anyone. "What the fuck are you talking about? I didn't try to kill anyone," I shouted in vain.

But that wasn't entirely true. If they'd have arrived ten minutes later, Cojo might have died.

"The victim's husband is on the scene, but so far we have not been allowed to speak with him. He appeared to be upset when he was allowed into the room. . . ."

"Right. Get Merlin out here. He'll tell you this is all just a big misunderstanding," I yelled, but no one was paying me any attention. I couldn't understand why I could hear them so plainly but my voice was being ignored. My brother had plenty of reasons to dislike me, but I was so sure he wouldn't want me to go to jail. Or would he? In the past, he had always shielded me. But this time it was his wife. Chances were he might not feel the same way he did for the random chick that got killed.

I couldn't believe the cops had found us so fast. We hadn't been in the room long before they came bursting through the door. How did they find us? Somehow I needed to get my brother alone so I could explain to him what happened. Cojo was his wife, but there was also a good chance she was the mother of my child. I banged on the window again, trying to get someone's attention. I needed to speak to my brother.

I had thought that by bringing Cojo to the motel, she would not see me as her husband's brother but as her man. So I'd made a mistake, but I was sure we could work it all out if they would just give me a chance to talk to them.

"Gavin Mills, a bartender at Tiffany's, a well-known strip club in Decatur, Georgia," the reporter droned on.

They were telling all my business. If I'd wanted the world to know I worked at the club, I would have done my own infomercial. Things were happening so fast, and I needed everyone to shut the fuck up so I could think.

"If they are taking me to jail, they need to hurry the fuck up," I shouted, but there was no one around to hear me. The officer who had brought me to his car had gone back inside the motel room. I didn't want to be around when they brought Cojo out of the room. I didn't want to see the fear in her eyes. This was not the way I wanted to remember her.

I watched in disbelief as they wheeled a stretcher into the motel room. This was certainly overkill, and I thought they were doing it because of the media attention. "Oh, come on," I shouted. This bullshit was not necessary. Cojo was perfectly capable of walking out of that room by herself. "I'll bet that bitch Gina put her up to it." Thinking about Gina made my head hurt, as I recalled the nasty words she'd hurled at me as they were leading me out of the room. I didn't understand why she was there in the first place. Last I heard, she hated Cojo, and Merlin didn't want anything to do with her. When did Gina become friends with Merlin and Cojo? Gina claimed she hated them both, so why was she up in the motel, all hysterical, like she'd lost her best friend?

I slumped back in the seat. Nothing was making sense. How had they found us in the first place? As the events of the night replayed in my mind, I recalled Gina's final words. Maybe I was insane. If they hadn't come into the motel room when they did, maybe I would have killed Cojo. As soon as the thought settled into my head, I shook it away. I was upset with Cojo, but I didn't want to kill her. Did I?

Chapter Two

GINA MEADOWS

I sat in the car a few minutes before I gathered the nerve to knock on Merlin's door. Even though we'd mended our fences, I still wasn't entirely comfortable around him and his wife. Cojo really was a sweet woman, and I felt bad for misjudging her. Thankfully, she wasn't a bitter woman, or she wouldn't be giving me a second chance to be a part of their family.

I got out of the car and paused while I got myself together. I was still suffering from an upset stomach, but at first I attributed it to all the craziness going on around me. I wasn't eating, and when I did manage to get something down, it came right back up. I smoothed down my top and walked up the short path to Merlin and Cojo's apartment.

Cojo answered the door when I knocked. "Hey, Gina. Come on in." She was smiling brightly, and it eased some of my fears. I could not believe how good she looked. She was positively glowing.

"Cojo, you look amazing. Your skin is radiant, and this belly fits your small frame."

Obviously pleased with my compliment, Cojo patted her stomach and led the way to the sofa. "Thanks, Gina. You made my day, because I spend most of my days feeling fat and unattractive."

"Hell, I wish I looked as good." I looked at my own belly, which could easily be confused with a pregnant pouch.

The look Cojo gave me would have been hysterical if I had said something funny, but it was exactly how I felt at the moment: fat and unattractive and totally confused. I thought I was having phantom symptoms because of Cojo's pregnancy, but I came to the realization it was something more than that. Either I was deathly ill or I was pregnant.

"Is there something wrong?" Cojo's brow was wrinkled with worry.

I panicked. I didn't know for sure what was going on with me, so I wasn't ready to share it, whatever it was. Right now my focus was on repairing my relationship with my son and his wife. "No, girl. I'm fine. Just a little tired. Gavin has been calling the house day and night, trying to get me to come and visit. I told him the night they arrested him, I was finished with him, but I guess he didn't believe me."

Cojo's face visually paled at the mention of Gavin's name. I could only imagine what she was feeling, and I didn't even know the entire story. One day I was hoping she'd feel comfortable enough to confide in me about the true nature of her relationship with my other son. She shook her head and grimaced, as if she tasted something really bad in her mouth.

"Thank God he hasn't called here. I don't want to hear from him ever again."

"I know, but you're going to have to go to court and testify whenever they set a date for his hearing."

She absently rubbed her belly, and I felt a twinge of envy.

"I know, but I'm still not looking forward to it."

We fell into silence, but it wasn't strained.

"Where's Merlin? I didn't see his car," I finally said.

"He had to report to the base. He should be home soon. He's sticking closer to home these days."

Silence again.

I looked around the room, trying to think of something else to say. "So when are we going to have your baby shower?" I didn't know who was more shocked by my suggestion, her or me. I wanted to attend her shower, but planning it? I didn't think so.

Cojo laughed. "Merlin and I haven't even thought that far. We just want to have a healthy baby."

I heard what she was saying, but I wasn't buying it. Why wouldn't she want a shower? I thought about it some more and decided I should be the one to give it to her. Especially since I had treated her so badly in the beginning. "Nonsense. You have to have a shower. This is your first baby. Just leave everything to me, and if you have someone you want me to invite, let me know so I can send them an invitation."

Cojo looked as if she wanted to cry. I didn't mean to make her upset. I had thought my offer would make her happy.

I moved over to the sofa and put my arm around her. "Honey, what's wrong?" I wasn't used to this emotional Cojo. Now that I was getting to know her, it was hard for me to see her crying.

"I'm all right. Lately, I seem to cry at the drop of a hat."

I understood what she meant. When I was pregnant, I cried all the time, even though my pregnancy was short lived. "You scared me. I thought I did something wrong."

"No, actually, I'm overwhelmed by your thoughtfulness. I always wanted this type of relationship with you." She wiped her nose with the back of her hand.

I went into the kitchen and grabbed a paper towel for her. It wasn't as soft as a tissue, but I didn't feel comfortable enough in their space to look for anything else. Her candor touched me in ways I hadn't felt in years, and it was a feeling I couldn't describe, even if I had to. "Cut that out. There is nothing cute about a snotty nose," I said as I walked back into the living room. I felt giddy and needed to do something to expel the nervous energy I was feeling. "Hey, since I'm here, is there anything I can do for you?"

"Gina, I'm fine. Merlin hasn't allowed me to lift a finger since you guys rescued me."

I didn't see the black cloud enter the room, but I damn sure felt it. "Wow, what a buzz kill." I was trying to be funny, but I'd never been so serious in my life.

"You ain't kidding a bit. I just wish I understood what was going through Gavin's head. Part of me wants to forgive him for what he did to me, but the other side of me would like to castrate him for scaring the shit out of me."

Absently, I patted Cojo's hand as my mind drifted off. I understood exactly what she was saying, but on a deeper level. I was beginning to believe my dream wasn't just a nightmare and Gavin had actually fucked me. And to add insult to injury, I could be carrying his child. How twisted was that? I felt like my life had become some low-budget movie, and I was terrified of the ending. I wanted to confide my fears to Cojo, but I was afraid if I said it out loud, it would come true.

"Gina?"

"Huh?" I'd been daydreaming and wasn't paying attention to the conversation.

"I asked if you were okay. You got this weird look on your face. Kind of scared me."

I patted her hand again and shook off my thoughts. I hadn't decided what I was going to do, and until I did, I would keep my fears to myself. "Sorry, dear. I guess I was off in la-la land. Hey, I could use something to drink. I'm feeling a little parched."

She got up, but I stopped her before she could leave the room.

"I don't want you waiting on me. I can fix it myself. Do you want something? Water? Milk?" I assumed she had plenty of milk, or at least I would if I knew for sure I was having a baby. I looked down at my own stomach, which was protruding before any thoughts of being pregnant had entered my mind, and smiled. If this turned out to be a false alarm, I was going to have to get my ass in a gym with a quickness.

"No, I'm good. I'm so sick and tired of going to the bathroom. I try to limit the amount of fluids I drink so I'm not running myself crazy."

She had given me something else to think about. Perhaps I wasn't pregnant, after all. It could also be stress, since I hadn't noticed any changes in my bathroom habits. Surely if I were pregnant, I would have noticed something by now. I went in the kitchen, grabbed a glass from the cabinet, and got some water from the tap, but the instant I turned on the faucet, I felt the urge to pee.

"Damn. Cojo, where's the bathroom?"

"Down the hall, first door on the right."

I noticed a pregnancy test on the shelf of their bathroom caddy. I picked it up to read the directions. It had been a long time since I'd used a test, so I was unfamiliar with the manufacturer. I shook the box. It was a twin pack, and one of them was missing. Without giving it too much more thought, I used her test.

Comparing my symptoms to Cojo's was one thing, but with this test, I'd find out for sure and put my mind to rest. I closed the top of the now empty box and placed it back on the caddy. With any luck, they wouldn't think to look in the box before I'd had a chance to replace the contents.

"Gina, is everything okay?" It sounded like Cojo was standing right in front of the bathroom door.

I jumped, splashing urine all over my hands and the seat.

"Uh, um, I'm good. My stomach's a little upset, though." I wasn't lying. My nerves were getting the best of me, because I honestly didn't know what I would do if I was actually pregnant.

"Oh, okay. I'm going to hit the other bathroom. You got me going too."

I allowed a small chuckle, which sounded fake even to my ears. "I'll be right out." I cleaned up the mess I'd made, and slipped the used test inside my shirt. It felt like it was burning against my skin, but I knew it was just my imagination. I rushed back to the living room, hoping to slip the test in my purse before Cojo finished in the bathroom. Suddenly, I wasn't feeling social. I wanted to go home and view my results in private. The walls began to close in around me.

Chapter Three

ANGIE SIMPSON

The bandages were going to be removed from my legs and arms today. I had been in a fire and had burns over 70 percent of my body. I wasn't under any illusions of what I would look like once they took them off. The doctor had advised me there would be scaring, and he'd suggested I watch several movies dealing with burn victims. He'd also had me talk with a counselor several times in an attempt to get my mind right. Even though I wasn't expecting much, I was still impatient to have the bandages removed. My wounds itched, and I couldn't wait to scratch them.

I also missed taking a bath. The first thing I was going to do when I got back home was take a long hot bath. A delicious bubble bath with my favorite read, soaking till my skin looked old and withered. That was my plan.

The doctors didn't want to do any of the cosmetic surgery I wanted because of my pregnancy. If it was up to my mother, I would wear my scars like a banner as punishment for my sins. What I wanted didn't matter. They would talk about my options in front of me like I wasn't in the room. Since I didn't have a pot to piss in or a window to throw it out of, I had no say. My father thought I needed to see the scars on a daily basis as a reminder of the dangers of the world. As if I could fucking forget I'd slept with a man I didn't know who'd tried to deep-fry my ass with gasoline!

But they didn't know all that. They thought Gavin had forced his way into the house, raped me, and set the house ablaze to cover his tracks. Although parts of my story were embellished, it was my story, and I was sticking to it. Regardless of how it happened, I was pregnant and my parents didn't believe in abortion. I spoke to the counselor about it, but she couldn't advise me. It was my body, but I was completely dependent on my parents until I could afford to pay the cost to be the boss.

I didn't want a child. Period. And I damn sure didn't want one by a nut like Gavin Mills. But once again, I didn't have a choice. My parents were going to make me have this baby, even if it killed me! My mother said this to me at least once a day, and I was sick of hearing it.

"Angela, come on. We're going to be late," my mother called up the stairs. She used her nice voice, but I wasn't fooled.

I tossed a couple of pain pills in my mouth and swallowed. As I put the cap back on the bottle, I contemplated taking the rest of them, but thoughts of wearing this body in hell deterred me from taking such drastic measures. Once the baby was born, I would have my plastic surgery, and with any luck, the scarring would be minimal.

"I'm coming." I paused at the top of the stairs, anticipating the pain. Going down was torture, but coming back up was pure hell. Bending my legs hurt the most, but I moved as fast as I could, because I didn't want to piss my mother off. These days, if she wasn't yelling, she wasn't talking. She said I was a big disappointment. I felt like she was more concerned about what the ladies down at the church were saying than how I felt. I heard the front door slam. If she thought it would hurry me up, she'd wasted her energy. I could move only as fast as my bandages allowed. My mother would see it if she bothered to look at me. But she wouldn't. She never did.

Even though she didn't come right out and say it, I knew my mother didn't believed my account of what happened to me. She said I must have done something to make that boy bust up in their house and shame the entire family. She never acted all crazy around my father, but the second we were alone, it was on. I couldn't wait until I was able to move out of their house and get on with my life.

"You're getting a sonogram today," my mother announced as I closed the car door and buckled my seat belt.

"For what?" I didn't know how I was going to make her understand I couldn't care less about this baby who lived inside of me.

My mother shot me a look that closely resembled hatred. It was so powerful, I felt like it was pressing me back against the seat.

"The child you carry is innocent. You are not going to punish this child because you . . ." She threw the car in reverse without finishing her sentence. Even though she didn't finish what she was saying, I knew exactly where she was going. I had heard it all before and had it memorized. For several blocks I seethed, until I couldn't take it anymore.

"Because I what? Couldn't keep my legs closed? Is that what you were going to say to me, Mother? Seriously?"

This was as close as she'd come to calling me a liar in my face. The good Lord only knew what she said when I wasn't around. I was so mad. Some of what she was thinking was actually true, but I was still mad at her for automatically blaming me. I was so mad, I was shaking. The problems between my mother and me started long before Gavin Mills came into my life. And she seemed hell-bent on using this incident to punish me for whatever resentment she'd felt toward me over the years. We'd never discussed her apparent hatred of me, but it had never been so blatant, either.

"Who the hell do you think you're talking to?" My mother's foot found the brake, bringing the car to a shuddering stop on the access ramp to the freeway.

Dumbstruck, I looked around. Was she out of her fucking mind? Stopping on the ramp was like painting a damn sign on the car saying HIT ME. I started babbling. "My bad, Mom. It's the hormones, you know? Kinda makes me crazy. Uh, could we just get going? This can't be good, you know?" Big balls of sweat trickled down my skin, irritating my sores. As much as I wanted to confront my mother about why we never got along, now was not the time.

She looked at me again, and I wished I had not bothered to meet her eyes, because for a split second she looked as though she wanted us both to die. I tore my eyes from her noticeable glare of hatred. Gavin Mills might have fucked up my present situation, but he didn't have anything to do with my past.

My relationship with my mother had been going downhill for years. She didn't have a motherly bone in her body, and part of me believed she was jealous of me. She resented the bond I had with my father, and had done everything she could to destroy it.

I exhaled when my mother resumed driving, but I knew we weren't finished yet. We were going to have it out. Hopefully, it wouldn't be in a car, where she could kill us both and I wouldn't be able to do a damn thing about it.

If it wasn't for my father, I might have run away from home years ago. I stayed because I was worried my mother would neglect my father if I wasn't around to supervise his care. My dad lost his right leg from complications of diabetes when I was eleven. I didn't even know he had the disease until he went into the hospital. When he came home, he was never the same. He'd get so depressed, he'd cry. He was used to being the breadwinner of the family. Now we had to make due on his Social Security and mom's meager check. I hated it when he cried.

"Are you going to sit here all day, or are you going to carry your ass inside and take this damn test?"

"Huh?" We'd arrived at the hospital, and I hadn't even realizes it.

"Hurry up, dammit. I can't leave your father at the house by himself for long. Lord knows what that man will do if I'm not around to keep an eye on him."

My mother was such a hypocrite. She was one of those part-time Christians. Half the time on her knees, praying for salvation, and the other half raising hell and talking shit. Telling my mother what I was feeling was pointless, because she didn't care. She'd told me so a gazillion times. As long as I was living in her house, I had to do what she told me to do. The only silver lining in this whole thing was the insurance money. When I turned eighteen and was released from the doctor, I was going to get paid. I was going to take the money and move as far away from her as I could possibly go. If my mother didn't get her act together, I'd take my dad with me too!

Chapter Four

COJO MILLS

"Okay, this is weird." I shook my head at my reflection in the mirror. I was enjoying the peaceful relationship with Gina, but I was still cautious of our newfound friendship. I had seen the flip side of Gina and didn't like her one bit. I was looking forward to getting to know this Gina better. "Gina, are you sure you're feeling okay?"

She came back into the living room, looking like she'd seen a ghost or something.

"I'm, uh, I don't know. I'm feeling a bit dizzy."

Horrified, I watched her pitch forward onto the sofa and roll on the floor.

"Oh my God, Gina!" Her eyes rolled up in her head before they closed. I didn't know what else to do, so I grabbed my phone and started to dial as I kneeled down next to her.

"Nine-one-one."

"Help, my mother-in-law is unconscious. My address is one twenty-three Sycamore Street."

"Is she breathing?"

"Uh, I don't know. Please help me."

"I'm dispatching a unit now, but I need to know if she is breathing."

I put my face near her mouth. I was breathing so heavily, I couldn't tell if I was hearing her heart beat or my own. I placed my hand on her heart, trying to feel her heartbeat, but something was in my way.

"What's this?" I paused for a second, unsure whether or not it would be appropriate to look down her blouse. My curiosity got the best of me. Reaching my hand inside her blouse, I pulled out the object stuck in her bra. "Well, I'll be damned." I immediately recognized the wand and its telltale signs. Stunned, I dropped my phone without answering the dispatcher.

"What—" Gina's eyes blinked and came into focus as her words were cut off. Her eyes traveled from my face to the wand in my hand.

I dropped the offending stick like it was made of fire instead of plastic. "Thank God you're okay. You scared the shit out of me." I was sure my face had turned a deep shade of red as I realized the implications.

She closed her eyes again and let out a deep breath. To me, it sounded like her last, and it scared me again.

"Gina, please," I shouted as I lifted her head from the floor and started patting her face. Thoughts were leaping around in my head, but none of them made any sense. Was Gina pregnant?

"Stop hitting me. I'm okay."

The bitch was back. I withdrew my hand and pushed back to give her room to sit up. "Oh, Jesus, I called nine-one-one and left them hanging on the phone."

"Shit."

I picked up my phone to let them know everything was okay. "Hello?"

"Nine-one-one."

"Yes, I'm so sorry. I need to cancel the call to my address. It's one twenty-three Sycamore Street."

"I already called it in, but I will try to stop them. Hold on please." A swift knock sounded at the door, and I realized it was too late.

"If this had been a real emergency, I'll bet you any amount of money you wouldn't have been able to get them on the phone," Gina said glumly.

"Stay there. Since they're here, they may as well check you out." I picked up the wand and handed it back to her.

Her eyes searched mine before she accepted it. I wanted to tell her that her secret was safe with me, but there was no time. The knock came again with a tad more force.

"So I guess I have some explaining to do," Gina said with a slight chuckle after the paramedics left.

"No, not really. You're a grown woman, so you don't have to explain anything to me." I was lying through my teeth, but I tried to act as if the suspense wasn't killing me. I really wanted to know what the deal was, but I'd be damned if I was going to ask.

"True, but I did steal your test, so I kinda owe you."

"Huh?" For a moment I thought that Gina might have bumped her head in the fall, because I didn't have a clue what she was talking about.

"You had a pregnancy test in the bathroom. I used it."

I laughed. I hadn't even thought about where the test had come from; it hadn't even crossed my mind. I was concerned only about the results. It would be weird being pregnant at the same time as my mother-in-law. "Oh, you can keep it."

She didn't laugh at my attempted humor. It was an awkward moment for both of us. She said, "I've never had any children. I was pregnant before. . . ."

I waited for her to continue. My husband had already told me Gina wasn't his biological mother, but he'd never gone into any details. This part of his life was taboo and was pretty much off-limits unless he brought it up. This might be the only opportunity I would get to learn more about the dynamics of their family.

"Gina, we don't have to talk about this if you don't want to." I didn't want to appear too eager. If she was going to shed some light on my husband's life before me, I wanted to hear it.

"Stop lying. You're as nosy as I am, so cut the shit." She started laughing in spite of the somber mood in the room.

"Okay, you got me. But if it's going to ruin what we're building here, I don't want to risk it." I sincerely meant it too.

"That's sweet."

She appeared to be off in a world of her own, and I didn't know what, if anything, I should say. I knew how it made me feel when folks tried to rush me when I was telling a story, and I didn't want to be accused of doing the same thing.

"Merlin's father never wanted me to have children. He was a selfish bastard."

"Really? I never met the man, so I don't know what to say."

"That's okay. I wasn't looking for you to agree or disagree. Regardless of what you could say, I knew the man for what he was, and the man was, and is, a selfish fuck. He never wanted me to have children, because he didn't want me to care about anyone more than I cared for him."

"Wow, that's pretty fucked up." I didn't mean to be so blunt, but the truth was the truth. I also thought bearing children was a blessing and a gift. A symbol of their love. If Merlin's father didn't get it, I was glad not to have met the man.

"There was a time I would have been ready to fight you over those words, but now that I know the truth, it doesn't hurt as much. But God knew what he was doing. See, I wanted a child because I thought it would bring Ronald and me closer. I told myself if I gave him a son or daughter, he wouldn't run the streets like he used to do. Thought it would keep his selfish ass at the house. But God knew I wasn't doing it for the right reason, either, so He took the only thing I cared about more than Ronald." Tears began to fall from her eyes.

I felt like Gina needed to get this off her chest, so I didn't want to stop her, but I was uncertain about what I should be doing as she unburdened her soul. Should I just ignore her tears, or should I try to console her? She must have read the indecision on my face, because she used her sleeve to dry her tears and lay back on the sofa like she was a patient in the doctor's office, purging her sins.

"I feel like we should be drinking." I didn't know about her, but I could've used a shot.

"I know, right?" She chuckled.

A comfortable silence fell over the room. Not wanting to break the silence, I sat back in my chair and waited. I had so many questions to ask Gina, but I was afraid to push too hard. However, if Gina didn't start talking soon, I was going to need another potty break.

"How much has Merlin told you about his father?"

I was scared. I didn't know Gina well enough to discuss what Merlin and I talked about behind closed doors. I felt like I should ask his permission before I did, but the desire for answers outweighed my better judgment.

"He doesn't really talk about him. I don't think he likes him very much, and I know he doesn't respect him. He's said that on numerous occasions."

"Hmm. That doesn't surprise me. Merlin was always the sensitive one."

When she didn't elaborate, I started to get upset. She hadn't told me anything I didn't know. Merlin's sensitivity was one of the main reasons I fell in love with him. When we were dating, we'd devote one day a month to Lifetime. We'd plan the entire day around the television, pigging out on junk food and made-for-television movies. He used to say the fellows would disown him if they knew he was a sucker for a Lifetime movie. I loved this about him. He wasn't faking it to get in my pants; he enjoyed them as much as I did.

"So Gavin takes after his father, I take it?" I really didn't want to discuss Gavin, but he was another part of the puzzle that didn't fit. The fact that Merlin kept his existence hidden from me spoke volumes at a time when I thought we shared everything.

"Humph. I doubt that. But then again, what do I know? Perhaps I'm to blame for the way he acts, because Ronald wasn't around long enough. Funny, I never thought about it until now, but that motherfucker was gone more than he was there, and I'm talking about before he moved to Detroit."

"Detroit? I'm so confused. Gina, Merlin hasn't told me anything about your husband, so I don't really know what to say."

She looked at me strangely, as if she'd forgotten I was even there. "Don't worry about it. I was just saying stuff out loud," she said.

Gina was really starting to scare me. Her mind appeared to be wandering.

"Do you want me to call Merlin and ask him to come home?"

"For what? I'm okay. Just got a lot of things on my mind, you know?"

I didn't know. That was my point. Gina and I were just getting to know each other. Things might have been different if Gina and I had had a relationship before all this mess with Gavin happened, and since we didn't, I was winging it. I wanted to know what she was going to do about the baby. It was kind of creepy knowing we were both about to be mothers. A slow shudder started in the small of my back and worked its way up to my shoulders.

She said, "I guess I should make an appointment to see a doctor."

It wasn't a question; it was more like a statement. Once again, I didn't know what to say. She didn't say what her intentions were, so I didn't even know if I should suggest a doctor for her. I hated feeling uncertain. If I knew whether or not she was going to keep the baby, things would be better, but I was afraid to ask.

"Guess that explains why I've been feeling so yucky too. Damn. I don't remember feeling this way before," Gina mumbled, lost in her own little world.

"This is my first child, so I don't have anything to compare it to."

"Figures." Gina snickered.

What the hell was that supposed to mean? Was she trying to insult me or something? I didn't want to over-react and take things the wrong way, but Gina was making it difficult. I was ready for her to leave. She'd already been here too long as it was.

"It's a good thing you got with Merlin instead of Gavin. Gavin would have swallowed you up whole and spit out the pieces."

She laughed, but I didn't see a damn thing that was funny. If she only knew how close I came to falling for Gavin's charms, she might not be joking about it.

I said, "Thank God. The last thing I would want would be to have my child's father in jail."

Gina jerked back as the blood drained from her face. Her eyes were wide and unfocused, and for a second or two, I felt sure she was about to pass out again.

"Are you okay?"

"What?" She was looking right at me, but she acted as if she didn't even see me.

"You don't look so hot. Can I get you something?" I felt cold, like the temperature in the room had suddenly plummeted.

Gina continued to stare, but for the life of me, I couldn't imagine what she saw. I couldn't sit there and allow her to continue to stare at me. It was creepy. The whole day had taken a turn for the worse. I was ready to start it all over, minus the drama. I went in the kitchen and got two glasses of milk.

"Girl, if I drink this, you're probably gonna want to leave the room," Gina said as I handed her a glass.

I took the glass back. She was not about to stink up my house.

"I haven't drunk milk in years. Thought I was done nursing these bones." She started laughing.

Everything about Gina was making me feel weird. If I were a genie, I would have blinked her away. "Have you told Ronald about the baby?"

She didn't answer, and I wasn't sure if she was ignoring me or if she actually didn't hear my question. Unsure, I waited.

A full minute later she said, "For what?"

All of her body movements let me know she was angry, and I regretted asking her anything. I should have just sat back and let her talk, but I had to open my big mouth.

"Oh." What the hell else was I supposed to say? This bitch was crazy. No wonder her kids hated her.

"Hey, don't judge me. You haven't walked in my shoes. I might not have been the best mother I could have been for those boys, but I did the best that I could do at the time. "

"Uh . . . I . . . I wasn't judging you. You have to understand this is very difficult for me, and I don't know what to say to you."

"Exactly. Folks need to mind their own business, anyway. What I do, who I fuck, ain't nobody's business but mine and my God's."

Oh God, how could this be happening? How did we go from sugar to shit in a matter of minutes? Of all times for the phone not to ring! I would have gladly taken a call from a telemarketer trying to sell me dog shit as a dietary supplement than this slow torture. *Lord, it's me, Cojo, and I could use a little help. Pretty please, get this bitch out my house.* I knew God was in the miracle business, and I sure could use one right about now.

"Wow. What am I saying? Cojo, it's the hormones. Do you get all crazy like this?"

I looked up at the ceiling, amazed at how quickly He worked. I was going to have to remember to pray in the future, especially when dealing with Gina. "Yeah, I'm driving Merlin insane."

I wasn't exactly lying. I was supersensitive these days, but I didn't think it had anything to do with being pregnant. We were still walking sideways around each other after the whole Gavin incident. Now that he and Gina appeared to be getting along, the last thing I'd want to tell him was I had a beef with his mother. I finished my milk and drank hers too.

Gina got up and walked toward the door, and I quickly followed her so she couldn't change her mind. For a split second, I worried about letting her drive but decided she was better out than in. If she was about to self-destruct, I'd prefer she do it away from my home. I tried to hide my relief as I dogged her steps to the door.

"Can you not tell Merlin about this right now? I haven't made up my mind what I'm going to do."

I didn't think her request was unreasonable, but I knew my rationale was twisted. I was thinking only of myself and what would be easier for me. "I wouldn't have said anything, anyway, Gina. It really is none of my business."

She smiled for the first time since she came out of the bathroom. "Thank you, honey. Maybe we can get together sometime next week and do some shopping."

"Sounds like a plan." I knew it would probably never happen even as I said it, but if it was going to get her on the other side of the door, so be it.

"Bye," she said.

I didn't relax until after the door was closed and locked behind me. With my back pressed against the door, I took several deep breaths before I could even move. Emotionally drained, I stumbled back to the living room.

"What was that?" I shook my head. Part of me felt sorry for Gina because either way things went, she was in a difficult situation. Whoever said pregnancy was a cakewalk was a lying-ass fucker. Gina had several strikes against her: her age, her single status, and the fact that she was crazy as all outdoors. Not to mention the reaction she was going to get when she finally told Merlin and Gavin.

Just thinking about Gavin made my heart race. I tried to ignore the anger and lust I felt each and every time he crossed my mind. Anger for almost ruining my marriage and lust for the way he handled his business when he had me. Those thoughts woke me up in the middle of the night, ready to fuck a duck. Merlin, of course, was excited with my new aggressive behavior, but I was sure he'd be crushed if he knew it wasn't because of him. He might as well have been farting in the wind for all the good he was doing. If anything, he frustrated me even more, because he had the equipment, but he just didn't know what to do with it.

Chapter Five

MERLIN MILLS

I was about twenty feet from my car when I noticed Captain Jamison coming from the parking area. She wore an evil scowl on her face, so I debated whether or not it was a good idea to speak with her. Part of me wanted to rush up to her to make sure everything was okay in her world, but the rational side of me thought it could also be a big mistake. Every time I saw her, I had to remind myself she was my ranking officer.

No matter how personal our relationship had become, I always had to err on the side of caution. Especially when approaching her in public. The army frowned on fraternization and wouldn't understand our friendship. Since she was the senior officer, it could cause a lot of trouble if it was perceived that our relationship went beyond the chain of command.

If I continued at my current pace, I would reach my car before she cleared the parking area. Since I was concerned, I slowed down. If she didn't want to talk, I would keep it moving. But if there was anything I could do to help her, I wanted her to know I was there.

"Evening, Captain Jamison." I saluted and stood at attention, but she breezed past me like I wasn't even there. This was definitely out of character for the captain, and it bothered me, probably more than it should have.

"Is everything okay, Captain?"

She whirled around, as if only now hearing my voice for the first time. "What?" she snapped.

Something was definitely wrong, and I hated the protocol that prevented me from any physical contact with her. It wasn't just anger that I saw in her eyes; I also saw pain.

"Sorry, Captain," I mouthed, wanting to get as far away from her as I could before she decided I should feel her wrath. I wasn't trying to create a scene, but I thought our relationship was better than this. As I turned to walk away, she stopped me.

"Specialist Mills, can I have a word?"

Her tone was stern, so I approached cautiously. I stopped in front of her and saluted her again, just in case she didn't see it the first time.

"At ease, Mills." She stepped closer to me, making sure our conversation wouldn't be overheard. "I'm having a very bad day. Didn't mean to be rude."

"No problem. If there's something I can do, please let me know."

A small smile flickered around the edges of her lips, and her face looked softer. She was a very beautiful woman, and a smile did her body good. However, the nature of her job dictated the stern countenance the rest of the army saw. I was lucky enough to have seen the other side of her.

"Thanks. How's everything?" She looked around, being careful to maintain a practical distance from me.

"It's going." I shrugged. I didn't want to talk about what was going on with me. I really wanted to know what or who had taken her out of her game.

"You got time for a drink?"

I was surprised she'd made such a suggestion, since we were both in uniform. Although it wasn't uncom-

mon for a private and a captain to have a drink together, it became suspicious when they were of the
opposite sex.

"Seriously? Do you think that's such a good idea?"
The last thing I needed to do was to get either of us in
trouble, but if she needed me, there was no way I was
going to turn her down. However, I would be less of a
friend if I didn't try to at least warn her of the potential
problems this could present for both of us.

She was slow on the uptake. I snapped my shoulders
back to attention. She was about to cross the line, and
she knew it, but she knew I would've crossed it with
her, if she really wanted me to.

"Wow, you're right. It's been a long day, and I'm not
thinking clearly."

"Hey, Cojo is putting some steaks on the grill. How
about coming by the house for dinner?"

She looked like she was seriously considering my
suggestion, but after several seconds of indecision, she
shook her head no.

"You know what? Thanks for the offer, but I think I
should take this body home and shut it down for the
night. I'll talk to you later."

We were close enough to ensure no one overheard
us.

I said, "Are you sure you're okay?"

"I'm fine. Go home, and enjoy your dinner. That's an
order."

She forced a smile, but her face haunted me as I left
the base. What could be so bad that she would risk her
position by associating with me? As I drove home, I
toyed with the idea of calling her. She'd given me her
number when my brother got me in some trouble, but
if I used it now, when all was good with me, it would be

different. Wouldn't it? She'd told me she was okay, but I still couldn't get her off my mind.

I pulled my phone from its clip as I drove. If I were a civilian, I honestly believed Captain Jamison and I would be more than just friends. She was unlike any female I'd ever met, special, and I owed her big-time. She'd stepped up to the plate when I'd needed her most, and she hadn't even known me. She'd taken a chance on me, and I was grateful to her.

When I first transferred to her unit, she had the authority to ship me back out again after my two-week leave, but she asked me if I wanted to stay. Somehow she knew I needed to be close to home. I turned my car around. I had to be sure.

I stalled for a full five minutes before I got up the nerve to knock on the captain's door.

"Merlin. I mean, Specialist Mills, what are you doing here?" She stood in the doorway, looking good as ever.

I could see the confusion on Captain Jamison's face, but she didn't appear to be upset to see me. Nervously, I fingered my hat. If I'd misunderstood her earlier discomfort, things could go very badly for me.

"Begging your pardon, Captain. I was concerned about you. I wanted to make sure you were okay." I could feel sweat trickling down my back. I didn't want to get sent to Timbuktu or bum fuck, Egypt, because I'd misunderstood what was going on with her.

She stepped back from the door and allowed me into her home. I relaxed somewhat, relieved she didn't start fussing and issuing orders to me. She had changed from her uniform and was wearing a purple velour jogging outfit. She had a drink in her hand. I followed her into the living room.

"That was nice, but you didn't have to come all the way over here." She sipped from her glass again, seeming to forget I was in the room.

"Am I at liberty to speak freely?"

"You're here, aren't you?" She was angry.

"Hey, I didn't mean to intrude. I thought you might need to talk. You've been a good friend to me, and I wanted to return the favor." I hadn't come over here to take any shit. So if that was what she had in mind, I would leave before the shit started popping off.

"Merlin, I'm sorry. I've got a lot of shit on my mind. Can I get you something to drink?"

"I can fix it myself."

I went into the kitchen and poured myself a drink. I debated about calling Cojo to let her know I was going to be late, but I didn't plan on staying long. Things between Cojo and me were still a little shaky, and I didn't feel like explaining to her why I felt the need to stop here before coming home. I decided I would deal with her when I got there.

She said, "I signed my reenlistment papers today." She finished her drink in one swallow as I came back into the room.

I waited for the sucker punch I was sure would follow. I was hoping she wasn't going to tell me they were transferring her from our base. Due to the nature of our jobs, this was always a possibility. She fixed herself another drink. Her silence pretty much confirmed my fears.

"Why do I feel like this is a trick?" I couldn't shake the "damned if you do, damned if you don't" feeling.

"No tricks, no surprises." She raised her glass in a mock toast.

I didn't understand what was going on, but she was obviously upset about something.

"Yeah, job security," I said, laughing because if all else failed, the army would always need bodies, which was one of the reasons I'd enlisted. If everything went right, I could do my twenty-something years and get me a nice cushy desk job somewhere, collecting two pensions.

"Yeah, that's true, but it also means I can say bye-bye to having a kid, or even a husband, for that matter."

I got it. The captain had joined the army at a young age for pretty much the same reasons I had. The economy was bad, and the only place offering consistent employment with benefits was the military. Unfortunately, her husband wasn't willing to wait it out. She told me he found someone else and pretty much fucked her out of her money until she was able to come home and fix her allotments.

"That's not true, Captain, and you know it. There are plenty of men looking for a good woman." I wasn't even going to touch the baby thing, because it would definitely be hard for a woman to raise a child in her position.

"Name one. You and I both know that the youngest officer on base is fifty-five, gray haired or bald, with a serious case of dicky doo. Fuckers poking me with their stomachs before their dicks know it's a pussy down there," she said and emptied her glass.

She pointed to the kitchen, and I went and got the bottle for her. I was holding my hand over my mouth to keep from laughing. I'd never heard the captain go off before. She was hilariously funny, but it scared me too. These kinds of outbursts had a tendency to change quickly from laughter to tears. I'd been through enough of them with Gina, so I knew firsthand. My only hope was she didn't become a mean drunk; that was my biggest fear. Suddenly, I regretted not taking the time to phone home.

"Shit."

"See, what I tell you? I'm fucked." Her words were slurred. She must have been going at it hard to be inebriated so quickly.

"I didn't mean it that way. It's just the knuckleheads I know on base don't deserve you."

She cocked her head and stared at me. Her look was so intense, I started to feel like I'd said something wrong or out of line.

"It's a good thing I like you're wife, or I'd be on you like stank on shit."

She said it so calmly, you would have thought she was commenting on the weather. Inappropriate or not, I was flattered by her words. I'd feel the same way if it weren't for Cojo, but I wasn't about to tell her. Not only was her comment outrageously funny and flattering, but it also wasn't something I needed to know. I liked our relationship just the way it was and didn't want any complications.

"Relax, Specialist. I may be a little drunk, but I ain't crazy. I saw the way you look at your wife. Besides, I ain't trying to get my feelings hurt."

Thank the Lord. I felt like I should say something, but I didn't know what would be appropriate. I didn't have game and was afraid if I said something to compliment her, she might misconstrue it and think she had a chance. "You're right. When it comes to Cojo, I wear my emotions on my sleeve."

"You wear your emotions, period. That's what I like about you, but it could also be your Achilles' heel. You're not afraid to feel, and if something upsets you, it's written all over your face. But in combat, your face would tell your enemy where to strike. You've got to work on that."

She was spoke softly, but I heard every word, as if she delivered them directly into my ear. She was on point with what she said. It was something I had struggled with since childhood. My brother, Gavin, called me Mr. Sensitive. I used to get teased by the guys at school, some of whom assumed I was gay. Gavin fed into those theories, making my teen life a living hell. It was another reason I hated his trifling ass. But even after all he put me through, I never lifted a hand against him until he started fucking with my wife. It took a lot to get me to that point, but I would never be that fool again.

"I don't want to be alone for the rest of my life," she whined as her head rolled down to her chest. Tears rolled down her face, and I felt her pain. I felt like I was reading the same page in an old book. My stepmother, Gina, would go through the same anguish while she pined over my father. She was another good woman gone bad over a no-account nigga. I had promised myself I would never be like him.

"Who splashed water on my face? Did you splash water on my face?"

Captain was drunk, no ifs, ands, or buts about it. "That's not water, Captain. They're tears. You've been crying."

"Humph, I don't cry, Specialist. I'm army." She jabbed a finger in her chest hard enough to leave a mark.

"You're army, Captain Jamison, but you're also human, and it's okay to cry."

The captain had a reputation for being a hard-ass, and very few people had seen her at her weakest point like I had. Perhaps if she showed this side more often, guys would be more inclined to approach her.

"If you tell anyone I was crying, I'm gonna have to kill you." She chuckled, but she continued to weep.

"Your secrets are safe with me, all of them."

We sat in silence as I tried to think of a way to get out of there before things got ugly. I was fairly certain she wasn't finished with this conversation, so I really needed to leave.

"My ex-husband called me. Said he made a mistake and wanted to start over again." She turned up her glass, drained it, and poured another. One thing was for certain: at the rate she was going, she was going to feel pain come morning.

"Really?" Even though I knew it was wrong, I felt a twinge of jealousy. The feeling caught me by surprise because, to my knowledge, I didn't have any romantic notions about my captain.

"Yeah, he laid it on pretty thick too. Sent roses to the job and everything." She laughed.

I was confused. Minutes ago she was complaining about being alone for the rest of her life, and now she was saying she had a nigga who wanted her back. Personally, I would have told the nigga to eat shit out of the crack of my ass, but that was just me. You got only one chance to piss on me. "And you believed him?"

She cocked her head again, as if she was trying to figure me out, and I realized she didn't have game, either. We were like two pitiful peas in a pod.

She slammed her glass down on the table, sloshing its contents around and wasting some of it on the table. She struggled to sit up straight and looked me directly in the eyes. "Hell to the motherfucking no! I don't believe him." She burped and giggled. It was a funny and feminine sound, and it made me smile knowing she made it. "Sorry." She giggled again.

"Good. He don't deserve you, either." I wasn't flirting; I was telling the truth. As far as I was concerned, he had had his chance and he'd blown it.

"You ain't never lied! The prick thinks I'm stupid. He knows I get a reenlistment bonus, and he probably wants to get his hands on it."

"Dag, I didn't even think about that bonus." I had so long to go on my first stretch, I hadn't even given much thought about what I would do come reenlistment time if the economy changed. Now that we were starting a family, it might make more sense to find a job that allowed me to be home with my family without the threat of deployment. It was certainly something to think about.

"That's a smart, dumb nigga. He got me once. He damn sure won't get me again."

Her head started rocking, and I could tell it wouldn't be long before she succumbed to sleep.

"Captain, you wear your pain on your sleeve too. Your husband hurt you, and it shows. If you want to change, it's not too late."

She attempted to sit up straight again, but she was fighting a losing battle. "Sounds like you've got something to say. Go on and say it."

"I hear the guys talking. They all think you're a beautiful woman, but most—if not all of them—are afraid to say anything to you. They think you're going to shut 'em down." I was nervous about speaking so frankly with her, and I hoped she wouldn't turn on me because of it.

"I will shoot them down if they don't come correct. Shit, I don't have time for any bullshit. Did you know

I'm almost forty? I'm at my sexual peak, and I spend every night alone with a fucking vibrator. I've got battery burn, for Christ's sake."

Damn. Way too much information for me to know about my captain. One of us was going to regret it in the morning. I needed to get the fuck out of there before I learned anything else I didn't need to know. "Captain, I think you should get some rest, and I've got to get home to my wife." I stood up.

"She's a lucky bitch."

I didn't take offense. She was talking out her head and speaking from her heart. Part of me wanted to get her a blanket or perhaps a pillow to make her more comfortable, but the other part of me told me to run as fast as I could for the door. "I'll let myself out. Have a nice weekend."

I flipped the latch on the door as I closed it and quickly walked to my car. I was glad I went over to her house, even though it got kind of thick. I just hoped there would be no regrets in the morning and that the captain remembered I came because I cared about her.

The lights were on in my apartment despite the late hour. Cojo was going to be mad, and she had every right to be. I should have called her. I sat in the car for a few seconds, trying to get myself together. Even though I hadn't done anything wrong, I still felt bad.

"You've been drinking." Cojo stopped short of kissing me and walked into the bedroom, leaving me standing in the living room.

"Honey, don't be mad. Something came up, and I had to handle it." I followed her into the bedroom.

"Something or someone?"

I stopped moving. It wasn't Cojo's nature to be jealous, so I was momentarily stunned. "Whoa. Where did that come from? I know I'm late, but I have a perfectly good explanation if you give me a second to tell you."

"Whatever. Dinner is on the stove. I'm going to bed." She flung the comforter off the bed and positioned two of the pillows in the center of the bed, making a little wall. I wasn't amused. She was acting like a two-year-old, and it wasn't making sense.

"Cojo, stop. Captain Jamison was going through something tonight. I stopped by her house to check on her. We had a few drinks while she talked it out."

I could literarily see the fight drain out of Cojo, because she felt the same way about the captain as I did. If it wasn't for her, I would be sitting in a military jail somewhere over some bullshit.

"Is she okay? Why didn't you call me?"

I walked over to my wife and held her in my arms. "It all happened so fast. I saw her when I was leaving the base, and she didn't look good. I thought somebody had died. That's how scary she looked to me. I followed her home to make sure she got there okay."

"So what happened? Why was she so upset?"

It felt like I had a "get out of jail free" card in my back pocket, because all vestiges of Cojo's anger were gone. I followed Cojo into the kitchen, where she warmed up my dinner.

"I think it was a lot of things all at one time. She made a decision to reenlist today, but she's scared she will end up old and alone. She wants to have a child one day, and she thinks her time is running out."

"We should see if we can fix her up with someone. Don't you have any friends?"

"Hold on, honey. It's not that simple. If we start messing around, playing matchmaker, we might end up doing more harm than good."

"What? Why do you say that?" She raised her brow.

She placed my food in front of me and sat down. Since she'd fixed only one plate, I assumed she'd already eaten.

"What if we fix her up with a bigger asshole than her ex-husband? Then I'd have a pissed-off captain to deal with, and who will she be mad at? Me."

"But what if it turns out good? Did ya ever think of that?" She gave me a peck on the head.

She was right. It could be a good thing, but the problem was I didn't have any friends other than . . . Braxton. A slow smile crawled over my face.

I said, "Hmm, we'll just have to think about this some more."

"What are you thinking? Oh, I know. Braxton."

"Yeah, he's not a bad guy. A little wild at times, but he could be trained if he had the right woman."

"See? Problem solved."

Chapter Six

ANGIE SIMPSON

"Well, you've passed the first trimester, and everything looks good. Would you like to know the sex of the baby?"

My doctor had just finished her exam and was doing a sonogram. She seemed excited, but I didn't share her joy. How could I? "Doc, I don't mean to bust your bubble, but I couldn't give a rat's ass what it is. About the only thing I do care about is when it's coming out of me."

"Not the healthiest of attitudes, but given the circumstances, I can understand where you are coming from. Have you given any thought to what you are going to do after the child is born?"

"My mother wants to keep it, but I'd much rather give it up for adoption. I don't want to have the child around as a constant reminder of my rape. Besides, I'm too young to have a kid. I can't even take care of myself, let alone a child."

Tears burned the back of my eyes, but I refused to let them fall. I'd shed enough tears over that night. And I was living for the day the nightmare would end.

"You may feel differently once the baby moves. Have you thought about that?"

"Obviously, you've never been raped before, or you wouldn't have asked me." I wasn't trying to be mean to my doctor, but I couldn't help it. How could I make her, or anyone else, for that matter, understand how violated I felt? It wasn't enough that my attacker raped me, but to add insult to injury, he set our house on fire and left me for dead. I had burns over 70 percent of my body. How could I make them understand I believed a beast was growing inside me? I felt like the child was snacking on me, eating away at my heart and soul.

"Get dressed. I will see you in my office."

The doctor left the room, and I wiped the gel off my stomach and put my clothes back on. I felt ashamed of myself for feeling the way I did. Normally, I wasn't combative, but every day seemed to bring out a different emotion, and it was driving me nuts. I fought back the urge to cry as I finished getting dressed.

"I want you to consider going to group counseling," the doctor said when I joined her in her office.

"For what?" This had to be something else my mother had cooked up with the doctor to humiliate me.

"Well, I think it would help you to be around other people who have been through the same type of experience. It's always helpful to know you aren't the only one going through it."

"Thanks, but no thanks. I'm not into sharing with a bunch of strangers." Fuck that. I was not about to sit in a room, trading stories with a bunch of bitches. I got enough of that shit at the house.

"You're mother thinks it's a good idea."

I was pissed. I thought it was against the law for her to discuss me with my mother. Whatever happened to doctor-patient confidentiality?

"If I wanted my mother in the room, I would have invited her in here."

"Your mother made the suggestion, and I happen to think it's a good idea. You're harboring a lot of pain and resentment. It's not healthy for you or the baby."

Fighting with the doctor was a big waste of time, because it was clear they'd already made a decision for me. They could make me go, but they couldn't make me participate. If it would get my mother off my ass, it might be worth it.

Chapter Seven

GAVIN MILLS

"Gavin, my name is Meredith Bowers, and I've been assigned to represent you."

I looked up from my chair at a slim, brown-skinned woman with an angelic face. She was short, about five-two, and couldn't have weighed more than 115 pounds. Perfect. She wore her light brown hair in a loose bun on the back of her head. I wanted to let it loose and run my fingers through it.

"I'd shake your hand . . ." I lifted my hands so she could see they were cuffed to the arms of my chair.

"I understand." She took a seat in front of me. She had a large mole next to her nose that would have been a real eyesore if her face wasn't otherwise so perfectly put together. The mole enhanced her beauty.

"Love the mole."

"Are you trying to be funny?"

She was obviously sensitive about it, so I regretted mentioning it. The last thing I needed to do was piss off the person charged with either getting me out of jail or making sure I didn't spend the rest of my natural life behind bars.

"No, honestly, I wasn't. It looks like God put his stamp of approval on your face. It's sexy to me."

She blushed, and I could feel the tension immediately leave the room.

She said, "I assume you know why I'm here."

"Well, I doubt you stopped by because you liked my personality." I laughed.

She pulled a folder from her briefcase, and the smile slid off my face. The seriousness of my situation practically smacked me in the face.

"You're right. Have you spoken to anyone else about your cases?"

"Uh, no. You're the first person that's come to see me."

"What about doctors? Anybody in your cell? I don't want any surprises when we get in court."

She got down to business quickly, and I appreciated it.

"No, I haven't said anything to anybody."

"What about the arresting officers?" she barked as she flipped through the pages of my file.

My head slumped on my shoulders as my heart slammed against my chest. "Shit, I don't remember what I said, but I don't think it was anything bad."

She read through the pages. Her ruby lips moved over each word. If it wasn't my life she was reading about, I might have considered the visual alluring. She frowned as she read.

"What did I say?" I asked.

"Nothing relative to the charges, but there are some notes here about a possible altercation with a Gina Meadows."

"That bitch," I mumbled.

Gina's parting words were fresh in my mind. I couldn't wait to get out of here so I could give her a piece of my mind. I had tried to call her several times, but she wouldn't accept my call.

"Who is she?" Meredith asked.

"My stepmother. She ain't never had anything good to say about me, and trust me, the feeling is mutual." I was bitter about it, but there wasn't a damn thing I could do about it in jail.

She pushed the file away and stared at me. Her look made me uncomfortable, because it felt like she was looking directly into my soul. "So I guess I shouldn't call on her as a character reference?"

"Hell no. Not unless you want me to sit in this jail for the rest of my life." I laughed, but there wasn't a damn thing funny about spending the rest of my life in jail. I'd been locked up before as a juvenile, but this was different. There were some seriously bad motherfuckers up in this camp, and I was ready to get the hell out of here.

"What about your father? Will he be willing to speak on your behalf?"

I didn't even try to hide the scowl that I was sure crossed my face. My father was the last person on earth I'd call. "Let me be real clear about this. The only reason my father could pick me out of a lineup would be because I look like him. But if my brother was next to me, he wouldn't know the difference. He never did anything for my ass while I was on the outside, so I don't suspect he'll do anything now."

If she was surprised by my response, it did not show on her face.

"Anybody else?"

I'd never given it much thought before, but I didn't have anyone on the outside who cared whether I lived or died. It had never bothered me before, but this time it did. I didn't have a dime on my books, and prison life was tougher without money. Money brought safety and security. "No, there's no one."

It sounded worse when I said it out loud.

"So tell me what happened with Angela Simpson?" She took a legal pad from her briefcase and a small tape recorder and placed them on the table.

"What's the recorder for?"

"In case I forget something. You never know. Something you say may not be useful now, but it might be useful later." She shrugged her shoulders and pressed RECORD.

I didn't like being taped, but I wasn't about to piss off the one person who could help me out. "Who?" I feigned like I didn't know the name of the girl from the fire. I was mad at myself for not making sure she was dead before I started the fire.

"That's the name of the lady who was burned in the fire. She claims you raped her and set the fire to cover it up."

I tried my best to get up from the table. That was how mad I was. I didn't take too kindly to people lying on me. "I didn't rape nobody. Are you serious? She really said that?" I was furious, and if I could have gotten out of those handcuffs, I would have found that lying bitch and finished her off for good.

"Sit down. If you start showing your ass in here, you're going to find your ass in lockup. They don't play that shit up in here."

I was shocked. Meredith appeared to be so prim and proper, so it was hard to imagine her cussing. Contrite, I sat back down. "I'm sorry. I hate folks lying on me. I spent my whole life having folks lying on me. Shit. I'm sorry. I didn't mean to go off. I should be used to it by now."

She didn't look like she was offended, and chances were she'd heard it all before from some of her other clients.

"Mr. Mills, if you have something I need to hear, I suggest you tell it to me now, because time is like money. I have none to spare."

I liked her and believed she could handle her own. This was a turn-on to me. There was nothing worse, in my opinion, than a weak woman. Weak women reminded me of my stepmother. "I picked her up around Cleveland Avenue. Something told me to leave her ass right there on the street, but she practically threw herself at my car."

Meredith was busy writing, so I continued talking.

"She said her boyfriend roughed her up and she was running when she found me. She begged me to take her home before he found her again."

"So you were helping her out?"

I searched her face to see if she was being facetious. If she was, I couldn't tell. "Yeah. She said he had been drinking and she was afraid of him."

"Did you happen to see the boyfriend?"

"No, she was alone when I saw her."

"Did she look like she'd been in a fight?"

"Yeah, her eye looked like it was turning black, and she was crying and shit," I lied. She might have cried at one point, but by the time I got to her, she was done crying and ready to suck dick.

"What about her clothes? Were they torn?"

I thought back because I couldn't remember. The last time I saw her, she wasn't wearing anything. "I can't recall. Does it matter?"

"Guess not. Just trying to cover all the bases. Go ahead. What happened next?"

"She got in, and I drove her home."

"That's it? Did you go inside the house?"

Her pen was poised over the paper as I debated how much more I should tell her. I didn't use a rubber when

I fucked her, so I couldn't deny sleeping with her. I didn't know why Meredith was questioning me about Angela, but it was obvious she knew something, or else she wouldn't be probing into an unrelated case.

"Yeah, and we had sex. But I didn't rape her." I was gambling on the fact they had tested her for rape and had my DNA.

"She never said no? Or was she unconscious when you asked her?"

"Fuck, you mean?" Outraged, I pushed back from the table, forgetting I was shackled. If I could have gotten my hands around the attorney's neck, I would have choked the shit out of her. I hated smart-mouthed motherfuckers, and she was really pissing me off.

"Don't you think they are going to ask you this when we get in court? I was testing you to see how you'd react. I'm telling you now. Don't you dare do anything foolish like that in court, or the judge will haul your ass right back to your cell."

I sat back in my chair, feeling stupid. "I don't do tests. Didn't like them in school, and I don't like them now, either. Especially if that bitch is trying to make herself look good while making me look bad. I'm not trying to stay up in this place, so I need you to help get me out of here."

"So what happened after you had sex?"

Now was not the time to be boastful. In my head I did the damn thing, but Angela thought I was lacking, and that was why I'd choked the shit out of her.

"Nothing. I left. I mean, after I hit it, she was worried her folks were going to come home and catch us, so I got the hell out of there."

She closed her pad and switched off the recorder. "Are you certain there isn't anything else you need for me to know? I can't stand losing, so if there is, you'd better tell me now."

"No, I swear. That was it. Hell, she wasn't even good, if you know what I mean." I regretted saying it almost as soon as the words left my mouth, but I couldn't help it. I could still hear the bitch taunting me in my head.

"I'm going to prepare some paperwork for your signature. I'll be back in the next few days to go over it with you. In the meantime, keep your mouth shut." She put her things back in her briefcase and got up from the table.

"What about the other charge?"

She hadn't asked me anything about Cojo, so I was worried that they'd given that case to someone else.

"We'll talk about it when I come back. I'm going to prepare a motion to have the two cases combined under an insanity plea. With the limited funding the courts are operating with, I think I can get a judge to agree."

"Okay. Thanks so much for your help. I really do appreciate it." I conjured up a tear and allowed it to fall from my face without wiping it away. If I'd learned one thing from my brother, Merlin, women liked sensitive men, and I intended to play into that. What did I have to lose? "I hate it here," I said in a low voice as the jailer came to get me.

"I know. We'll get you out. In the meantime, play nice. You don't need any more trouble while you're here. I'm also going to set up an appointment for you to speak to a doctor," Meredith said.

"For what?"

"Do you want out of here?"

She was dead serious, and so was I. I nodded my head.

"Good."

As the gate slammed shut, I felt a glimmer of hope.

Chapter Eight

TABATHA FLETCHER

"Don't look now, but your nutty friend just walked in," LaDena whispered over the top of my cubicle.

"Huh?" I looked up from the listings I'd been pouring over to see what LaDena was talking about. "Stop playing, Dena. Gina wouldn't come here. She hates this place."

"If that ain't her, then she's got a twin."

I peeked around my cubicle, and sure enough, Gina was waiting in our open-aired lobby. I tried to keep my annoyance off my face as a feeling of dread washed through me. I didn't have time for Gina's foolishness today. I had a new client coming in, and I had to figure out where I was going to take them. The housing market was in such a slump, I couldn't afford to lose any prequalified buyers.

"Fuck."

"Do you want me to get rid of her?"

Eagerness was stamped on Dena's face. She would have been happy to escort Gina out of the building, but it would be a surefire way to start a huge catfight in the middle of the lobby. My car was in front, so Gina knew I was in the office.

"No, sit your ass back down, and mind your own business," I whispered.

LaDena didn't like Gina, and I wasn't about to get in the middle of a fight between my oldest friend and my coworker.

"Well, excuse me. I was only trying to help." Her head disappeared from view.

I could tell I'd hurt her feelings, but I didn't have time to do much about it now. I didn't know what had made Gina stop by unannounced, but whatever it was, it couldn't be good. "Dena, don't be like that. I didn't mean it. Can you cover for me while I find out what she wants?"

"Oh, now you need my help, so you want to act all nice and shit."

Sometimes I couldn't stand working with a bunch of women. You always had to worry about who was on their period and how they were going to fuck up your day. "Stop it. You know she's going through it," I whispered back.

Not waiting to see if Dena would cover for me, I grabbed my purse from the bottom drawer of my desk and hurried out into the reception area. I grabbed Gina's elbow and practically dragged her out of the office behind me. "What are you doing here?" I demanded when I was out of LaDena's hearing range.

"Hi to you too, heifer," Gina snapped back as she yanked her arm from my fingers.

I could already tell this wasn't going to go well, and that was exactly why I tried to keep Gina from my office. When she got in one of her bitchy moods, she didn't care who heard her.

"Hi," I replied. I tried to keep the irritation out of my voice as we walked, but I couldn't help it. It was completely selfish of Gina to show up at my job, as if I didn't have shit else to do.

"Where are we going?" Gina whined.

"Coffee. I need coffee."

Actually, I probably could use a joint, but I hadn't smoked in years, and the only place I knew where to find one was off-limits to me. Gina followed behind me like a timid child until we reached McDonald's. I got us both coffees and sat down across from her.

"Now, would you please tell me what was so important you had to show up at my office without a phone call?" I was beyond pissed. I hadn't seen or heard from Gina in months, and I was not in the mood for some bullshit.

"Can't I just stop in to see my friend? Jeez, someone got up on the wrong foot today."

"Cut the shit, Gina. It's too damn early for this crap."

Gina didn't look so hot. The clothes she wore were dirty, and it looked as if she hadn't combed her hair in weeks. I'd seen this crazed look before, and I was immune to it. If Gina came to me for more sympathy for the sorry-ass man who'd had her nose wide the fuck open for fifty billion years, she stopped at the wrong office. I was done. And if she knew what was good for her, she'd be done too.

"You always said you'd be there for me. I guess that was a bunch of bullshit. Silly me for believing you when I really need your ass."

I hated it when she tried to use reverse psychology on me. "You need to stop right there. I said I would be there for you, but that doesn't mean you can keep doing the same thing over and over and expect me to repeat the same sick pattern. Enough is enough. Haven't you ever heard of the definition of *insanity?*"

"Are you calling me crazy?"

Her voice got loud. The last thing I wanted to do was to have a scene in fucking Mickey D's.

"I didn't say you were crazy, but if you keep doing the same things over and over, expecting different results, that's insane. Now, tell me what's wrong, 'cause I've got to get back to work, and you, my dear, need a damn bath, because this street urchin shit is played."

She looked down at her clothes, as if she wasn't even aware of the way she looked. For a brief second, my heart went out to her. If I ever ran up on another dick that made me act the way she was acting, I would start switch-hitting for the other team.

"I think I might be pregnant. No. Scratch that. I took the test, and I'm sure of it," Gina practically whispered.

Since she'd been speaking so loudly just moments before, it took a second before her words sank in.

"Sweet mother of Jesus. Please tell me it isn't so." It wasn't my most tactful response, but it was certainly off the cuff and real.

"I don't know why I thought I could tell you this," she mumbled.

What the hell did she want me to say? We'd been down this road before, and each time nothing good had come of it. The only thing different about this time was she was older, but apparently none the wiser. I was ready to leave. I couldn't sit there and pretend everything was okay when it wasn't. I was done fooling myself, and if this heifer wanted to sail off in la-la land by herself, it was on her.

"What do you want me to say, Gina? Third time is the charm? Or maybe this time you'll keep the baby?" I went too far, even for me. But even though I regretted the way I said it, I had spoken no truer words. Each time Gina got pregnant, she convinced me to be there for her, love her child for better or worse, and each time Ronald made her give it up. I was not going down that road again. This time she was going to have to take this journey alone.

"You witch." She picked up her hot cup of coffee and threw it at me.

Thank God my intuition told me to stand, or the bulk of it would have landed in my face. In all the years we'd been friends, we'd never intentionally set out to harm each other. Even though I was madder than I could ever recall, I was also afraid my friend had finally lost her damn mind.

"I'm not going to put my hands on you, because you're clearly crazy. I'll holla." I looked down at my favorite blue linen suit. It was ruined. "You don't know how lucky you are right now. I'm sending you the bill in the morning. And you better be glad that shit wasn't hot."

I grabbed what was left of my dignity and left her standing in the middle of Mickey D's. If she cared, I couldn't tell. I practically ran out of there, but with each step I took, the harder it was to keep it moving. Gina needed me. I didn't want to wake up one day and read about my friend, dead of an apparent overdose or some other shit. I had to help her stupid ass. I turned around and rushed back to the restaurant, but Gina had already gone.

I did not want to go back to my office, especially with coffee stains all over my clothes, but I didn't have any choice. My clients were due within the hour, so I didn't have time to go all the way home and change without being late for our appointment.

"What the hell happened to you?" Gayle Jackson, the office manager, broadcasted when I walked through the door.

So much for slipping in unnoticed.

"I don't want to talk about it." I wanted to get to my cubicle and check to see if I had a suitable pair of slacks in the closet.

"LaDena, you win." Gayle pulled a five-dollar bill out of her purse and walked it over to her sister, LaDena.

"Told ya." LaDena tucked the five in her bra and keep on working.

Curious, I stopped walking. "Bet? What bet?"

LaDena was always betting on something. If it wasn't the lottery, it was who'd get the first walk-in or when the weatherman would finally get the forecast right. She walked out of her cubicle with a big Kool-Aid grin on her face.

"Damn, Gayle, you can't hold water," LaDena joked.

The sisters and I shared office space. The space was small, two cubicles and a waiting area. LaDena and Gayle shared one cubicle, and I had the other. We'd been in business together for about five years, and most of the time we got along well. It had started out as a part-time gig for me, but I was finally able to cut my ties with corporate America and go into business with the sisters. At the time, they were having trouble making the rent. Every now and then the sisters would gang up on me, but those times were few and far between.

"If I had fifty cents for every dollar you threw away on your stupid bets, I wouldn't have to work every day," I said.

"Well, this stupid bet paid off, thank you very much." LaDena waved the bill in my face and placed it back in her bra.

"'Bout time you won something," I mumbled.

Unfazed, LaDena laughed. "And if your nutty friend comes back, I might get me enough to pay for my lunch at Red Lobster."

"Don't you have people coming in this morning?" Gayle, the peacemaker, asked with a semi-worried expression on her face.

I looked down at my clothes in disgust. I felt like every granule of sugar from the coffee was sticking to my skin. "Don't remind me. I think I have some clothes in my gym bag. It'll be okay." I didn't have time to fight with LaDena, so I decided to drop it.

"You want me to do the showing for you?" Gayle said.

Gayle's eyes were glistening, but I shut her down quickly. She might be all smiles, but if Gayle took my clients out for me, she would want to split the commission if it resulted in a sale. I needed my money.

"No, that's okay." I grabbed my gym bag out of the closet in my cubicle and took a pair of jeans and a shirt from the bag. It wasn't my outfit of choice for meeting new clients, but it was better than the caffeine-splattered outfit I had on. I would make up some excuse as to why I was dressed so casually. "You still didn't tell me what the bet was about."

The sisters were back at their desks, as if nothing had happened. Since they weren't talking, I assumed the butt of their joke was me.

"It wasn't nothing. We were just being silly," LaDena answered.

She locked eyes with her sister, neither speaking. I laughed as I made my own mental bet that Gayle would spill the beans before the clock struck two. She always did, and I didn't expect today to be any different. Gayle couldn't hold water in a bucket.

Out of habit, I dialed Gina's cell. As pissed as I was, I could not get the hurt look on her face out of my mind. The phone continued to ring until the answering message came on. I didn't leave a message. She would see my name on the call log, and if she was still speaking to me, she'd call me back. I'd give her a few hours, but if she didn't call by the end of the day, I would go by her house to apologize.

When the bell rang over the door, I assumed it was my clients, because we rarely had walk-ins. For continuity, each of us listed our clients on a community calendar so we could back one another up if necessary. When I saw it wasn't my clients, my smile faltered for a moment.

"Merlin, what are you doing here?" I asked. My surprise was tempered with fear. Did he know about me? Or was he here to bring me news about his mother? Closing my eyes, I braced myself for the worst.

He said, "We have an appointment."

I relaxed and opened my eyes. He was smiling, and I exhaled loudly. I didn't notice the pretty brown-skinned woman standing next to him until he pulled her forward. She had to be his wife, and from the looks of her she was pregnant.

"I don't know what's wrong with me. Merlin, I looked right at your name and didn't make the correlation. I thought Gina told me you'd enlisted in the army and moved away?"

"I did, but I'm back now."

Merlin looked great, and I beamed with pride. He had grown into such a handsome man. My heart swelled, but I also felt sad. I pushed my emotions aside and put on my professional face.

"Hi. I'm Cojo. Merlin speaks highly of you." She took my hand and rapidly shook it.

I was surprised Merlin talked of me at all. I didn't do half the things I should have done for him, and I hadn't seen him in years. I knew he'd got married, and I remembered something about him enlisting in the service, but that was it. About his wife, I'd heard next to nothing. The only thing I knew about her was that Gina hated her guts.

"Wait. So you picking my firm wasn't a coincidence?" I was really confused.

Merlin laughed. "No. When I told Gina we were looking to buy a house, she told us where you worked."

LaDena was perched on the edge of her sister's desk, watching our exchange. The only thing missing was popcorn and soda. If they were waiting for an introduction, they weren't going to get it today. I was trying to sort all of this out in my head, and I didn't need their added interference.

I said, "Well, let's go, then."

Normally, I would have sat with my clients before we went out on the street to find out exactly what they were looking for, but I wanted to get Merlin and his wife away from the sisters as quickly as I could. As the door closed, I saw Gayle hand LaDena another bill. I didn't even want to know what they were betting on this time.

Chapter Nine

MERLIN MILLS

Excited, I grabbed Cojo's hand as we followed Tabatha to her car. It was good seeing her again, and I could tell by the expression on her face she was surprised to see me too. I had known her most of my life and had fond memories of her.

"So, when did you make the move to real estate?" I sat in the passenger seat, while Cojo sat in the back.

"I've been doing it for about five years on a part-time basis. I went full-time about two years ago."

"How's it working for you with the economy the way it is?" I said, wondering where she would take us first.

"Well, I wish it was better, but I was tired of punching a clock, so I can't complain. I still can't believe you're here with me. I knew you got married and all, but I didn't know you were having a baby. Congratulations to you both."

"Thanks. We're excited." I leaned over the seat and smiled at Cojo. She was being very quiet, but then again, she didn't know Tabatha.

"Did he tell you I used to change his diapers?" Tabatha said to Cojo while looking in the rearview mirror.

"No, he didn't. He told me you were a friend of the family, but Merlin doesn't talk much about his life prior to meeting me."

"Friend, hell! Him and his brother spent about as much time at my house as they did at their own. I'm more like an aunt."

Just mentioning my brother was like throwing water in hot oil; it started popping. I heard Cojo take a deep breath, but I chose to ignore it. We rode in tense silence for a few minutes. Tabatha knew a lot about the dynamics of my family. These things I hadn't discussed with my wife, and I wanted to keep it that way. The truth about my life was embarrassing and difficult for me to talk about.

"When's the baby due?" Tabatha said, nosing the car through the city.

Grateful for the diversion, I replied, "The doctor told her May, but I think she's going to drop in April, close to my birthday."

Cojo said, "Hey, I wouldn't mind going early. I'm already tired, and I've got another four months to go."

"Tabatha, that's why I need to have her settled into a house before the baby comes. At first I thought we'd leave Georgia, but Gina wants to be close to her grandbaby, so we decided to stay here for a while, or until we know for sure where I will be stationed." I was looking at Tabatha as I spoke, so when the car veered suddenly to the right, it scared us all.

"Watch out," Cojo yelled.

Tabatha righted the wheel, but I could tell she was shaken up by the near miss.

"Are you okay?" I asked, my heart beating faster than a motherfucker.

"Yeah, I'm sorry. I'm a better driver than this. I just need to concentrate on one thing at a time." She chuckled.

"Well, I could drive if you want me to. That way you can concentrate on the road," I said it in a joking manner, but I was so serious.

"I'm good. Relax. I might've zoned out for a minute, but it's okay now." She reached across the seat and patted my knee.

I was going to give her the benefit of the doubt, but if she pulled another stunt like the one she just pulled, Cojo and I were getting out. If something were to happen to my wife or my child, I didn't think I could live with myself. We'd been through too much as it was.

We drove in silence to the first house. Tabatha appeared to be all right as she showed us around the home. It was an excellent starter home in what appeared to be a good neighborhood. We were looking in the Roswell area, because Cojo wanted to be close to her job and it wasn't far from the base.

"What do you think?" Tabatha asked as we exited the house.

"It looks good. It's also child friendly," I said.

"All houses are child friendly until them little buggers learn how to walk. I remember when Merlin was little, he was in everything." Tabatha laughed, caught up in her own little world.

"Oh yeah? Merlin was a bad boy? Tell it. Tell it," Cojo said, clapping her hands together.

"No, not him. He was just curious as all get out. Now, that other one, he was bad."

I felt a flash of anger at Tabatha. She should have known my brother was still a sore spot with me. As children, we never got along, and things hadn't changed much since then. I was pretty sure Gina had told Tabatha about Gavin's latest stunt, so I wasn't sure why she would bring him up.

"We'll be okay, because we're going to have a good baby," I said.

"There is no such thing as a good baby," both ladies answered at the same time.

"I was a good baby." I was beyond annoyed. I was mad.

"You might have been, but that damn brother of yours made up for it," Tabatha replied.

Once again the mood of the group changed. I knew what my problem was, and even Cojo's, but I didn't understand Tabatha's reaction. She had practically thrown her professionalism out the window. Gone was her smile and sunny disposition, leaving a mean scowl in their place. Whatever Gavin did to piss her off, it was his problem and not mine.

We saw three more houses, but we didn't like them nearly as much as we did the first one. It was perfect for our needs, and I loved the neighborhood. I wouldn't worry about Cojo going to bed at night in the house alone when I was away on duty. I kept this thought in the forefront of my mind, because there was a large probability I'd be shipped out any day without much notice. I had to be secure in the knowledge she'd be okay without me.

I was feeling pretty good about using Tabatha to buy our first home because I knew she had my best interests at heart. She had been through a lot with my family and had saved my ass on many occasions.

"Gimme a hug, boy. I'm so glad you're back."

We were back in front of her office. Giving Tabatha a hug felt so natural and brought back some of the happier memories I had of my childhood. There weren't many, but in most of them Tabatha was there. She had always stepped in when Gina went too far, but she hadn't been there 24/7. Tabatha was a bit of a mystery to me, because I had never once heard her talk about man troubles. Gavin thought she was gay, but I didn't believe it.

She moved closer and gave Cojo a kiss on the cheek. "I'm going to submit the offer to the sellers today. Hopefully, we'll hear from them soon. I'll let them know you are looking to do a fast close, which should motive them to accept the offer without countering. Keep your fingers crossed."

"With you on our side, Tabatha, I'm not worried. Thanks for everything," I said.

She was still standing by the curb as I put the car in gear, but just as I was about to pull away, she rushed toward the car.

"Merlin, wait. I think Tabatha forgot something." Cojo powered the window down.

I said, "Something wrong?"

"No. No, nothing like that. I was just wondering if you've spoken to Gina lately."

"Not in a few days. Why?"

She looked almost frantic to me, and I felt like she wanted to say something else but was afraid.

"Oh, no reason. I was just asking. If you see her, tell her I said to call me." Tabatha waved.

"That's odd. I thought they talked every day. Did that sound strange to you?" I said.

"No, not really." Cojo stared out the window but didn't say anything else.

Women, sometimes I just couldn't figure them out.

"Where are you going, babe?" Cojo said when she saw me preparing to leave.

"I've been trying to reach Gina since we got back from Tabatha's office, and she's not answering the phone. I'm going to run over there just to make sure she's okay."

Cojo stumbled and I reached out and grabbed hold of her arm to steady her. "What's wrong? Are you all right?"

"Uh, I'm fine. Just felt dizzy for a moment. I'll be okay."

I was torn. I kept getting this nagging feeling in my gut that something wasn't right with Gina, but I was afraid that if I left, something could happen to Cojo and the baby. I sat down across from her on the sofa, because she was freaking me out. She wouldn't look me in the face, and she seemed unable to sit still.

"Is the baby moving? Are you in pain?"

"I'm fine. Well, maybe the baby is moving a little bit. Can you get me some water?"

I jumped up off the sofa and ran into the kitchen. Once there, I couldn't decide whether to give her water straight out of the tap or to put some ice in it. "How do you want it?"

"Huh?" I heard her say.

I stopped. Something didn't feel right. I went back into the living room as Cojo slipped her phone back into her pants pocket.

"All right, Cojo. What's going on?" I was nervous. Ever since Cojo accidently slept with my brother, I was having a hard time with trust issues. I was suspicious of every little thing, and it was taking a toll on both of us. She hung her head, and I waited for what I believed was going to rip my heart into shreds again.

"Promise me you won't get mad?"

I counted slowly in my head as vivid images assaulted me. After all the things we'd been through, I couldn't believe she had the nerve to twist her lips and say that to me. I didn't answer her right away, because I knew there was a good chance it wouldn't come out right. In my heart, I knew she was about to tell me the child she was carrying was not mine but my brother's. I sat down and gripped the sofa for support. No matter what she said, I would try my damnedest not to hit her dead in her mouth.

"What is it?" I kept my voice low and my tone even. I wanted to hear what she had to say, and I could tell she was scared to say it. Whatever it was, it was better than living a lie, or at least I hoped it was.

"I've been keeping a secret from you."

Duh, I had figured that shit out for my damn self. I wanted to reach over and choke the shit out of her. Thank God we'd put down only a thousand dollars on the house, or I'd really have to kick her ass, baby or not. I pulled out my phone, ready to call Tabatha to see if it was too late to get my money back.

"Wh—what are you doing? Who are you about to call?"

Cojo looked terrified, but I didn't care.

I said, "What do you have to tell me?"

"I didn't tell you Gina came over here last week. She asked me not to."

Relief rushed through my body like oxygen as I slid my phone back in my pocket. "Honey, is that all? I thought it was something major. You scared me." I felt ashamed for thinking the worst and vowed to be a little more tolerant, especially since she was pregnant. I moved over and wrapped my arm around her shoulders. Her head dropped down; she was trembling. "It's no big deal, honey. You two didn't argue, did you?"

It wouldn't have mattered to me if they did, but I wanted to know. This was the only reason I could think of that Cojo would keep it from me. But even if they did argue, it was okay as long as Gina didn't disrespect my wife. Cojo and Gina had just started talking, so I didn't expect things to be perfect between them right away.

"No, not at all."

She kept ringing her hands together, which let me know something else was bothering her. I slowly pushed her away so I could see her face.

"Then what's wrong?"

Her lips were quivering, and my heart was pounding.

"She took a pregnancy test, and it came back positive. She asked me not to tell you." She sat perfectly still with her eyes closed.

Her words were slow to register, but what resonated deep inside me was the thought of Cojo once again aligning herself with someone other than me. I felt something inside of me shift, and even though I knew I was acting irrational, I became angry.

"I didn't want to keep it from you, but I didn't want to fight with your mother, either. I thought she would have told you by now, but she seemed so desperate to keep it a secret until she decided what she wanted to do."

Distrust fueled my suspicions. I thought back to when Cojo had been kidnapped by my brother and when Gina threw up. She had said she wasn't feeling well then and had made an offhand comment about being pregnant. She was probably pregnant then. The more I thought about it, the madder I got at both Gina and Cojo. Women had the power to change a man's life in the blink of an eye. For a split second, I wondered who the father was and felt sorry for him, especially if he didn't have a clue his life was about to be forever changed.

I turned on Cojo with a vengeance. "You're married to me, and this means I come first. What part of that do you not understand?" It was a stupid argument, but it was how I felt.

"Merlin, stop. I wasn't trying to keep something from you. I was trying to build a relationship with your mother. Can't you understand why it would be important for her to trust me?"

"And what about me? Isn't it important for me to trust you?"

"What are you saying? Since when did you stop trusting me?"

I ignored her questions. "So you decided what I should and shouldn't know? Who gave you that right?"

"I was trying to respect her wishes. For crying out loud, don't turn this into something it's not."

"I'm not turning it into anything. I'm just saying your alliance is with me, not my family."

"You're not making a lot of sense right now. Can you stop and think about this rationally? I thought I was doing the right thing."

"I can't tell. You don't know how Gina is when she's pregnant. You don't know anything about her at all except for what I've told you."

That seemed to shut her up a bit, and I was glad, because every time she opened her mouth, I got angrier. For some unexplainable reason, I felt Gina's pregnancy had diminished the joy I should be feeling about the birth of my first child. I didn't want to share it with another brother or sister. I had spent my entire life sharing and couldn't understand why, for once, it couldn't all be about me.

"I'm sorry, Merlin."

Cojo started to cry, but it didn't faze me one bit. The only thing I could think about now was her willingness to lie to me.

"I need some fresh air."

She reached out and tried to touch my shoulder.

"Don't."

Her fingers felt like icy clamps, and I pushed her hand off me, then walked to the door. I could hear her loudly crying behind me, but I closed my ears to her heartache. She had no clue how I was feeling inside, and it hurt me even more. I shut the door, and it slammed against the frame, shaking a little, but it did nothing to quiet my racing heart. I knew I was not being rational, and I needed someone I could trust to talk to before I did something I would regret.

Chapter Ten

MERLIN MILLS

I drove aimlessly for about an hour. My gut instinct told me I should go over to Gina's house and confront her, but if she really was pregnant, things might not go well. Women tended to get emotional. In Gina's case, it would be toxic, and I wasn't ready for it. Undoubtedly, something I needed to say would come out wrong and ruin whatever chances we had left to form a healthy relationship. I couldn't do it Rambo style and run up on her, because she'd more than likely bust me in the mouth, or worse, stab me like she did my father. I had to be logical in my approach to the situation.

I pulled up in front of Tabatha's house and felt a sense of relief to know I made the right decision by coming to see her first. I was certain Tabatha would be able to help me decide how to best handle this situation with Gina and my wife.

"Merlin, what are you doing here? Is something wrong?"

Tabatha stood back from the door and allowed me to come in. I could see her concern written on her face.

"I'm sorry to drop by without calling, but I really need to talk to you." It had been a very long time since I'd been to Tabatha's house, and it was certainly the first time that I'd come on my own accord, so I was uncomfortable.

"It's okay. Come on in. I was about to have a drink. Would you like one?"

"Thanks. I could really use one."

"Uh-oh, I have a feeling I can kiss my commission check good-bye. Do I need to bring the whole bottle?"

She was smiling when she said it, but she didn't know how close to the truth she was, because I was seriously having second thoughts about buying the house.

When I didn't answer, the smile disappeared from her face. I followed her footsteps through her all-too-familiar living room and into her kitchen. Gavin and I had spent many a night sleeping in that living room while Tabatha and Gina hung out in her bedroom. Tabatha was my stepmother's only friend, so if Gina was pregnant, I was sure she would know.

"I haven't been over here in ages. It still looks the same."

She didn't respond, but she didn't have to, because I was sure she was also taking that walk with me down memory lane.

"I think I know why you came," she said as she handed me my drink.

On my way over here, I kept hoping Cojo was wrong, but if Tabatha knew too, it had to be true. I felt like there was this big conspiracy and everyone knew about it but me. "Great. Everybody knows about this but me." I drained the glass and reached for the bottle. Even though I was upset, I didn't want to take my anger out on Tabatha.

"If it makes you feel any better, I just found out about it today."

In a way it did make me feel better, but my relief was short-lived. "Actually, it does. I'm so mad at my wife right now for not telling me, I don't know what to do. I had to leave the house." I held up my hands in surrender. My head was pounding like there was a miniature band playing inside of it.

"Why are you mad at her? Don't you think Gina told her not to tell?"

"I could give a flying fuck what Gina told her to do. She's my wife." I thumped my fingers on my chest for emphasis.

"And what does that have to do with the price of tea in China? Just because she's your wife doesn't mean she has to tell you everything. Some things don't need to be said, even between a husband and a wife."

"Oh, that's great. Now I'm getting marital advice from someone that has never been married."

Tabatha's head jerked back, and her eyes appeared to change from molten brown to a deep amber color. If I could have sucked the words back into my mouth, I would have.

"Tabatha, I'm sorry. Damn, hit me. I deserve it." I held my head down, ashamed of my actions.

She took a deep breath. "You know something? I should bop the shit out of you. But you're lucky I know where it's coming from. But that doesn't excuse bad behavior. I didn't tolerate it when you were a kid, and I'm not about to tolerate it now." She poured herself a drink, and we sat in silence for a few awkward moments.

"There has been so much shit going on for the last couple of months, I don't know if I'm coming or going. I can't deal with this new shit. I feel like I'm going crazy."

"Well, taking this shit with your mother out on your wife isn't gonna make it any better. This has to be difficult for her as well, especially since she is just getting to know Gina. If Gina told Cojo not to tell you, you and I both know Gina would have lost her damn mind if Cojo didn't do as she asked."

She was right, and deep down inside I knew it, but it still didn't take the sting away. I also knew that part of my problem was a trust issue, but I wasn't in the mood to be reasonable.

"Excuse my French, but this is fucked up. I'm going to have a brother the same age as my child."

"That's if she has this one." Tabatha finished off her drink and topped off both our glasses.

I said, "With her history of miscarriages, I'm sure her doctor will order her to be on complete bed rest. What scares me the most is what will happen to her if she is unable to carry the baby to term. She almost went crazy with the last one."

Tabatha banged her glass on the table so hard, I thought it would break. She looked like she had something she wanted to say and was trying to decide whether or not to say it. I didn't push, because I knew whatever it was would come out if I waited on it. I didn't have to wait long.

"Weren't no miscarriage. She aborted those babies."

"That's not true! I was there, and I remember the pain and the tears she cried." This couldn't be true. It just couldn't be.

Tabatha stared at me with tears in her eyes as she nodded her head.

"I don't believe you. You don't know what you're talking about. Why would she do that? She wanted a child of her own more than anything in the world. She used to tell us that every damn day!" I was up on my feet and pacing the room. Nothing was making sense, but in the back of my mind, there was a small part that believed.

"She did want children. She wanted them more than life itself," Tabatha cried.

Tears were running down both our faces. We both remembered. I fell down on the chair, too drained to stand any longer, too weak to front.

"Your father."

She spat out *father* like it was a four-letter word. I wasn't expecting the hostility on her face. She said it like she despised the ground my dad walked on.

"What are you saying?"

"Ronald didn't want her to have children. The motherfucker told her if she bore a child, he was going to leave her. She gave up her children because she loved that bitch-ass man, and he kept throwing it back in her face. It was okay for him to bring home his little bastards for her to raise, but he didn't want none by her. I can't stand that man."

I recoiled from her words, especially since I was one of those little bastards. I couldn't be mad at Tabatha for saying how she felt, but it hurt nevertheless. Fragments of conversations from my childhood came at me with the speed of bullets. Some of the comments were made by Gina, some I overheard, but my brother and I bore the brunt of all her pain. I thought she couldn't have kids, because we were such horrible children. I tried so hard to be good; I really did. I took all that shit from Gavin for her, and it still wasn't enough.

"Merlin, I didn't mean to piss you off. I was only telling you how I felt. Are you okay?"

I didn't know if it was the pain she saw written on my face or the shakes that were trying to take over my body, but Tabatha could tell I wasn't taking her news very well. "No, I'm not. I don't think you can understand what we went through as children. How she

made me feel. How they made us feel! It's too much."
I found myself getting mad at Gina all over again. It
didn't matter how long ago it was, it seemed like only
yesterday, and I was struggling not to hate her for it.

"Gina was wrong. I'm not going to lie to you. I told
her this time and time again, but the person that was
really responsible for the travesty was Ronald. For the
life of me, I cannot understand how he walked through
all this shit unscathed. Every time I think about that
nigga, it makes my blood boil."

Ronald might have been my biological father, but he
was a stranger to me. He was never around, and when
he was, he didn't spend any time with us. Gina had told
us fathers worked, so it was okay for him to be gone—
he was working. Hell, what did I know? I was a kid. He
came around and gave us money. Every now and then
he would beat our asses if we did something he didn't
like, and then he was gone. But he wasn't the one I saw
on a day-to-day basis, and he certainly wasn't the one
who dished out the majority of our punishments. Gina
was.

I probably should have been ashamed to cry in front
of Tabatha, but I wasn't. I couldn't have stopped my
tears if I wanted to. I cried for Gina, and I cried for
myself. I had had no idea of the pain she'd endured
because of my father, and it just made me sick inside.

"How can I hate somebody I don't even know?" I
whispered. I never knew my real mother, didn't even
know her name. Gina was the closest thing to a mother
either one of us had.

Tabatha said, "I don't have the strength to fight with
Gina anymore about Ronald. She's told me time and
time again that she can't help who she loves. I got that,
and as much as I disapprove of her having his child, I
will not try to persuade her not to have this one. It will

kill her, because she doesn't have too many more times in her. So, as much as I hate it, I'm going to be supportive one more time."

"What should I do?" Tears were still rolling down my face. Wiping them away would've been useless, because more kept coming.

"Gina looked a hot mess when she came by my office today. Be there for her when she calls on you. She's going to need you now more than ever. But first, go home to your wife. She needs you too. Be a better man than your father ever was."

She didn't know I'd been trying to do that my entire life.

"Should I tell Gina that I know about her being pregnant?"

"You're going to have to play that by ear. I've been calling her all day, and she won't return my calls. She must be really pissed at me, but she'll get over it. I hope."

Chapter Eleven

ANGIE SIMPSON

"We have a new member to the group. Would everyone please welcome Angie Simpson," the group moderator announced.

A smattering of clapping ushered me into the group counseling session. I wasn't sure what to expect, so I was surprised to find a lot of women who looked just like me. It did not lessen all my fears of meeting with a bunch of strangers, but I did feel a little better. At least my mother didn't come in with me. That was a relief.

Ever since the fire I had had no privacy. The only time I was alone was to take a shit, and even then, I'd better not take too long, or she'd come knocking on the door. I heard her tell one of her friends that I might be suicidal. That was so far from the truth, it wasn't funny. The only thing I wanted to kill was the child growing inside of me, but unless I found a method that didn't hurt, I wouldn't be doing that, either.

My mom monitored all my phone calls and had me blocked out all the social networks on the computer. My dad had asked her to lay off, but she wasn't paying him any mind. I felt like her sole purpose in life had changed to make mine miserable. I wanted to scream at her and tell her to leave me alone. I was sorry for fucking up, but my pride wouldn't let me. I took an empty chair toward the back of the room, hoping to disappear.

"Angie, we're an informal group. There are no rules here, and everyone will get a chance to share, if they want to. We do ask that you respect each woman's pain and privacy."

We sat around for a few more minutes as other people filed into the room. Some of them seemed at home and spoke to their friends, but a lot of the faces looked as miserable as mine. A few of the ladies were noticeably pregnant, but most were not. I just wanted to do my time there and go home.

"Hello. My name is Andrea, and I'm a victim. Six months ago I was robbed, beaten, and left for dead. I can't sleep at night. I spend most of my time being afraid. About the only time I feel safe is when I am in this room with you guys." Andrea smiled, but it didn't look genuine.

This wasn't what I'd expected. The next person started speaking almost immediately. She was already crying.

"I can't sleep at night, either. My name is Lee, and I was attacked sixty-six days ago. It was my birthday, and someone kicked in the front door to my apartment. I was tied up and raped. I'm afraid to go home, and some days I feel like I'm losing my mind. The sad part about this whole thing is I used to think the person who raped me was my friend."

One of the ladies scooted over and gave Lee a hug. Hell, I felt like hugging her too, and I didn't even know her.

"I'm Caroline. Things didn't go well for me in court today, and we have to do the whole thing again because the jury could not make up its damn mind. I can't go through this again. Once was hard enough. I said no! It doesn't matter when I said it. I said no. So if the state decides to dismiss my case, I'm not going to fight. I can't do this again."

"Caroline, I know how difficult this has been for you, and I can understand how you feel, but you can't give up. Each time one of us goes to court to defend our rights, it's either a win or loss for women around the world. Somehow we've got to be able to drive home the message to men everywhere that no means no. It's unconditional with no prequalifies. When someone crosses the line after we've said no, it's rape," another lady said.

A small round of applause followed her comment. The woman called Caroline did not appear to be impressed, as she continued to hug herself and cry.

"I was raped by a group of guys. I never got to see their faces. I lost count after the third person. I don't remember how many there were, because I passed out. They took my virginity and gave me AIDS. How's that for sharing? What am I going to do about that? I don't even know who to hate, so I hate myself."

One by one, the ladies shared their pain. There were so many, I forgot their names. However, I was not ready to open my mouth. Part of me admired their courage, but the other part of me felt ashamed because part of my story was a lie. I was moved by their painful memories, but none of them were being forced to have a child they didn't want. On this note, I stood alone.

"This is a waste of time," I muttered under my breath. I was there under false pretenses, and I thought it'd be a matter of time before they found me out.

"Angie, did you have something you wish to share?" When the moderator called her out, all eyes turned to Angie.

"Uh, no. I was clearing my throat."

Got to be more careful. I almost busted myself. I spent the rest of the time listening, and by the end of the session, I felt better. None of the ladies were perfect, but they weren't giving up. I also realized that sometimes bad things happened to good people too, and I needed to hear it, because my mother had convinced me God had put me on ignore.

"How did it go?" my mother asked when she picked me up from the meeting in her pink Cadillac. It was the only remaining relic from her once thriving Mary Kay business. The same business she gave up to have me.

"It was okay."

"Okay? Just okay? Well, I sure hope you don't think I'm going to keep driving you all the way across town to these stupid meetings if the only thing you can say about them is that they are okay. Do you know how much gas is these days?"

"Mom, I—"

"Of course you don't know how much gas is. You're too busy trying to look cute, while your father and I stress out over bills, trying to keep a roof over our heads. The same darn roof that you practically burned to the ground."

"I didn't start the fire, Mother." I should have kept my mouth shut, but I was sick and tired of my mother badgering me. I didn't know what she wanted from me. I'd said I was sorry. Why couldn't that be enough?

"You started something, or we wouldn't be in this predicament. I told your father you were just selfish. You don't even have the sense to say thank you after all we've done."

The more she talked, the faster she drove. I eased into my seat belt and fixed my eyes straight ahead. I didn't think she even noticed I was tuning her out. I had to for my own sanity.

She accelerated through a stop light five seconds after it had turned red. I heard the loud crunch before I felt the flash pain. It was horrifically intense for maybe a minute, and then it stopped. It happened so fast, I didn't have time to scream as I watched my mother fly through the windshield. She wasn't wearing her seat belt. Her Bible, stuffed with leaflets, stayed on the seat and served as a symbolic reminder that God wasn't done with me. I reached for it and held it to my chest.

A MARTA bus had stuck the driver's side of the Caddy, catapulting my mother's lifeless body from the car and trapping me inside. I was not ever going to have to ride in this car again.

Chapter Twelve

GAVIN MILLS

Last night my dreams were very vivid, and I woke up feeling hopeful for a change. I dreamed Cojo had come to visit me and had decided to give us a chance. In my dreams, there were no bars, so it kind of busted my bubble at little bit when I opened my eyes and the harsh reality of where I was stared me back in the face. Despite my dismal circumstances, I refused to allow the harsh reality of prison confinement to ruin my day.

I wasn't allowed to contact Cojo, but there was nothing wrong with her contacting me, and for some reason I believed she would do it soon.

"Nigga, I don't even want to know what you were doing in your bunk last night, but whatever it is, you need to keep that shit away from me," my cell mate said.

"Huh?" I hated this cell mate's shit.

"All that damn moaning and groaning shit. You must have been up all night fucking something, but you can't be making those kinds of noises up in here. All it does is attract attention, the wrong kind. If one motherfucker runs up on me because he heard your punk ass last night and thinks it's that type of party, I'm gonna bust you dead in your face."

"Man, fuck you and them niggas. You ain't heard shit. I wish the fuck you would get up in my motherfucking face." I was embarrassed, but I wasn't about to let it show. Weakness was not an option in this bitch, real or perceived.

"Yeah, well, fuck you too," my cellie answered.

"Mills, visitor."

The guards rarely spoke in complete sentences to us. I assumed the position, because they would tell me only once. I put my back up to the gate and allowed my hands to be cuffed. Even though there was little to no chance my dream would come true, my heart leaped with optimism at the possibilities. I tried to wipe the grin off my face as I was led away from my cell. However, my excitement was replaced with skepticism when I learned who my visitors were.

"Gavin, this is Dr. Leona Harrison. She is going to be assisting me on your case. Right now she's here to listen and make observations," Meredith Bowers said.

"'Sup?" I asked as I gripped my lawyer's hand and subsequently the doctor's. I was disappointed, but I refused to let it show. I didn't know Meredith well, but if she thought seeing a doctor was going to help me get out of this bitch-ass hotel for convicts, I was going to do what I had to do to make it happen.

After signaling the guard to remove my custom cuff links, we were all seated around a scarred aluminum table.

"Gavin, let me remind you that everything we discuss in this room is subject to attorney-client privilege for purposes of providing you with the best defense available. Do you understand?" Meredith pulled a yellow pad from her brown leather briefcase and put it on the table. She opened a pack of Juicy Fruit gum and handed me a stick.

I smiled my thanks, because gum was a luxury we weren't allowed to have. "Yeah, I understand."

Meredith said, "I've got some good news. The judge has agreed to hear both your cases on the same calendar day and to grant our request for a speedy trial."

"I like the speedy trial part, but did you get a chance to review the other case?"

"Yes, Dr. Harrison and I have both reviewed the files."

Thus far Dr. Harrison hadn't said a thing. She was starting to make me feel nervous. I knew she had a purpose for being there, but the jury was still out on what it was.

"Okay." I felt like they were waiting for me to say or do something, but I wasn't sure what it was. This was their dog-and-pony show, so I was prepared to wait. I would go in any direction they led me as long as the final destination was out the damn door.

"As you know, Gavin, you are facing multiple charges for some very different cases. This is one of the reasons why I brought in Dr. Harrison."

"I don't understand," I said.

"Well, in my experience, if you have a person doing violent crimes, such as rape, arson, and attempted murder, they are usually consistent behavior-wise. The nature of their crimes tends to escalate. But in your case, it's flipped, which we can use in your favor."

"I told you I didn't rape that girl. She was fine when I left her." I hocked up some saliva and spat on the floor.

The ladies exchanged glances.

Meredith said, "No need to get all hyped up, Gavin. We're on your side."

The ladies exchanged glances again.

"Did you get a chance to speak to Cojo?"

Again, the look exchange. Their secretive behavior was getting on my nerves. If they motherfucking had something to say, then they should just say it.

"I've filed a request for a deposition on your behalf, but I haven't spoken with her yet."

"But don't you see, she can clear all this shit up? Man, this is some bullshit."

I didn't want to talk anymore. I felt like I'd been locked up long enough for all of this to have been cleared up. I wanted to go back to my cell, possibly dream again. Anything was better than sitting through this shit.

"The way I see it, Cojo is the least of your problems. The more serious of your charges involve Angela Simpson."

"I did not rape that girl." I was pissed at myself for not finishing the job I'd set out to do.

"But your car was seen leaving the scene of the fire."

"They arrested my brother, Merlin, for that crime. Hell, we look just alike. I didn't do it."

"And your brother was cleared. He had an alibi. The good news is that Angie has not identified you yet. You got caught up because someone saw the car you've been driving leaving the scene right before the fire."

This was news to me. I thought I had gotten away without anyone seeing me or my car. "Who the hell told you that?"

They obviously knew more about the case than I thought they knew, and I needed to find out what information they had before I started lying and fucked myself even more.

"Turns out it was a friend of your brother who initially told the police about the car. Your brother told the police he'd given the car to you," Meredith said. Meredith held up her hands and sat back in her chair. Her expression challenged me to contradict the facts, but from the smirk on her face, I knew I couldn't.

"So, I told you I was there, but I didn't do nothing to that bitch she didn't want me to do."

"That may be true, but we've got to prove it. What else can you tell me about that night?"

I was getting frustrated, and that wasn't good, because I tended to react impulsively when I was mad. Once again the ladies exchanged looks.

"Shit, man, there is nothing else to tell. I picked the bitch up, drove her home, we fucked, and I left."

Meredith exchanged another look with Dr. Harrison.

"What you keep looking at her for? I'm the one talking," I muttered.

"Stay focused, Gavin. I told you Dr. Harrison is here merely for observation. I am watching her reaction because I'm trying to get a feel for how a jury will react if I have to put you on the stand."

Finally, this was making sense to me, and I started to calm down. All she had to do was explain it. I hated it when folks did shit and didn't tell me why. I wiped my forehead and wished I had a cigarette. I didn't even smoke on the regular, but situations like this were stressful. Especially when I was lying my ass off and my freedom depended on it.

"Tell me about Cojo."

"Me and Cojo are in a relationship. Everything was fine until my brother came home and messed things up. Now Cojo wants to act all brand new and keep things a secret. That's how things got so fucked up. They made up all this shit just to get me out of the way." I spread my hands wide and above my head.

"Cojo, she's the lady you are accused of kidnapping?" the doctor asked.

"How many other Cojos do you know?" *Damn, is this bitch dumb or what?*

Dr. Harrison said, "I'm just making sure. There's no need for sarcasm."

Once again I had to remind myself to take it down a notch. If Meredith could get me out of this shit, I'd fuck her too. She acted like she needed it. "I'm sorry. I just get so mad sometimes and I say things I don't mean."

"Do you *do* things you don't mean too?" The doctor raised a brow, like she was on to something.

"Don't we all?" I realized I'd fucked up as soon as I said it. "Hey, wait. That shit didn't come out right. I mean, sometimes I do things I don't mean, but nothing serious. I mean, I would never hurt nobody or nothing like that." I started biting my fingernails, which I had already chewed to the quick. When I realized what I was doing, I stopped, because I thought it made me look guilty.

"So let me make sure I understand you. All of this started because of your relationship with Cojo Mills?" Meredith asked.

"Yeah. That's my baby too," I said with pride.

"Which baby?" Meredith asked.

"Fuck you mean, which baby?" I was beginning to believe this heifer rode on the short school bus on the days she made it to class. Either that or she wasn't fucking paying attention, and to be honest, I didn't know which one of them was worse.

Meredith closed her pad and stood up. She nodded to the doctor, and she stood up too.

Confused, I asked, "Where y'all going? We done?"

Meredith said, "Y'all is leaving because you obviously don't know how to talk to women."

Her face was so serious, I knew she wasn't playing. I had to think of something quickly to make things better.

"You ever been in jail, Meredith?"

"No, of course not." She huffed.

"Stuff be messing with you in here. Stuff that don't faze you on the outside, it messes with you bad in here." I jabbed my finger against my head repeatedly so she could understand where I was coming from. "I don't mean no disrespect. I just say things. . . . Don't be thinking." I allowed a tear to fall out of my eye. It was something I'd learned to do as a child, cry on demand. When they both sat back down, I knew it had worked like a charm.

Meredith stared at me hard and said, "Okay, as long you understand I will not tolerate your speaking to me in any kind of manner. Do we understand each other?"

"Yeah, I understand. I'm sorry."

"What is your relationship like with your brother, Merlin?"

I wanted to ask this bitch if she was kidding me. Hell, I fucked my brother's wife, so how did she think things would be between us? Instead I answered, "He's always been jealous of me, so we didn't get along much." I ignored the looks and continued talking. "When Merlin got popped, I was at their house with Cojo. Ask her. She was going to leave Merlin because she realized how crazy he is. He beat her up too. Ask her about that while you're at it."

"Okay, Gavin, I think we have enough for now," Meredith said. "We're going to brainstorm on all of this, and I'll figure out a course of action. Again, stay out of trouble, okay? I should be back in a couple of days."

They both stood up to leave.

"All right, then. Tell Cojo I love her and I'm not mad. I just want to come home to her and our baby," I said.

Meredith nodded. "I will."

She signaled for the guard as her phone buzzed. She sat back down and took the call as I was being escorted back to my cell. I felt happier because I thought things were starting to move in the right direction. I didn't notice the concerned look on Meredith's face as she listened to her call.

Chapter Thirteen

MEREDITH BOWERS

I said, "Well, now you've met Gavin Mills. I've got my work cut out for me."

"Yes, you do. Are you sure you want to do this?" Dr. Leona Harrison looked at me.

"I don't have a choice. This is my last case as a public defender, and I refuse to go out with a loss."

"And you're willing to let a nut loose on the streets to do it?"

If that was supposed to be a morality question, she was barking up the wrong tree. I wasn't paid to decide whether or not a client was guilty. I got paid to provide a reasonable doubt in the minds of jurors, if the case went to trial. If we didn't go to trial, it was my job to cut our losses and save the county the expense of useless court proceedings. I felt sure I could win this case, or I wouldn't have wasted my time.

"Fuck 'em. If he gets in trouble again, he'll call me and become a paying client, because I delivered when he wasn't."

"Damn. Well, all right, then. At least you're honest."

I said, "So what do you think about him? Do you think he's nuts?"

"Hell no. That loopy motherfucker is as sane as you and I. He knows exactly what he's saying and doing at all times. I think he's a con artist, and because of his looks, he is used to getting what he wants."

"So how do I go about getting him off?"

"You say the bitch is crazy," Leona said.

I laughed, but I was completely serious. I was going to get Gavin Mills out of jail if it killed me. Not because I gave a rat's ass about him, but because he came into my life when I was having an I-don't-give-a-fuck moment. "Then let's make it happen. If we can get the charges reduced to temporary insanity, a few months at the hospital, it should be good to go. In fact, if you make this work, I'll spring for a weekend trip at the resort of your choice."

"Girl, don't play. I'll have your boy wearing a plastic suit for the rest of his life with those types of incentives."

"Down, girl. I need him back on the street. Gavin will probably be our first client when I start my practice."

"Got it. I'll have my report to you within the week. Are you going to see the sister-in-law or the lady from the fire?"

"I'm going to handle them, but not right now. Gavin gave me an idea exactly how to do it, but I can show you better than I can tell you. I do want to speak to his mother."

"Why didn't you tell him Angela was pregnant too? Was that on purpose or what?"

"Yeah. I'm going to hold on to the information for a minute. I don't want Gavin to lose his damn mind while he's in there. I've seen guys like him before. If he realizes he will be spending the rest of his life making child support payments, he might decide to stay his ass in the clink and ruin my perfect record."

I was excited for the first time in months. I didn't want to tell Leona, but there was something about Gavin that turned me on. His sense of entitlement did it for me. He was like a thug without a gun—smoking.

Chapter Fourteen

MERLIN MILLS

"What are you doing here?" Ronald stepped out the door of his lavish house and pulled it closed behind him.

He obviously didn't want me to come inside, and even though it had always been clear to me how little he valued my brother and me, it still stung.

"Man, is that any kind of way to talk to your son?" I wasn't expecting my father to roll out the red carpet when I showed up at his house, but I definitely didn't expect his total indifference. If I didn't have something I wanted to say to him, I would have turned around and left, but I was determined to speak to him today, come hell or high water.

"Uh, man. I didn't mean it like that. I was expecting something else, and you caught me by surprise."

If I was twelve and still believed my dad walked on water, that shit might have sounded believable, but this was two thousand fucking twelve, and I wasn't buying it. "Whatever, dude. Are you going to invite me in, or are we going to have this conversation on your porch?" I could not help but feel some kind of way upon seeing how large my dad was living.

"Uh, I'm about to go out." Ronald pulled some keys from his pocket and locked the door, as if I had really caught him before he left the house.

Annoyed, I said. "Which one is it?"

"What?"

"First, you said you were expecting someone else, and now you say you're going out."

His face blazed bright red as he realized I had caught him in a lie.

"Fuck you want?" Ronald growled at me, like he was facing some random dude from the streets instead of his own flesh and blood.

Part of me was relieved that we didn't have to play nice with each other. I assumed he'd reached his tolerance level, but so fucking what? I'd reached mine too. I had promised myself I wasn't going to get angry before I rang his bell. I was going to try to be respectful, but all those resolves went right out the window. As far as I was concerned, to get respect, you had to give it, and this man had done nothing to earn my respect.

"Fuck you mean, what I want? I'm not some damn stranger riding your jock on the street. I'm your motherfucking son. Would it hurt your sorry ass to say 'Hi' and 'How have you been?'" I could tell he wasn't expecting my outburst and probably regretted not inviting me in, but if he wanted to do it on the street, I was going to go right there with him.

"Man, keep your damn voice down. You ain't in the damn hood no more, shit."

He looked around, as if he were expecting the neighborhood patrol to come up and give him a citation for loud talking. Which was highly unlikely, because his nearest neighbor was a quarter of a mile away.

"I can fucking see that. Yeah, it must be nice." Disgusted, I shook my head. Going to see him probably wasn't a good idea. I wanted him to be excited about seeing me. I wanted him to see how much I'd grown. I wanted him to know I didn't need his sorry ass now.

"Yeah, whatever. I worked hard for this shit too."

I had no doubt that he did work hard, but at whose expense? Even if he was young then and didn't want children, he made a decision to have us. He had a choice when we didn't, and I'd come to the realization I was better off without him in my life. He was a toxic man, and loving him had practically destroyed my stepmother.

I tried to ignore his indifference. "I'm having a kid. Did you know that?"

"Really?"

He didn't even bother to pretend like he gave a fuck, and it shouldn't have hurt me, but it did.

"Yeah. Got married too, but I guess you don't know that about me, either, right?"

"Well, I've been real busy."

I looked around so I wouldn't have to look at him, my fists itching to blaze a hole in his grill. "Did you know your father?"

"What?"

"I asked you if you ever knew your father. It wasn't a difficult question."

"What the fuck is that supposed to mean?" His fists were balled up by his sides.

I had a flashback to one of the few times he'd been around and whipped my ass. He used to hurt me, but I wasn't twelve anymore, so I stood my ground.

I ignored his question. "I'm excited about being a dad. I can't wait until it gets here."

"Okay." Ronald looked around like he was eager to be somewhere else, but I wasn't finished talking to him yet.

"I've been trying to understand why you didn't give a fuck about us. I figured if you didn't know your own dad and he didn't tell you how to be a man, then maybe I could give you a pass for being such a miserable fucker to us. So I ask you again, did you know your dad?"

"I ought to punch you in your motherfucking face," Ronald growled, but he didn't move. His eyes were wide, and his nostrils flared. I could tell he was furious, but he didn't raise his hand.

His outburst meant nothing to me.

"What about your mother? I never met her, either. Hell, I've never even met my own mother. Do you even remember who she was? Is she still alive? Or did you kill her slowly, like you're killing Gina?"

"You snot-nosed piece of shit. Fuck you come around here for?" Ronald charged at me, and I tripped him as he passed. He didn't fall, but I knew he got the message to back the hell up.

I said, "I wish the fuck you would. I will stomp a mud hole in that ass." It wasn't a threat; it was a promise. Years of repressed emotions were poking holes in my resolve to remain calm, at least until I found out what I needed to know.

Ronald regained his footing. "I don't have time for this shit. You ain't been coming around here, so what do you want?"

"Maybe it's because I didn't know where the fuck you lived. Last I heard, you were in Ohio. Did you know your other son is in jail?" I could tell by the look on his face he didn't know, but I wasn't surprised. It was also painfully clear to me that he didn't want to know. He obviously thought his job had ended the night he fucked my mother, whoever she was.

"Did Gina put you up to this?" Ronald demanded as he looked around wildly. He was breathing all hard, like he was ready to tear some shit up.

"No. She doesn't even know I'm here. One day you're going to need someone. You've pissed on everyone who loved you, and told 'em it was raining. When you make that call, I sure hope isn't to me, 'cause I ain't got nothin' for ya."

"Then why the fuck are you here?"

"I told you. I want to know who my mother is. I think you owe me that much."

He just looked at me as if I were crazy. For years I'd blamed Gina for my father leaving us behind. I thought if she'd been a better woman, he wouldn't have left. Over the years I began to realize I was wrong. A father didn't stay away from his children unless he wanted to. This man left because he didn't give a damn about us or her. I'd given him every chance to make things right and he hadn't.

I started walking to my car. I waited for him to stop me and tell me what I wanted to know, but he didn't. He didn't say a word as I drove away from his house and him. At the end of the day, it was his loss, not mine.

I walked into the house and hugged my wife. She was the most important person to me in the world, and I needed her to know it.

"Merlin, where have you been? Are you okay?"

"I'm okay. Just tired is all."

"You've been gone all night. I was worried sick about you." Cojo pulled away from me. She had every right to be upset with me.

I had acted like an ass.

"I know, and I'm sorry. I was upset, and I took it out on you. When I realized what I was doing, it was too late to call you."

"Where did you go?"

"I drove around for a while."

"Did you go see Gina?"

"No, I didn't know what to say to her. I went to see Tabatha. She told me I was wrong, but I already knew it. I just didn't know how to tell you."

"Merlin, if we're going to make it through this, we've got to find a better way to communicate with each other. We can't go off mad at each other, and we can't afford to hold grudges or keep secrets. I realized after you left I should have trusted you enough to tell you. I thought I was doing the right thing, but I was wrong too."

I loved my wife, and I thanked God for giving me such a loving and thoughtful wife. It wasn't going to be easy, but I was going to try to do better. I held her in my arms again. "I went to see my father too."

Cojo pulled back from me. "You did? How did that go?"

"Do you mind if we don't talk about it right now? I'm going to tell you, but right now I just can't."

"I can respect that."

Cojo pulled me by the hand and led me to the bedroom. She slowly took off my clothes. She pulled back the covers. "Get in and get some rest. You look like you can use it."

"Thanks." I was so grateful. As beautiful as she was, I wasn't in the mood for sex, and I think she knew it. I never believed I would ever say that, but it was true.

Chapter Fifteen

GINA MEADOWS

I did something today I hadn't done in years. I got down on my knees with my eyes closed and my head bowed, and I prayed. I stayed down there until my knees were numb, but I didn't find the answers I was looking for. I had no more tears left, and I was finally ready to accept the facts. I was having a baby, and my stepson could very well be the father. I wasn't the type to have meaningless sex, and my son was the only man I'd been around.

I had been drinking a lot and had times when I couldn't remember shit. The one thing I remember was waking up one night drunk as a skunk, with my panties and pants hanging around my ankles, and feeling like I had had the shit fucked out of me. There was no other plausible person. I did not believe I was pregnant by an alien or some divine being. So I was finally able to accept Gavin as the father of my child, however painful that might be, but I would carry the paternity of my child to my grave.

My circle of friends was very small, so there were only a few people who would have balls enough to ask me who the father was. My plan was simple. I would neither confirm nor deny the father's identity, because at the end of the day, it wasn't anyone's business but mine and God's. I felt like there was a lesson to be learned in all of this, but for the life of me, I couldn't figure out what it was.

Tabatha had been calling, but I wasn't ready. I was an emotional wreck, but somehow I believed things were going to get better. I started unpacking all the boxes I had stacked in the corner and getting my house in order while I was still up to the task.

A couple of months ago I thought I was going to move and finally be with the only man I'd ever loved. But it didn't pan out. Nothing in my life seemed to pan out. I suffered for a few seconds and thought I was going to cry again, until I heard the doorbell ring. I cautiously walked to the door. I wasn't expecting anyone, and there really wasn't anyone I wanted to see at the moment.

"Who is it?"

"Mrs. Mills?" asked a female voice.

She was looking for a Mrs. Mills, so of course it piqued my curiosity. I was certain she wasn't looking for my daughter-in-law, Cojo, so I had to see who was behind door number one.

"Yes. What do you want?" I asked, opening the door.

A smartly dressed woman stood at the door, carrying a briefcase in her hand. *This cannot be good,* I thought to myself.

"Mrs. Mills, my name is Meredith Bowers, and I'm representing your son Gavin, and I was wondering—"

I tried to shut the door, because I didn't have anything to say, but the woman used her briefcase to stop me. I assumed she was there about the baby, and I wasn't ready to discuss my child with anyone. "Get away from my door," I growled as I tried to push her briefcase out of the way.

"Mrs. Mills, please. It will only take a few minutes of your time."

My stomach chose that moment to revolt. Perhaps it was all the energy I was exerting trying to get rid of the heifer or the mention of Gavin's name. Either way, I had to throw up. I rushed away from the door and ran to the closest bathroom. I barely made it. I felt like my insides were being pulled out from the soles of my feet. Since I hadn't been able to keep much food down lately, it didn't last long, but the pain from the dry heaves was breath stealing.

"Mrs. Mills, are you okay?"

The bitch took my getting sick as an invitation to come into my house. I wiped my mouth with the back of my hand and threw open the bathroom door. It slammed against the wall, sure to leave a mark or dent.

"I did not tell you it was okay for you to come inside my house! Now, get the fuck out!" I couldn't believe the woman's nerve. I was all up in her face, ready to go to work. She didn't know me from a can of paint, but she thought it would be okay just to walk into my damn house. She'd better be glad that I didn't have a gun, or I would have shot her uppity ass.

"I know, and I'm sorry, but I was worried and wanted to make sure you were okay."

I could tell a lie at a hundred paces, and this bitch was lying her ass off. "Fine. Now that you see I'm okay, get the fuck out." Perhaps I could have been a little nicer, but she had tried my patience the second she crossed the threshold.

She started walking toward the door. "Are you moving?"

"Huh?" I stopped walking, confused.

"I see all the boxes, so I was wondering if you were moving."

"First of all, I want to know how you got this address. And second, it ain't none of your business what I'm doing."

"Oh, I'm sorry. I just thought with the boxes and all . . ." Her words trailed off.

I followed her all the way to the door. She annoyed me, and I didn't even know who she was. She said she was working for Gavin, but I wanted to know in what capacity. "You still didn't say what you want with me." I held the door tightly by the knob, with her ass on the other side. I was careful to keep an eye on that briefcase, just in case she decided to use it again to stop me from closing the door.

"Ah, yeah, that's right. I'm the attorney representing him, and I was wondering—"

"Oh." Wrong answer. If she were working for the prosecution, she might have a little more luck getting me to talk.

"Mrs. Mills, I know you and your son are having problems right now, but let me assure you that having him cool his heels in jail is not the way to handle it." She talked fast, her words flowing out of her mouth like she was used to saying a lot in a little amount of time.

"Excuse you? You don't know anything about me or my so-called problems." I was pissed. I didn't know who this bitch thought she was, but she could kiss my entire black ass. I slammed the door shut, but she wasn't done.

She started aggressively knocking on the door.

I yanked it open again. "If you don't get away from my door, I am going to call the police," I shouted. My stomach was beginning to hurt, and I knew I had only another few minutes before I would be throwing up again.

"Mrs. Mills, I think your son is sick, and I don't believe he will receive the treatment he needs behind bars."

Regardless of what hell Gavin had put me through, as his mother I could not bear the thought of him being sick. "Sick? What's wrong with him?" Visions of him hurt, bleeding, or worse floated through my head. I didn't want anything bad to happen to him.

"I think your son has some mental issues that need to be addressed. If I could just have a little of your time."

"Ain't nothing wrong with that boy's mind. He's as sane as you and me. Now, I think you need to leave." I tried shutting the door again. She almost had me, but I knew immediately where this was going, and I didn't want any parts of it.

"Perhaps you can tell me when I can speak with your husband, Gavin's father."

Once again I froze. This woman knew what buttons to push. I had to give it to her; she got my attention each and every time. "He don't live here." I started to tell her that I and Gavin's father had never married, but again, it was none of her business.

"Do you know where I can find him?"

"Yeah, I know, but maybe you should try finding him like you found me. Good luck with that." I shut the door for good this time, but I was chilled to the bone. I did not like the vibe I got from that woman, and I had a strange feeling I would be seeing her again.

Chapter Sixteen

MEREDITH BOWERS

Since it was still early, I decided to head back to the office. There were a few things I wanted to handle while they were still fresh in my mind. I was supposed to meet with a realtor later that afternoon to go look at office spaces. I had tried doing it myself but wasn't having much luck.

I put away my things and called Young, the newest member of our staff, and asked him to come into my office. Young was fresh out of college, hungry, and very easy on the eyes. I wasn't the type of person to fuck around with someone from work, but if I were, he would definitely be my type.

He knocked on the door but didn't wait for me to invite him in. He just walked in and took a seat. He had his iPad in his hands and was ready to take notes. The other thing about Young I liked was he exuded confidence. He had all the ladies running around the office, acting like fools, even the older white ones, who should have known better. Cracked me up.

"What's up?" Young inquired.

"I've got something I need for you to handle. Actually, it's two things. How's your schedule looking?"

"Depends. My days are pretty full. They got me posted at the jail, trying to pop fools before they fuck up and incriminate their own selves."

"I feel ya. I started out this way too, before I bit the bullet and went back to school. It may be tedious, but at least it helps make the day go by quickly."

He said, "Yeah, you're right about that. Plus, it gives me a chance to get back at the same motherfuckers who tried to take away my freedom."

"You like this kind of stuff, don't you?"

This was working out even better than I thought.

"Yep. I'm even thinking about going back to school too. It really pisses me off how the system will railroad you, and once they get you, they lock you down inside, man, trying to break you and shit. Oh, my bad. I didn't mean to cuss in front of you."

"It's cool, Young. I feel ya. Look, I got a case that might be right up your alley. I am going to try to get my client off because I think he's crazy as all outdoors. I need you to find out as much about him as you can." I pushed over the files I had created along with the case file from the jail I'd acquired.

"What type of stuff are you looking for?" He browsed through the manila folder.

"Anything that will help me. Read his file and the charges. I've already spoken to his mother, and she won't be very helpful, but I want to know why. I also need you to find out what you can about his father, and he's got a twin. Check him out too."

"Okay. Sounds pretty easy. Is that it?"

"No. There is another lady involved. It's in the paperwork I gave you too. Her name is Angie Simpson. She doesn't have a file, so I couldn't find out much about her except where she lives. I need you to serve her with this deposition notice and see what you can find out about her as well. I'm trying to find out something about her that will rattle her cage if I need to."

"All right, then."

He got up to leave, and I admired his ass.

"Oh and, Young, keep this to yourself, okay?"

"Uh, sure. I'll get back to you as soon as I know something. I'll try to get the notice of deposition served today."

"Wait. I think the girl lives with her parents. I'd like to have her served when they are not around, if at all possible."

Young raised his eyebrow, and I could almost see the wheels turning inside his head, but he didn't say anything about it.

"Okay, I'm on it."

I watched his ass as he left the office. Something about the young man did it for me. I loved his style of dress and his swagger. He had a unique fashion sense and wasn't swayed by the traditional stuck-up gear that most other men wore. It was hard to break my gaze, but I did. Young was definitely off-limits to me.

"Hi. I have an appointment to see Gayle Jackson." I was standing in a modest mortgage office with a nice view of the public square.

"Gayle went down the street to get some coffee. I'm her sister/partner, LaDena, and you must be Mrs. Bowers."

"It's Miss, and yes, I am." I looked around the office as I took a seat. It was a nice, and something just like this would definitely suit my needs. I needed something around the same size, with one exception. I needed my own private office.

I didn't have long to wait for the person whom I assumed to be Gayle to return to the office. She was carrying a brown tray with three cups of coffee from Starbucks.

"Your appointment is early." LaDena nodded in my direction.

Gayle said, "Oh, man, I'm so sorry. I thought I'd timed it right. I love coffee, and we can't seem to make a decent cup between the three of us."

Gayle had an infectious laugh, and I instantly liked her.

I said, "That's quite all right. I just got here."

"Do you want some coffee? You can have mine. I didn't put anything in it." Gayle walked toward me with a cup in hand.

"No, I'm fine. I can't drink coffee this late in the day. If I did, I'd be up for the rest of the night."

"Shoot, it don't bother me. I drink it all day. It's when I don't have it that I become a problem."

"You ain't never lied." LaDena came toward me, carrying a cup of coffee she'd taken from her sister. She gave that cup to a lady in the other office who was on the phone. "That's Tabatha. She mainly shows residential properties, while Gayle and I specialize in commercial listings."

I followed Gayle into her office area and took a seat in front of her desk. As far as privacy went, there wasn't any in these cubicles, but it obviously worked for them.

"Thanks for coming in. I have some paperwork for you to fill out, and then we can go look at some properties." Gayle pushed a clipboard toward me with a pen.

I was a little irritated, because I thought shopping for real estate would be more like car shopping. Find what you want; then fill out the paperwork. Obviously, I was wrong.

"Your office is so quiet, it would drive me nuts." I could actually hear the ink coming out of my pen as I filled out the financial questionnaire.

Gayle laughed. "Trust me, it's not like this all the time. You just came on a good day."

"You ain't lying. We're being good because we have company. We have our fights, but it's all love," LaDena added, which reinforced my desire to have a private office.

I couldn't afford to have personal information floating around an office without the privacy of walls and doors and continue to practice law. I would be setting myself up for a lawsuit. I could tell LaDena was a handful and had her two cents to say about everything. But again, different strokes for different folks. I pushed the completed paperwork back to Gayle and glanced at my watch. I didn't know about her, but I had a million things I still wanted to get done in my day, so I was eager to get going.

"Now, tell me what you're looking for, and we can get started." Gayle turned away from her computer and perused my paperwork.

I noted she was checking her Yahoo account.

"I am opening a small law firm, and right now I need space for, say, two, maybe three offices with a receptionist area. I'm really not interested in buying right now. I'd rather lease the property and see how things go from there."

"That's a very good idea. You said over the phone you liked this area, so I've already picked out a few locations for us to see. Give me a few minutes to get the keys together and we can go."

"Okay."

I tried not to eavesdrop on the conversation in the cubicle next to me, but my curiosity was piqued. Since I wasn't doing anything else, I listened. The lady named Tabatha was speaking to someone who was obviously upset. I might not have paid attention to the call, but I heard the chick say my name. My name wasn't uncommon, but I could go weeks without meeting anyone with the same name.

If I could have moved into the cubicle next to me without making a total ass of myself, I would have. My gut told me she was speaking to the same lady I'd met with earlier today, and Tabatha confirmed it when she called the person she was speaking to Gina. I couldn't believe my luck, because the odds of this happening were incredibly small. But it was happening, and whatever was being said had Tabatha upset too.

I pulled out my phone and pretended to be absorbed in responding to an e-mail, but I really was texting Young to add Tabatha Fletcher to the list of people I wanted to know more about.

"You ready to go?" Gayle cleared her throat, and I feared I'd been busted.

"Uh, yeah. I'm sorry. I was lost in my own little world."

Gayle said, "I see."

I heard the censure in Gayle's tone, but I chose to ignore it. We gathered our things and went to the parking lot. We rode in silence, which was a good thing, because I was deep in thought. There was something from that phone call I needed to hear, and it pissed me off to have missed it.

"You seemed a little interested in Tabatha's phone conversation."

I inhaled deeply. I hadn't expected Gayle to boldly call me out, and I realized I'd underestimated her. "No, it wasn't her conversation. I wasn't paying attention to it. I just happened to tune in when I thought I heard my name, that's all." I hoped she'd be satisfied with my response.

"Oh, okay. I was going to say that's one of the problems with using cubicles for offices . . . no secrets. They look nice as hell, but everybody is all up in your business."

"Yeah, I see. I'm gonna definitely need some doors in my office and some thick-ass walls too."

We both laughed.

Gayle made me uncomfortable. I felt like she was looking right through me, and I couldn't wait for this little excursion to be over with. "How long is the typical lease for commercial properties?"

"Oh, they vary upon location for obvious reasons. You wouldn't want to lease a property for a restaurant for a year and have to move the following year because the owner wouldn't agree to renew, now would you?"

"Uh, I guess not." I despised mindless chitter chatter.

"Of course you wouldn't. A restaurant's location is almost as important as the food and the decor. If you take a nice five-star restaurant and move it into the hood, chances are most, if not all, of your customers will be looking for somewhere else to dine."

She had a point. I wasn't trying to duck and dodge bullets or possibly get carjacked just to eat.

"I never thought about it that way, but you are so right. Luckily for me, I won't have those constraints. Eighty-five percent of my business will be conducted somewhere other than my office. I chose Covington for my office because it's close to my home, but I have a large Atlanta client base, and I know they won't want to travel all the way out here."

"Exactly. When are you looking to open up your office?"

"I don't have an exact date in mind yet. I am winding down the last few cases I have on my current job so I can concentrate on the office. I'd like to get a place and start setting it up so that when I'm finished with my cases, I can start work right away without delay."

My phone chirped, signaling to me that I had a message. Gayle looked like she was annoyed by the interruption, but I couldn't have cared less. The text from Young read, She got served, but I need to talk to you ASAP. I smiled. Not only was Young good-looking, but he was also fast. Gayle continued to talk, and I tried to pay attention, but my mind was a thousand miles away.

Chapter Seventeen

TABATHA FLETCHER

If it were possible to have a monsoon in my head, it would adequately describe how I was feeling at the moment. It felt like someone had taken all my thoughts, emotions, and good sense and thrown them up in the air. I was being assaulted with memories that I thought I had buried in my backyard. I imagined my brain cells crashing into one another, exploding against a solid bass drum inside my head. The pain was so intense, I wanted to cry out. But I couldn't without letting everyone know something bad was happening.

I clutched the phone to my ear, afraid if I let one finger go, I'd lose my grip on reality. My hands trembled, adding to my pain, because each time my body shook, its tremors bounced off the drum echoing in my mind.

"Gina, calm down. I can't understand you when you get like this."

Gina was babbling, and the only thing I understood for sure was it involved Gavin. Whatever it was, it had to be major, because it obviously made her forget she had cut me off and hadn't spoken to me for the last several days. I was relieved our tiff was over, but I wasn't sure I was ready for this new battle that was brewing.

"What?" I was in so much pain, I hadn't been paying attention to what she was saying.

"I said she wanted to know where to find Ronald!" Gina shrieked.

I gasped for air. "Did you tell her?" I felt like I was sucking oxygen from an air bag with holes in it. I placed my hand over my heart; it was beating very fast. It felt like it was about to leap out of my chest, despite my feeble attempt to keep it inside.

"Hell no. I told the bitch to find him the same way she found me."

Her words were muffled. It sounded like she had a wad of gum in her mouth and she was trying to speak around it.

I said, "Whatever it is that you are doing while you're trying to talk to me, I'm going to need you to stop. I can't make out what you are saying. Who was this chick, and why was she there?" Part of me wanted to rush over to Gina's house and get the information from her face-to-face, but the other part of me was scared she would see right through me. I willed myself to calm down so I didn't overreact and rat my own self out.

"She said she was an attorney. I forget her name, but she was working for Gavin."

"An attorney or a public defender?"

"What the hell difference does it make? They are both lawyers, aren't they?"

"Yes and no. An attorney is someone you pay for, and a public defender is appointed by the court."

She said, "Well, I don't give a fuck which one she is. All I know is the bitch came to my house and I don't like it."

"Right. What did she want?" I knew how Gina was, and she could go on for hours about nothing if I didn't keep prodding her along in the right direction.

"She made it sound like I was the reason Gavin was in jail. Said I was hurting him because he really needed help and he wouldn't get it in jail. How am I to blame? I did everything I could for that child."

Gina kept fussing, and it was a struggle for me not to get annoyed, especially since I believed she was part of the problem with Gavin. She was as much to blame as everyone else when it came to why Gavin was acting out. However, I didn't want to hear about Gavin right now. I wanted to know what all this had to do with Ronald.

I lied, "That's ridiculous, and you know it." I wondered how much of what Gina was telling me was actually said and what was imagined.

"But what if he is crazy and needs psychiatric help?"

I felt like I had been punched in the gut, and I practically choked. I was outraged. "She said that?"

"Well, no, but she implied it."

Just as I thought, Gina was overacting. It still couldn't be ignored, since the woman did take the time to come and see Gina in the first place. My head felt like it was going to explode. I wanted to choke Gina for dragging this out, when she could have just told me what I wanted to know without the drama.

"What did she want you to do?"

"She didn't get a chance to say. I kicked her out. I was sick to my stomach and didn't feel like dealing with her."

"You should have at least found out what she wanted." *Open up mouth and insert foot*. Damn, sometimes I hated that about myself. I tended to say exactly what was on my mind, without stopping to think how it would be received.

"I don't know why I called you. I forgot I wasn't speaking to you." Gina hung up.

I said to myself, "Great. Nice going, asshole."

Before I could get myself together, LaDena wheeled her chair over to my cubicle.

"What's going on now?" she said.

LaDena had made popcorn and was munching down on it like someone was going to take it from her. When she saw me looking at the bowl, she offered me some.

"No thanks." I got my purse from my desk drawer.

"Where are you going?"

"Damn, can't I have a little privacy around here?"

"Honey, please. You knew there were no walls when you signed on with us. If you ask me, your friend Gina is two Fruit Loops short of a box. I don't know why you fool with her siditty ass, anyway."

"No offense, but ain't nobody asked you." I was on the verge of getting pissed.

"You don't have to get all mad. I'm just saying. And I ain't forgot how you came in here the other day with coffee all over your clothes. Humph. Gonna get mad at me." She rolled her eyes.

"So I'm a klutz. Sue me." I was not about to get into a barb-trading exercise with her, because when this was over with, I still had to work there.

"Okay, if that's your story."

LaDena scooted out of my area, and I left before she decided to return. Her words were still ringing in my ears. But it wasn't her words that had me rushing out of the office; it was fear. If this lawyer was able to track Gina down, it would only be a matter of time before they tracked me down as well. I needed to know what to do about it.

"What the fuck you doing out here? I thought you gave up the pipe." Ronald rolled a joint and pressed it

closed with his large lips. He stood on his block like he
was the king of fucking Georgia.

"Screw you. I'm not here for no dope. I needed to see
you, and I knew where to come to find you."

"Well, you found me. What the fuck you want?"

He was angry, but I didn't give a fuck. I was angry
too. I never wanted to see his miserable ass again, but
this time it was necessary. I knew phoning him wasn't
going to work, because he'd ignore my call. It pissed
me off that he still looked the same and didn't appear
to have aged much. I couldn't believe I had once loved
him.

"I don't know why you got to cuss at me and shit. I've
done everything you've asked me to do," I said defen-
sively.

"No, you haven't."

"Yes, I did," I shouted. I knew I was loud, but I didn't
care. He plucked my nerves.

"Keep your damn voice down. You're going to scare
my people away."

Ronald was a smug bastard. He used people and
their addictions to get what he wanted in life. I hated
that about him. Part of me wanted to walk away and let
the shit hit the fan, but since I was involved, I couldn't
afford to do it.

"What haven't I done? Huh? What?"

"You're still friends with Gina. I told you I didn't like
it."

"You are not my fucking father, and you can't run my
life."

"You asked me what you didn't do, and I told you."

He turned his back, as if I were no longer visible,
and this infuriated me. He was so lucky I didn't carry
a weapon in my purse, because he would have been a
dead motherfucker.

"She was the only friend I had. You took everything else. Why couldn't I at least have that?"

He slowly turned around and looked me up and down like he were seeing me for the first time. "You looked better when you were sucking on your glass dick. At least it kept the weight off. You sure you're not here to score some more shit? I got it right here, and it's good too. I can even cook it up for you—just the way you like it."

He smiled for the first time, showing his pearly whites. Motherfucker didn't even have tartar buildup on his fucking teeth. His voice, smooth as butter, appealing as chocolate . . . and deadly for me, because one hit always led to another and another.

"I hate you." My words were forced between clenched teeth. Even though I knew what dope could do to me and everything I'd accomplished, my mind told me I could do just one. My body craved it. I realized my mistake too late. I'd awaken a sleeping giant by coming on the block and confronting my enemy.

"Then why are you here?"

Ronald twirled a plastic bag full of crack cocaine in front of me. Taunting me with it. I shut my eyes, but I could still see. I needed to get away from him as fast as I could. I needed to run, not walk, to the nearest meeting.

I said, "Ask Gina."

I laughed when he rubbed his neck, with a grimace on his face. He bore the scar from the fork Gina had planted in it.

"We don't talk. You, of all people, should know that."

"Tough. I was going to tell you, but since you wanted to be a shit, find out for yourself. But know this. I won't lie for you. Not again. Not this time. I'm done." I turned and ran back to the safety of my car before I broke down and gave in to my addiction. My drug of choice called me by name, but I was determined not to listen. I couldn't afford to.

Chapter Eighteen

COJO MILLS

I was worried sick about Gina. She said we'd go shopping, but I hadn't heard from her in weeks. I'd called her several times, but she hadn't returned any of my calls. I didn't feel comfortable just showing up at her house, but she was leaving me very little choice.

Without giving it a second thought, I picked up the phone and called my husband on base. "Merlin, have you spoken with Gina?"

"Sweetie, why didn't you ask me this while I was at the house? I could get in a lot of trouble if they catch me on the phone."

He didn't sound like he was angry, but these days I never knew what was going on in his head.

"I'm sorry. I didn't think about it till now. I've got too much time on my hands. I think I need to go back to work."

Dead silence followed.

I wondered if Merlin had hung up on me. I had not been back to work since his brother tried to kidnap me. Merlin had gotten used to me being at home and was watching me like a mother duck. He wanted me to stay home until after the baby was born, but it was slowly driving me crazy. I thought it was a temporary thing and maybe things would go back to normal. Thus far they hadn't. Merlin didn't even want to discuss my returning to work.

"Are you there?" I whispered.

"Yes. Somebody walked by. Listen, I can't talk now, but I don't want you thinking about going to work now. There will be plenty of time for working after the baby is born. Right now I wish you would relax and take care of yourself and our baby."

Merlin could be so sweet, and I was so fortunate to have him, so it baffled the hell out of me why I couldn't get his brother out of my head. Gavin was like a damn drug. I thought about him all the time. I had to be nuts. In my head, I knew the only reason why Gavin wanted me was that I belonged to his brother, but it still didn't stop me from lusting after him.

"Okay, babe. I'll see you when you get home."

He said, "All right, then."

I hurried off the phone, ashamed of my thoughts. I didn't realize he hadn't answered my question until after I'd hung up, but I didn't dare call him back. I rubbed my stomach, but I wasn't comforted. I had an ache deep inside of me, and I had no way to satisfy it. They say an idle mind is the devil's playground, and my mind was stagnant. I replayed every second I spent with Gavin over and over in my head like a warped VHS cassette.

I knew this behavior was crazy, but I couldn't help it. I even relived the night he abducted me. In my heart, I knew he would not seriously harm me, and I knew I'd overreacted when the police showed up. But I didn't have a choice, especially when I saw Merlin standing in the doorway. His eyes had asked what his lips dared not, and it had nearly broken my heart.

But I couldn't get the thought of Gavin being locked up because of me out of my head. I began to believe it was my fault. This type of stinkin' thinkin' could lead only to more pain, but I seemed incapable of stopping it. It wasn't like I was trying to ruin the life Merlin and I were creating, but I began to wonder if it would be enough.

It was unfortunate that I didn't have a circle of friends I could talk to about what I was feeling. Even if I did, I didn't know if I would confide in them. I was ashamed of my feelings because most of them involved sex. And if I allowed myself to think logically about the situation, I'd realize that without sex there really wasn't anything between Gavin and me. It wasn't like we enjoyed the same movies or had something else in common. I didn't know anything about him, other than the fact that he did what he wanted when he wanted to. He fucked better than I'd dreamed possible. He was an opportunist who saw what he wanted and took it. Was that a crime?

I turned on the television, hoping to get my mind off my problems, but turned it off after several minutes. Two hundred channels and I couldn't find a thing I wanted to watch. I tried reading, but that didn't work for me, either. My eyes kept seeing Gavin's face on the pages. I felt like I was being tormented, so I slammed the book closed.

"Fine. Fuck it." I went into the bedroom and started getting dressed. I was going to go do some shopping for the baby. In the past, shopping had a way of taking my mind off my troubles. I was hoping it would work for me today too. I had been holding off doing it in hopes of having Gina go with me, but with each passing day, it seemed as if it was not going to happen. I dialed her house one final time before I left and was about to leave a message when she picked up the phone.

"Hello," Gina answered.

"Uh, Gina, hi. It's Cojo. I thought I was going to have to leave another message. How are you?"

"I'm doing okay."

I waited a second or two to see if she would elaborate, but she didn't. "Good, good. I am bored out of my mind. Merlin won't let me go back to work, and these walls are closing in on me."

"I feel you, but I welcome the break. When you've been working as long as I have, you learn to appreciate the small stuff, like peace and quiet."

"Yeah, well, we'd better stock up, because it will be over with before we know it." I laughed. I could have kicked myself in the ass for even alluding to her pregnancy. For all I knew, she might have had an abortion, and my stupid ass brought it up.

"Yeah, you got a point," Gina said.

She didn't sound upset, and I was glad that I hadn't said anything to piss her off. If her emotions were raging out of control like mine, we'd have been arguing by now.

"I'm about to go do some shopping. If I don't get out of this house, I'm going to go nuts." I twirled my car keys on my finger.

"Shopping? That sounds like a great idea. What are you looking for?"

"Well, I haven't done any shopping for the baby, and it will be here before you know it."

"Do you mind if I tag along? I could use a few things myself."

This was the confirmation I needed, so I assumed she was going to go ahead and keep her child. "I would love for you to go with me. Would you like for me to pick you up?"

"Uh, I can come get you, if you don't mind driving with me. I'm not a good passenger. I have this control thing going on."

I tossed my keys on the table. "That's fine with me, because I hate to drive. I'll see you when you get here."

I hung up the phone, happy to be getting out of the house. I almost called Merlin to let him know but didn't. Even though I was fairly certain Gina would be keeping her baby, I knew she hadn't told Merlin, so I refused to get in the middle.

"Gina, I never knew shopping could be so much fun. Thanks so much for going with me," I said, sitting my bags on the floor between the couch and the coffee table.

"I had just as much fun. It's been a long time since I've spent time just hanging at the mall."

"Hell, we didn't have a choice but to hang. We both got tired."

We busted out laughing. We'd spent the entire day shopping and talking about folks, and not once had a dark cloud passed over our heads. What surprised me the most was I didn't have to work at finding something to say to her. Gina was really a nice lady, and I was glad to finally get a chance to spend time with her.

Gina said, "I know that's right. My ankles are all swollen, but I think we got some good deals."

"I'm going to hide this stuff before Merlin gets home and take me a nice hot bath."

"Boy, that sounds good too. I can't remember the last time I actually got in the tub and soaked."

"It's the best. I try to do it at least once or twice a week. It's great for swelling and relaxing." I was pumping myself up and was eager for Gina to leave so I could get to my bath.

"Well, I won't hold you up. If you ever feel like going shopping again, give me a call."

I was touched. "Careful, Gina. I'm one big hormone. If you're not careful, I'll be crying like a baby."

"Who you telling? I haven't cried this much in my entire life. I hope it doesn't mean I'm having a girl. I've got a box of clothes I saved from Merlin and Gavin that I would love to put to use again."

"I'm not mad at you. I wish we had something like that, especially since Merlin won't let me return to work yet. I don't want him stressed out about bills."

"Child, don't you worry. If Merlin told you he got it, it's all good. That's one thing I can say about that boy. He knows how to handle his business, and he's very responsible. Of the two, Merlin was always the more reliable."

As much as I wanted Gina to leave so I could take my bath, I also wanted to hear what she had to say about the brothers. I was tired of all the closed mouths, so I invited Gina to stay a little longer. "Do you need to rush home? I am pining for a cup of tea. Would you like some?" I held my breath, because I didn't want to push this truce, but I couldn't resist.

"Yeah, sure, I'd like some, and if you've got anything chocolate and sweet, I'll take some of that too."

"Here I go again, treating you like company. The next time you come over, you're family." I went into the kitchen and prepared our snacks.

"We don't have to wait until next time," Gina said as she followed me into the kitchen.

"Good. Look in the cabinet. I've got all types of junk food. I know it isn't good for my waistline, but, hey, I won't tell if you don't."

Gina said, "Chile, chocolate is soul food. Didn't you know?"

We both started laughing. It was so natural, and it was hard to believe that mere months ago we were mortal enemies. I set out the tea, and Gina grabbed a little bit of everything and arranged it on a plate. It was a fat woman feast, which I was sure I'd regret later.

I said, "I'm so glad Merlin isn't here to see this. He would have a stroke."

"I don't mean no harm, but until a man can do what we do, I don't want to hear it. You and I both know if a man had to have a child, the human race would cease to exist."

"You ain't lying. I don't think they could handle being a woman, period."

Gina said, "Yeah, we got the short end of the stick too. We have to work harder and get paid less both in and outside the home. Monthly cramps would make a grown man cry, and thong underwear . . . Jeez, don't get me started on thongs. Our opinion doesn't count for shit, and we're usually right. The only place our name is listed first is on the damn birth certificate, which makes sense when you think about it, because at the end of the day, we're probably the only one who sticks around. Men can turn off the switch and walk away, while a woman is stuck like Chuck."

Gina's joke started to sound like a tirade. I knew she was speaking from her own personal experience, and my heart went out to her. I was also glad my reality was not hers. Gina had confirmed that Merlin was a winner and not a quitter.

I didn't know anything appropriate to say, and I damn sure was not going to question Gina about the father of her child. I assumed it was Merlin's father, but if I'd learned one thing in life, it was never to assume anything.

"This chocolate has got me talking crazy. Used to be alcohol, but go figure, now it's chocolate."

She gave a humorless laugh, and it sounded like she was on the verge of tears. I was torn. I didn't want to say or do the wrong thing.

"Gina, I don't have many friends or much experience with other women, but I like you, and I think I would even like you if you weren't my mother-in-law." I paused. I didn't know if she was going to turn on me, so I waited for a few beats. "I feel like you're hurting, and I want you to know if you need me, I'll be here for you. I'll try to stay in my lane, so tell me what you need and I'm there."

There was so much more I wanted to say, but I didn't know how to say it. I wasn't trying to make a long, drawn-out speech. I was just trying to let her know she didn't have to do this on her own.

Tears glistened in both of our eyes, but they didn't fall. Not only was I telling Gina what I was willing to do for her, but I was also silently asking her to do the same for me. I didn't know what was going to happen, and I needed her guidance and support.

Gina said, "Come over here and give me a hug." Gina opened her arms wide, and I fell into them, unashamed. "I didn't come over here to get all sappy and shit," she said and sniffed.

"I'm sorry." My voice was muffled, as I was trying to get her shirt out my mouth.

"Shut up. You spoke from your heart, and I've got your back too."

I didn't get the answers I wanted, but I felt like I opened the door of opportunity.

Chapter Nineteen

MEREDITH BOWERS

Young caught up with me as I was leaving the office for lunch. It was perfect timing, because it had been a couple of days since he said he needed to talk to me and I hadn't been able to catch up with him. He called me a couple of times. I was going to call him back, but I kept getting distracted.

"Have you had lunch yet?" I asked.

"No. You buying?"

He gave me a fifty-megawatt smile, which I couldn't resist. There was something about a man and a beautiful smile that would get me every time. I didn't know much about Young, but I could tell that he lived on the edge and thumbed his nose at authority. I could tell as much by the way he dressed and often times by the way he spoke. Depending on his environment, he could change his persona. One minute he would be straight hood with baggy jeans and a hoodie, which went over very well at the jail, but then he would switch up and get boardroom savvy in a New York minute with a bow tie and red suspenders.

I said, "I guess so. What do you have a taste for?"

I saw the way his eyes twinkled at my provocative suggestion, but I didn't flinch. I wasn't trying to mix things up with him, but I needed to make sure I got what I wanted from him before I dismissed his fine young ass.

He said, "I'm not picky, and since you're driving and buying, I'll take whatever you want to give me."

I wasn't the only one teetering on the edge of impropriety. It was somewhat refreshing after dealing with all the stuffed shirts in the office. There were six black people working for the Newton County DA's office. The other four, in my opinion, weren't worth the breath God gave them. Two of them knew they were token niggas and played the role of office snitch and bitch. I had no use for them, because I had no respect for a person who was willing to throw someone else under the bus just so they could get ahead. Not cool. The other two black people were older and more subservient. They would do only what they were told to do and would never think of trying anything outside the box. They were sure to keep their good government jobs without any aspirations for anything better than punching a clock. Pathetic.

"I'm fiendin' for some pancakes."

"At two o'clock in the afternoon?" Young said, laughing.

"Sure. We can go to IHOP, and you can get what you want. They serve all kinds of stuff. And I can get my sugar rush on. Does that sound all right to you?"

"Like I said before, I'm good with whatever."

He winked at me, and I found myself smiling back at him. It was all in good fun, and as long as he knew not to cross the line, I'd play along.

"How did your meeting go?" He looked at me.

"Meeting?" I frowned since I didn't remember talking to Young about any meetings.

"When I texted you, you said you were in a meeting."

"My bad. I've been going at it so hard, I don't even remember what I said to you."

He said, "I take it things went well, then?"

"Better than expected, actually." I was not about to share too many details about what had actually transpired. Although I thought he was a pretty cool dude, I still didn't know him enough to trust him with those details.

"Good. I'm glad it worked out for you. I made a mental note to be in the office when you came in, but I forgot about it."

"Maybe you need to go digital and leave the mental shit alone," I said, laughing.

"Oh, so you got jokes? All right, then. It's all good."

He wasn't offended, and I liked that. I enjoyed people who didn't take themselves so seriously that they forgot to laugh, if only at themselves.

We didn't talk again until after we reached IHOP and ordered our food.

I said, "So have you found out anything I might be interested in?"

He pulled a small notepad out from the inside pocket of his suit jacket, which he'd laid over the seat next to him. His tie was flipped over his shoulder, and he'd also rolled his sleeves up slightly above his wrists. He wore a band of some sort on his wrist.

I'd noticed the bands before, because they always matched his suits, but I'd never asked him what they symbolized. I could tell he took good care of his clothes. It told me that either he didn't have much and had to take care of what he had, or he just liked to look good. Either scenario worked for me. I couldn't stand a man with gravy-stained ties and scuffed-up shoes.

He wiped his mouth with his napkin before he spoke. "Where do you want me to start?"

"Let's start with Gavin. I need to go see him later this week."

I watched his perfect lips move as he read through a few pages from his notepad.

"Well, he spent some time in the joint and hasn't been back in Atlanta long. I don't know why he was sent there, because his records are sealed, but I have a friend working on getting me the scoop. Prior to his arrest this time, he worked as a bartender at a strip club. He's had no other arrests since he's been released from there."

"I knew all of that. What did you find out about his parents?"

He sighed. "I wish I knew exactly what you were looking for so I could tailor my search. You know what I mean?"

He had a point, so I couldn't get mad at Young.

"What else?"

"His father lives in Alpharetta, Georgia, with his wife. The mother, Tabatha, lives in Covington. They never married, and I don't think she's been active in his life."

"Wait, what did you say?"

"I don't think his mother has been active in his life."

"No, you said, 'Tabatha.' I thought his mother's name is Gina, at least that was the name of the woman I went to see."

He shook his head. "That's not the name on the birth certificate. Someone went to a great deal of trouble to conceal it, but Gavin and Merlin Mills were born to Tabatha Fletcher and Ronald Mills. You might have spoken to his common-law wife, but Georgia doesn't recognize common law. Ronald did marry another woman several months ago. From what I can tell, Ronald lived in Ohio until recently, but Gina raised his illegitimate children."

"Wow. You know what this means?" I said excitedly.

"I'm sure I don't have a clue," Young said, laughing.

"Right. Don't worry about it. This is good. Anything else?"

I was so excited, I wasn't even hungry anymore. I wanted to go see Gavin. I was pretty certain he didn't know who his birth mother was. I was also sure once he found out, the shit was going to hit the fan.

He said, "I still have a few more things to confirm, but I can have a full report on your desk by the close of business tomorrow. Is that good?"

"It's perfect. You just don't know."

"And you are so not going to tell me, right?" He stared at me.

"Right."

I really wanted to bring Young into the fold and tell him everything, but I wasn't sure how he'd react. He was new to the department and still green around the gills. He might not understand some of the hard tactics I was using in this case or my desire to walk away from the department with this win under my belt, regardless of whether or not it is warranted. I tried to get the waitress's attention to make our orders to go.

"Wait. I have some more info about the chick you wanted served."

"Oh damn, I forgot all about her. Were you able to serve her without her mother knowing about it?"

"Well, I guess you can say that. Her mom died in a car accident. I had to serve the papers while the chick was in the hospital."

"Are you fucking kidding me? Why didn't you tell me?"

"I told you I needed to talk to you ASAP, and I left you two messages. What else was I supposed to do?"

"Fuck. What happened?"

The whole time he was talking, I was trying to figure out how this could benefit my client.

"I was following them, and the girl's mom ran a red light and got clobbered by a bus. I stuck around and waited for them to be transported to the hospital. The mom went through the windshield and died instantly, but the girl was wearing her seat belt."

"What about the baby?"

Young shook his head no. I wanted to leap up from the table and kiss him, but I knew he would not understand. As tragic as the news was, it was the best news my client would ever receive. If there wasn't a baby, the case could disappear. I sat back in my chair.

He said, "You all right?"

"Yeah. I guess I'm in shock. How's the girl doing?"

"She's cool. Actually, I think she's relieved about the baby. She took the papers and didn't cuss me out, so what does that tell you?"

"Did she flirt with you?"

Young blushed, showing both his dimples. This boy was adorable.

He popped his collar. "Well, you know."

We shared a laugh. I was going to have to rethink my plans for Young. I might have to make some plans for this young man's future.

"You think you can get her to do the deposition this week in my office?"

"Which day do you want her?" He pulled out his phone and started scrolling through some numbers.

"It's like that?"

"Is nine o'clock tomorrow okay?"

"I'm cool with that."

"Good. Glad I could be of assistance."

Chapter Twenty

GINA MEADOWS

I was curled up in a knot in front of the television, trying not to get sucked into the soap operas playing nonstop on all the regular channels. They were good diversions from the real-life drama I was living, but I was tired of my life as a reality star. Cojo crossed my mind often, and I forced myself not to call and burden her with my troubles. My situation was so much different from hers. She had a husband who worshipped the ground she walked on, and I was confident he would be there for her when times got hard. I could feel the tide of depression rise around me like a shroud. I fought to push it back before it consumed me. Sometimes I was successful, but there were days when the only thing I could do was ride it out. I feared today would be one of those days.

A television commercial penetrated the fog surrounding me. Before I could talk myself out of it, I picked up the phone and made a call I hoped would change my life.

"Georgia Psychological Association. How may I direct your call?"

A huge knot grew in my throat, which prevented me from answering the question. I fought the urge to hang up the phone as my fingers began to tremble. I felt like

I was in a fight for my life and I was the biggest obstacle I needed to overcome.

"Uh." I hadn't uttered but two letters, and it felt like I'd recited the Gettysburg Address backward.

"Yes? How may I direct your call?" the voice repeated.

I expected to hear impatience and irritation, but I didn't. I attempted to push past the knot in my throat. It felt like every nerve ending in my body was screaming at me to give up, but I was determined to make a change. If not for me, I could at least do it for the sake of my child.

Speaking barely above a whisper, I said, "The television said I should call if I was feeling sad or lonely. It said I should pick up the phone if I felt like hurting myself or someone else."

"Excellent. You did the right thing. Let me get someone on the line to speak with you. Please don't hang up. It will be just a moment."

During the ten seconds I was on hold, I heard voices in my head telling me I was crazy. They said I was being stupid, but I refused to listen. Just admitting I had those kinds of thoughts empowered me and made me feel hopeful.

I was on hold for less than a minute, but it felt like hours as I fought my inner demons. I had probably seen the same commercial a million times, but today, for some reason, it spoke to me. It was almost like the actors had put down their scripts and had called my name.

Someone said, "Hello?"

"Yes, I'm here." I felt a great sense of urgency as an even bigger knot formed and blocked my windpipe. It was like drowning on land. I couldn't get enough air.

What if this lady thinks I'm crazy or, even worse, tries to take my child away from me? Suddenly, I was angry with myself for wasting time on the call.

"My name is Helen. I'm so glad you called."

This bitch doesn't even know me. Why the hell is she going to just lie in my face and shit? For all she knows, I might be a bomb-toting vigilante ready to blow her shit up! "I'm sorry to have bothered you." I was madder than a crippled crab without a crutch. I wanted to punch the shit out of something.

"Wait. Don't hang up. I know exactly how you're feeling right now."

"You don't know shit about me," I snapped. I felt a lecture coming on, and I was not in the mood to hear it.

"Oh, but I do. I was in your same shoes less than six months ago."

"And now you're a fucking authority?" I didn't know where all my anger came from, but I had no problem dumping it on the bitch who had answered the phone.

"No, but I believe I have walked in your shoes before. And I can do it again if I don't do the things I need to do to take care of myself," she calmly stated.

"I guess you're waiting for me to ask how you do it." I really did want to know, especially if she suffered the same way I did. But the voice warned she was pulling my chain.

She said, "I didn't know enough about what was going on with me to seek help. Thank the Lord, help found me before I was able to give in. But it cost me. I almost killed my child and myself too."

Her confession left me feeling a little numb, and I wanted to know more but was afraid to ask, so I just hung on the phone like a drowning man holding on to a life preserver in the middle of the ocean.

"Don't know if I will ever make things right again. Hell, I don't know if my child will ever look at me the same way, but I'm going to keep trying."

I could hear the emotion in her voice, and it zapped my anger, nipped it in the bud, and made me willing. I needed to hear what she had to say, because she was right. I'd been down that road before. Now, more than ever, I wanted to change. I couldn't afford to be reckless with my life or the one I carried inside of me.

Helen must have thought I hung up. "Are you still there?"

"I'm here." I wasn't sure what was supposed to happen next, so I waited.

"What's your name, sweetie?"

"Gina." My heart was beating so loudly, I wondered if she could hear it.

"Gina, where are you right now? We have a group discussion tonight that you might find helpful, but I thought maybe we could get together for coffee."

"I'm not sharing my life with a bunch of strangers."

"You don't have to share anything if you don't want to. I just want you to come and meet some of my friends. No pressure."

"I'll think about it. Give me the information, and I'll see. In the past I'd medicate myself when I was feeling bad, but I can't do it now with the baby and all."

This was as much of a commitment as I was willing to make. At least it was a start in the right direction. If they couldn't help me, it might be enough for me to know there were other people whose thoughts sometimes took them places they didn't want to go.

"Gina, if you're like me, it's easy to give in, especially if you're alone. I am here for you . . . if you need me."

One of the main reasons why I was ready for a change was I didn't want to repeat the same mistakes I made when I raised Gavin and Merlin. For the first time, I was ready to admit that something was wrong with me. Tabatha used to say I resented them because they were not my biological children. I disagreed, but now I was beginning to believe it went deeper than that. My feelings of low self-worth and depression went back as far as I could remember. There would be times when all I could do was go to school and come home. During those bad times, as I liked to call them, my grades would suffer, and I would virtually cut myself off from the world.

There was no rhyme or reason to those feelings. It wasn't like a menstrual cycle or something I could plan for. The feelings came and went like a slow-moving storm, and I couldn't get out of the way. As I hung up the phone, I felt the familiar tug of emotional warfare approaching, and it surprised me. In the past, I thought I was incapable of stopping it, but with this new awareness, I felt somewhat empowered. It was a little scary. But on a deeper level, I was ready for the fight. I tossed the phone onto the sofa and went to get dressed. I wasn't sure I was going to make it to the meeting, but I damn sure was gonna try.

Chapter Twenty-one

MERLIN MILLS

I was having one of those days when everything I touched seemed to turn to shit. The day had started out with a terrible migraine I couldn't seem to shake. I glanced at the digital clock sitting on my desk and winced. The Excedrin wasn't working, and I was tempted to ask the sergeant if I could duck out early, but I didn't want to answer any questions. The phone rang, startling me out of the mini daze I was in. I snatched the phone off the receiver to silence the ringing.

"Specialist Mills."

"Back that shit down a notch, nigga. It's just me," Braxton said, laughing.

I smiled through my pain. Braxton Harris was my oldest friend and was like a brother from another mother to me. "What's up?"

"I ain't want nothing. I was just checking on you. You know how we do."

He was right. Braxton was the one who kept the lines of communication open. If it was up to me, he'd never hear from me, because I wasn't much of a phone person. Lucky for me, he didn't take offense.

I said, "Yeah, it's all good. Cojo is driving my ass to drink. Other than that, everything is everything."

"Oh, say it's not so. Don't tell me there is trouble in paradise?"

I bristled at his remark, but I instantly let it go. I knew Braxton wasn't coming from a bad place, but it was uncanny how he was able to home in on my troubles.

"No, we're good, but you know with the baby and all, she's like a stick of dynamite. The littlest thing can light her fuse."

He said, "Yeah, I heard women can get a little sick in the head when they have babies."

"You ain't even lied."

I thought about the argument that had started my day, when I was leaving the house. I made the big mistake of drinking the last of the milk with my cereal. She said I wasn't being sensitive to her needs. Hell, she didn't even like milk, but I bit my tongue and took the abuse. We lived less than one block from the store, and she didn't have to go to work. It would have taken ten damn minutes to go get some more. So I got in the car and drove to the convenience store, even though it made me late for work, and brought her some milk, and that was when the headache started.

Braxton said, "So do you want to catch a drink before you head on in?"

"You throwing?" I laughed. This was my way of asking who was going to pick up the tab.

"Yeah, nigga, pitching all night long if you can hang."

This was another code, letting me know his day was probably as fucked up as mine.

"Oh Lord. Where do you want to meet?"

"Let's hit our old spot on Old National Highway. I haven't been there in a minute. I need one or two of their strong drinks in rapid succession."

I knew exactly where he was coming from. I just needed to call home and let Cojo know I was going to be late and hope like hell she didn't chose tonight to pitch a fit. I said, "All right. I'll meet you there by four, and if I get there before you do, I'm starting without you."

"Peace."

I glanced at the clock again. Two more hours 'til quitting time. I called Cojo to give her the heads-up. I wanted to hang with my friend, but I didn't want to spend the rest of my night paying for it. "Hey, baby. How are you feeling?"

"Fat, but otherwise okay."

I couldn't see her face, but she was definitely in a better mood than she was this morning. But these days you never could tell when it was going to change. One minute she'd be walking around the house singing, and the next she'd be acting like someone had shot her favorite puppy. I had no idea pregnancy did this to women. I hoped things would change once the baby was born. I had to keep telling myself this was only temporary, but sometimes doubts and insecurities told me something else was wrong. Our marriage was too new for it to be anything else, but tiny slivers of doubt tried to work their way into my mind. I refused to let them take root and grow, though.

"Hey, that's my child you're carrying around, and I think it's a beautiful thing."

"You just wait until you have to help me tie my shoes, and then you'll see how beautiful you think everything is."

She was huffing like she was out of breath. Part of me wanted to ask her what she was doing, but I didn't want to be the match to light her fire.

"I'll still think you're beautiful. Besides, I might like to see your cute little ass stuck up in the air while you tie your shoes." I chuckled as the visual came alive in head.

"Humph. That ain't cute."

I could tell she was ready to get mad, so I decided to stop playing with her. Cojo was a fitness buff, and she believed in keeping her body right, so I was sure the added curves were working on her nerves.

"Hey, I wanted to let you know I'll be late coming home. Braxton called and asked me to have a few drinks with him."

Too late, I realized I'd told her what I was going to do, instead of asking her if there was anything she wanted to do first. This was something new she threw at me last week, and I'd decided then I wouldn't make the same mistake again.

She said, "Well, I guess that's that. Thanks for calling."

So much for trying to do things the right way. I could have avoided this argument if only I'd phrased it differently. It wasn't that she minded that I wanted to spend time with my friend, because I knew that wasn't the point. The point was she was home all day by herself without a life, as she so eloquently put it, while mine marched on. I thought it was a trick to get me to agree to her going back to work.

"Honey, wait. That didn't come out the way I meant it to."

"Oh, I think it came out exactly the way you wanted it to. But that's okay. You go out with your boy and have some fun. You know where I'll be. My fat ass will be parked on the sofa, as usual."

"Baby, if this is going to start another fight, I won't go."

I was getting a little ticked off. I understood somewhat where she was coming from, but I didn't understand why she couldn't just come right out and say she
didn't want me to go. It would be a whole lot simpler
and would save us both a lot of time and emotions. I
could hear Cojo breathing over the phone, so I knew
she didn't hang up, but she also didn't say the words to
absolve me from any perceived wrong, either.

I sighed loudly. "Never mind. I'll be home right after
work." I felt like I'd been punked, and it pissed me off.

"Merlin, don't mind me. I swear, I'm driving my own
self crazy. Tell Braxton I said hi. Do you want me to
hold anything for you for dinner?"

This sounded like the woman I married, but I wasn't
sure she was telling me the truth. I honestly didn't
want to deal with the drama. It wasn't worth it to me.

"Cojo, I'm coming home. Don't worry about it."

"Nonsense. Go hang out. It's not like you do it all the
time. Shoot, you might as well do it now, because when
the baby comes, you might not get the chance."

She'd made a good point. I believed I was ready for
the child, but I hadn't really thought past the birth
of the baby. I didn't think about how the baby would
change our lives, but it was much too late to worry
about it now, because ready or not, the baby was coming.

"Fine. Do you want me to bring something back for
you?"

She hesitated before she responded, "No, I don't
think so."

She hung up the phone, and I felt my headache returning. As I continued to watch the clock, I calculated
the pros and cons of my going home right after work.
On the one hand, Cojo would probably be happy as a

sissy in boot camp, but I would resent her for making me change my plans. In the end I decided to go hang out with Braxton and take my chances.

Braxton was not at the bar when I arrived, which surprised me because he didn't have as far to travel as I did. The place was fairly crowded for a weekday, but I managed to snag a table far enough from the bar for privacy but close enough so our glasses would never be on empty.

The early afternoon crowd was a mixture of men and women of various ages. When we first started coming to this place, it was predominately white, but as I looked around the sea of faces, I didn't spot one white face in the bunch. I was okay with this as long as management didn't fuck up and start serving watered-down drinks and raise their prices.

A lone dark-skinned woman tried to make eye contact with me. She was a cute sister with a nice smile and a banging body, but I couldn't hang. I wasn't even going to front about it. I held up my hand so she could see my ring.

"So?" she mouthed, showing practically ever tooth in her mouth.

I was flattered by the attention, but her boldness turned me off. I was a big proponent of going after the things you wanted in life, but I respected the sanctity of marriage. Even when I was single, I never got involved with married women. There were too many other women out there for me to get involved with that shit. I didn't need the hassle of looking over my shoulder, and I wasn't about to play second fiddle to some other nigga. Not to mention, I didn't want to repeat the sins of my father, who had zero respect for women.

I shook my head no to the lady, and she turned her attention elsewhere. I could tell she had an attitude, but I didn't give a royal fuck.

Braxton said, "Damn, man, what's up with the face? You look like you're mad at the world."

I stood up to give my longtime friend Braxton Harris a pound and a hug.

"Nah, man. The chick over there was trying to push up on a brother, and I was trying to put her down easy," I said, laughing.

"Which chick? Where?" Braxton's head was swinging left to right like a pendulum.

"Damn, bro, slow down. You thirsty or something?" I'd never seen this side of Braxton before. He almost never publicly lusted after a woman. It was normally the other way around. Between him and Gavin, I was usually the odd man out.

"Nigga, please." Braxton gave an uneasy laugh.

My eyes slid to the woman, and he followed my gaze. She looked us both up and down and smiled. I didn't like her look. Her eyes implied something more was going on with Braxton and me than two friends getting together for a few drinks.

"Stank bitch," I mumbled under my breath, but apparently loud enough for Braxton to hear.

"Oh no, not the *B* word. What's up with you? I ain't never heard you use that word before."

He was laughing, but I could hear the concern in his voice. He was right; I never used the word. Women to me were the most beautiful creatures on the earth, and I believed they'd earned my utmost respect. This funk I was in was affecting me and had me talking all crazy.

"Man, that woman peeking over here like we gay and shit. Hell, just because a brother don't come on to her don't mean they gotta be gay. I hate that shit, and I feel like walking over there and telling her too."

Braxton looked around to see who all was looking. His eyes stopped on the girl, but she rolled her eyes at him and turned away. "Man, you right. She just might be one of those stank bitches, after all. Fuck her. You got a wife at home."

I started laughing, but my chuckles died in my throat.

Braxton said, "You all right, man? Things going good at home?"

I signaled the bartender to get a refill and to order a drink for Braxton. I wanted to talk to someone about what I was feeling, but I wasn't sure how deeply I should go with him. "We cool, but, man, she be tripping. I know it's the baby and all, but damn, sometimes she really works my nerves."

"Wow. I heard women go through some changes, but since I haven't even come close to being in that situation, I don't have any firsthand experience."

"It's deep, man. One minute she's cool as ice cubes, and the next she's like somebody from a horror flick." I tried to make light of the situation, but there were days when I didn't even know this woman I married.

"Hang in there. I'm sure it's going to work out."

It wasn't much by way of encouragement, but I appreciated the attempt, anyway. "So what's going on with you? I haven't seen your ass in a minute."

"I can't complain. Taking things one day at a time. Nothing too serious, if you know what I mean."

I cocked my head and tried to read through the words my friend had said. Braxton and I were a lot alike when it came down to our family values. We both came from dysfunctional homes, so things like family and friends meant a lot to us. I couldn't even begin to think where I would be if I didn't have him to lean on through my rougher moments. "I hear you. I've been meaning to holla at you, but you know how things can get. Plus, I'm still reeling from all the shit that went down with my brother."

"What's going on with that? I haven't seen his monkey ass on the news, so I assume he's still behind bars."

We shared a laugh. He wasn't too fond of my brother and didn't bother pretending he did care for him. I understood where he was coming from. Just because Gavin was my brother didn't mean I had to like him.

"He's still in there, as far as I know. I haven't heard anything from him, thank God."

Braxton said, "Nigga, you'd be the last person he would call. Especially since he tried to take your woman from you again."

"I know, right? I just don't understand him. I've never done anything to him, but he was always riding my ass about something. This thing with Cojo took the shit to a whole other level."

Braxton knew a lot about what had happened throughout my childhood with Gavin, and even some of the shit Gina had done, but I hadn't told him Gavin slept with Cojo. I didn't want my best friend to look at my wife any differently just because my brother was fucked up in the head.

Braxton said, "Yeah, man, that shit was wild. Honestly, I couldn't believe he would go there. Fucked me up that day when I went by your house and saw his ass posted up like it was his apartment, instead of the other way around."

I felt like a needle had scratched across my favorite record. The headache, which had finally abated, came back with a vengeance. "Say what? When did you see Gavin at my house?" This was the first time I was hearing about him going to my house when Gavin was there. If Braxton noticed my discomfort, he didn't let me see it. My fingers tightened around my glass, and it felt like my eyes were going to pop out of my head.

"I stopped by the house when you were locked up to see if there was anything I could do, and his stupid-ass answered the door. Nigga wasn't wearing a shirt, so it kinda caught me off guard."

He tossed back his drink, totally oblivious about how his words were affecting me. He ordered us another round as I tried to make sense of what he'd said. My head felt like it was about to explode. Cojo had never mentioned anything to me about Gavin coming over to the house while I was in jail. And she certainly had never mentioned him being there half dressed. Part of me wanted to race home to find out what the fuck was going on, but I knew better than to react before I had more information.

"Oh yeah? I didn't know that." I tried to keep my words light and even, but it was hard. Images of my brother with my wife played before my eyes in disgustingly vivid detail, and it was too much to take. I closed my eyes and tried to pretend I was okay with what I was hearing.

"I think I surprised Cojo, too, because she looked frightened. No doubt the fucker was threating her then and she didn't tell me."

We paused while the waitress replaced both of our drinks. I tossed mine back and ordered another before she could walk away. At the rate I was going, I was probably gonna need to find another way home other than driving my car. The last thing I needed was to get stopped for a DUI and wind up back in the slammer. I laughed to hide the tears I felt like shedding.

I said, "So what did she say?" My teeth were clenched, and I was afraid of what he was going to tell me, but I needed to know.

"Come to think of it, she didn't say much. She said he was just leaving."

"She didn't tell you what he was doing there?"

"No, and I didn't ask. I thought it was weird, but hey. I didn't know what was going on."

I nodded my head. He wasn't the only one who didn't know what was going on. If things were on the up and up and there was nothing to hide, why didn't she tell me? Why did I have to find out from my friend that my brother was even there? Cojo had told me she hated Gavin and never wanted him to come over, so why the fuck was he in my house, damn near naked, when I wasn't there?

There had to be a reasonable explanation for this. But for the life of me, I couldn't figure out what it was. I didn't want to go off on Cojo half-cocked, but all my fingers kept pointing back to her.

"Damn, dog, what's wrong with you?"

Braxton was snapping his fingers in front of my face, trying to get my attention. I had so many questions going around in my head, I couldn't keep my fears to myself any longer.

"You fucked me up with your intel. I wasn't expecting it."

"Why? Something going on I don't know about?"

I really didn't want to discuss it with him, but I had to talk to someone. "I'm gonna tell you, but I swear, dog, I don't need it coming back to me later. All right?"

"Hell, man, you know I got you. You my boy." He ordered another round, and not a second too soon.

"I never told Cojo I had a brother. I know it was wrong, but I never thought about him. He was gone, and I didn't think I was going to see him again."

"That nigga is like nasty drawers. When you least expect it, they start to stink." Braxton sipped his drink.

His analogy might have been funny if we weren't talking about such a sensitive subject for me.

"Well, his stankin' ass showed up at my house right before I came home, and he, uh . . ." I couldn't get out the rest of the sentence as I fought back tears.

"Ah, hell no! Don't tell me."

I nodded my head, unable to completely fill in the blanks. From the look on his face, Braxton understood where I was going with it. I felt sick to my stomach. I got this way every time I thought about my brother sleeping with my wife. I gagged. I looked around the bar to see if anyone was watching. If I was going to puke, I'd rather do it in private instead of in front of total strangers. Especially one stranger in particular, who was already looking at me cross-eyed. Thankfully, she had moved on to another part of the room and wasn't dogging my moves.

I said, "She told me she thought he was me." Bitter bile filled my mouth, and I attempted to swallow it. There was something else going on, and I was going to have to deal with it head-on.

"How the fuck did that happen? This is some bullshit, man. I would have killed that motherfucker if it were my wife."

"I was so messed up, I hit her, man. I thought I was going to kill her."

"Cojo? Why did you hit her if she didn't even know you had a twin?"

I was still struggling with the answer to that question myself, so I couldn't tell him.

"Oh, is that why y'all were having that trouble back a few months ago? How come you didn't tell me? Man, that's fucked up." Braxton shook his head.

I was still trying to clear the lump from my throat. If he only knew how difficult it was to tell him now, he'd understand why I couldn't tell him before.

"Shit, man, if you hadn't told me he was over at my house again, I might not have ever told you. I've been trying to put this shit behind me, but it just keeps on rearing its ugly head."

"Damn, dog, I don't know what to say." He shook his head again.

Braxton patted me on the shoulder and handed me a napkin from the dispenser. I spat into the napkin and blew my nose. I felt like a blubbering idiot.

"Gavin played it off like it was a joke, like he used to do. He said he didn't know we were married, so he thought it was okay." I choked out the words, because they tasted foul in my mouth. I'd handled the whole situation badly. I should have fucked them both up. I'd been good and mad, because I felt like they were playing me for a fool. I despised being treated like a fool. "She said it only happened once."

"Hell, once was more than enough, as far as I'm concerned. So he must have gone back for seconds or thirds while you were locked up. That's one dirty cat."

"Yeah, I guess so." I couldn't ignore what was right in my face. Ever since it happened, things hadn't been the same. I wanted to blame it on the baby, but Cojo and I weren't jiving right in the bedroom and we'd never had a problem before.

"Shit. Man, I stuck around to make sure he left. As he was leaving, he went to kiss her. Dude was going for the lips, but she turned her head and he got her cheek. At the time I didn't really pay it much attention, but now I'm not so sure it was an honest mistake."

I felt like my entire world was falling down around me and there was nothing I could do to stop it. How could I salvage any of it? Better yet, should I? "Dude, every muscle in my body is telling me to walk away, and the only thing holding me in check is the baby."

Braxton hung his head, and when he brought it up, he did not make eye contact. He looked all over the room, at everything but me. "Damn, man, is it even yours?"

"I got to go." I pushed away from the table and stumbled toward the door. I felt like I needed to throw up. Whatever was causing the commotion in my stomach acted like it was content to stay where it was.

Braxton grabbed his arm stopping him. "Nah, you ain't about to drive up out of here like this. Do us both a favor and leave your car here. You can crash at my place tonight, and I'll bring you back in the morning for your car."

"I got to go to work in the morning."

"And you wear a fucking uniform, so you wash your drawers and you're good to go. Don't act like you ain't done that shit before."

I could tell he was trying to make me smile, but it wasn't working. "You got anything to drink at your house?"

"Does a donkey got hips?"

"And a chicken got lips?" I said, finishing for him with a weak smile. He was right. I didn't need to go home feeling the way I did, so I allowed him to lead me out of the bar. He threw a fifty down on the table, and we left.

Chapter Twenty-two

TABATHA FLETCHER

Memories that I'd hoped never again to revisit overwhelmed me, and it all started with seeing Ronald again. I had told myself it would be okay, and I'd wanted to believe I was over him. But I'd lied to my damn self. Big mistake, because it seemed as if I'd awaken a sleeping giant, an addiction so powerful, it almost killed me.

I paced my apartment, trying to out walk the emotions that threatened to suck me into a dark vortex. After several hours of walking back and forth, I realized I was not going to be able to talk myself down from this without help.

I picked up the phone, but before I could finish dialing, the doorbell rang. Company never dropped by unannounced, so I was afraid to go to the door. I'd seen on the news that thieves were getting so bold, they were coming to homes in broad daylight and kicking in doors.

I was standing frozen next to the phone, unsure about what to do, when the bell rang again, followed by an impatient-sounding knock. Whoever was at the door wasn't going away, so I had no choice but to answer it.

"Who is it?" I shouted into the door opening. If they were going to kick it in, they would have done it by now.

"Girl, it's LaDena. Open the damn door. It's hotter than a witch's tit out here."

I couldn't understand why LaDena was outside my door. She never came by, and she'd picked the absolute worst time to start trying new shit.

"Did you get lost?" I blocked the doorway just in case she had it in her head she was coming inside.

"Lost? Why you blocking the door like a damn linebacker?" She pushed me aside and came in the house.

"Hello? Why are you at my house instead of your own?" My curiosity stopped me from getting upset with her.

"I'm here because I'm sick of watching you mope around the office like you've lost your last friend. And since you act like you don't want to talk in the office no damn mo', I decided to come by to see if there was anything I could do." She walked in my kitchen like she owned the damn place and poured herself something to drink. "Is this all the alcohol you got?" She held up the half-empty bottle like there was piss in the bottle instead of aged scotch.

I rolled my eyes. "You don't have to drink it."

She hadn't been here two minutes, and she'd already plucked my nerves.

"Humph. You don't have to tell me. I always carry my own." She pulled out a silver flask from her purse and poured a generous portion of the contents into a glass with some ice.

"Why don't you just make yourself at home?"

"I already did. Are you going to let me drink alone?"

I had never noticed this bossy side of LaDena, and I didn't know if I liked it or not. But she did take the focus off of me and the other, more dangerous things going on in my head. I poured myself a drink and followed her into the living room. "Where's your sister?"

"I don't go everywhere with my sister. I mean, I do have a life and a brain of my own."

"I'm sorry. Did I offend you? I didn't mean it like that. I was just asking because I always see you two together."

"She's at the house. She and me got a bet going that I won't get you to talk, but my money says you will."

"Another bet? You both are a trip. I keep telling you to stop wasting your money and do something worthwhile, like putting it in the stock market or something more productive."

"Child, please. Turn on the television. The stock market done crashed three or four times this week. Besides, I don't need you to tell me how to handle my money. It's just for fun. You make too much out of some things."

I didn't know how to take what she was saying to me. I had never considered talking to her about my problems, because I didn't want my business passed around the office like a sugar bowl. "I wasn't trying to tell you what to do. I was just saying."

Part of me wanted her to say what she came to say and leave, but the other part of me needed the company and wanted her to stay.

LaDena said, "So are you going to tell me what's going on? Or am I gonna have to camp out on your sofa like a relative?"

"I don't know what you're talking about," I lied. "I'm just taking a mini-vacation."

"Vacation, my ass. You got a counteroffer on the house you showed two weeks ago, and you haven't even been in there to check on it. What do you want to do? Lose the sale?"

I had forgotten all about the offer I'd made for Merlin and Cojo's house. It wasn't like me to mess up in my professional life. "Damn, I thought I had put my home fax number on the contract. I'll go by tomorrow and pick it up. What else is going on that I should know about?" I knew I had been antsy lately, but I didn't think it was enough for anyone to notice.

"I'm not trying to get all up in your business, but I can tell something is eating at you. Now, if you don't want to tell me, I'm good. But I think you'd feel better if you were to get it off your chest."

"Don't get me wrong, Dena. You and me are cool, but I can't put my private life out there like that." I played around with the ice in my glass so I didn't have to look at her.

"So just because I live with my sister doesn't mean I share everything with her. How do you know I don't have something I want to get off my chest too?"

"I thought—"

"Exactly. You're so preoccupied with your own drama, you didn't notice."

I looked up for the first time since she'd walked in the room and was stunned to see the remnants of a black eye. "What the fuck happened to your face?" I leaped from the sofa and rushed to my friend, but she pushed me back.

"See? That's what I'm talking about. My eye looks good now compared to how it's been looking for the last week. You came in the office the other day for a hot-ass minute and didn't say a damn thing. My eye was sticking out like a fuckin' shelf. Did you even notice?"

I felt ashamed because I didn't. I'd been so consumed with my own urges, I'd ignored everything going on around me. I opened my mouth to speak, but there was nothing to say.

"Close your mouth, because you're cold busted. Throw some shoes on. We've got to go to the store and get some more to drink. I got a feeling it's going to be a long night."

Dena grabbed the UTZ potato chip bag from the coffee table and set it on her lap. "I thought we were friends before you started working with us. Obviously, something has changed. What I want to know is, why?"

We'd been drinking pretty heavily and snacking on chips, doughnuts, and brownies.

"Dena, you are taking this way too personal. We are friends, but I have so much stuff going on in my life right now. I'm sorry."

"I don't think so. I made up this big-ass lie about my eye, and I waited for you to ask me and you didn't. What's up with that? At first I was, like, okay, don't jump the gun and assume the worst. But, damn, it's been four days and nothing. If you were me, what would you think?"

"I can see why you would feel that way, but honestly, it's nothing personal with you or your sister. It's my own shit I can't see through." I was getting tired of this conversation and was feeling like I wasn't shit, because I didn't notice her eye. Her timing was all wrong. I couldn't feel bad for her when I was too busy feeling sorry for myself.

"If we're friends, like you say, then how come I don't know any of the shit you're going through? And don't give me that horseshit about your personal business. Friends don't have personal business. It's community shit. You feel me?"

"Damn, girl, I said I was sorry. You know how you and your sister can go. I didn't want y'all talking about me like I had a tail, especially since we work together, so I kept it to myself."

She said, "You make us sound like a couple of old bitches who spend all day fucking talking about folks."

I opened and closed my mouth several times because I didn't know how to respond to her statement. The more I thought about what she said, the funnier it was to me, so I started laughing.

"What? I'm funny all of a sudden?"

"Yeah, you are. You and your sister do sit around talking about folks all day long. Now, close your mouth, 'cause you're busted." Even though we were having a serious conversation, I could not keep the smile off my face.

"All right, I can see where this is going. I came over here as a friend because I thought you might need a shoulder, but obviously, I was mistaken."

She was drunk and upset as she tried to get out of my oversized chair.

"Dena, calm down. I really appreciate you coming over here. You caught me by surprise, because we've never opened up to each other before." I didn't mean to start crying, but I really did need someone to talk to.

"Oh shit, please don't give me the waterworks. I'm a sucker for a good cry, and my eye is already swollen." Dena pulled a worn tissue from her purse and handed it to me.

"I've been going through a rough time right now, but it'll pass. It always does."

Dena said, "I hope so. You're one of the strongest women I know, and I hate seeing you like this."

I had never been good at receiving compliments, and her kind words made me feel like a fraud. I didn't feel like I was worthy of her praise, especially since she didn't know my history.

"Me, strong? Not hardly."

"Yes, you are. It's one of the reasons why I liked you in the first place. I can't stand a weak woman. You also have a heart, and I like that too."

I shook my head. "I'm not as strong as you think."

"You're a lot stronger than your nutty friend Gina. I don't understand why you hang out with the woman. She would drive me fucking nuts."

I bristled. Dena was passing judgment without even knowing what she was talking about. "Gina is a better woman than I'll ever be."

She said, "If you surround yourself with nutty people, don't be surprised if it starts to rub off on you."

If Dena heard me defending Gina, she chose to ignore it. At first I started to get pissed off, but I had to step back and take a look at myself. All the information they had about Gina came from me. They didn't know the whole story.

"Look, I know I'm hard on Gina, but you don't know our history. In the past, I've said some pretty mean stuff about her, but it was only because I was mad at her. If you knew the whole truth, you would think differently about her."

"Whatever. You don't have to defend your choice of friends to me. To each his own. Besides, I didn't come over here to talk about her." She fixed herself another drink.

I could understand that, but much of what was going on with me had a lot to do with Gina. I spoke before I lost my nerve. "I've done some things in my past that I am not proud of."

"Honey, haven't we all? And that's why it's best to leave the past where it is, in the past, and focus on the present. Because at the end of the day, it's all about who and what you are in the present. I mean, who hasn't done some dumb shit? The trick is to learn from your mistakes and keep it moving."

"Humph. Easier said than done. What if your past just won't go away? What do you do about that?"

"Tabatha, I'm forty-two years old, and I've made my share of mistakes too. Some of them I'm not proud of, but I've learned from all of them. The only way my past can come back and haunt me is if I let it. I found out the moment I threw back the sheets and exposed my secrets, they couldn't hurt me anymore."

I said, "I don't think I could ever do that."

"Have you ever read the Serenity Prayer?"

"It's been a minute."

"You should read it again." She fished through her worn wallet and produced a pocket-size card. "I carry this around with me. When things get too much for me to bear, I pull it out and read it."

I was skeptical as I reached for the card. It wasn't like I didn't believe in the power of prayer; I felt like my sins ran too deep for prayer. I read the card, and I was surprised by the relief I felt. The words *God grant me the serenity to accept the things I cannot change, the courage to change the things I can, and the wisdom to know the difference* resonated within my soul.

"Thanks." I was overwhelmed with emotions as I handed the card back to her.

"Keep it. I've got more at home," Dena said, smiling.

"Oh, so you walk around passing around scriptures?" I laughed to keep from crying. The card was so on point.

"Girl, don't get it twisted. I'm no Holy Roller, but a good message is worth sharing."

We sat in silence for a few minutes. I had a lot to think about. For the first time since I saw Ronald, I was thinking rationally instead of bashing myself.

"It's so hard sometimes," I whispered.

"Can I ask you a question?"

"I guess. I'm not going to promise you I will answer it."

"Fair enough. How do you expect God to forgive you if you can't forgive yourself?"

I felt like I'd farted in public and everyone in the room knew it was me. "I've forgiven myself, or at least I thought I did, but it's the other people I hurt that I'm having a hard time with." It was a hard admission to make, but it was the truth.

Dena said, "Did you knowingly go out of your way to hurt these people?"

"Of course not."

"Then I don't understand what the problem is. Everybody makes mistakes, even ones that hurt other people."

I had never seen this side of Dena before. I kept waiting for her to say something to piss me off so I wouldn't pay attention to what was really going on. She didn't know how close I was to telling her my darkest secret. But part of me was scared shitless of what she would think of me if she knew the truth.

"What's the worst thing that can happen if you told the truth? Are you going to go to jail? Did you kill somebody?"

I shook my head. "No, nothing like that. But I could lose a very good friend."

"Hell, there isn't anything you could tell me that would make me walk away from you. Who would I get to cover your share of the rent?"

It was a joke, or at least I took it as one. It did lighten the moment, but the feeling didn't last long.

"I wasn't talking about you." I had never considered Dena a good friend. She was certainly an acquaintance of mine, but we didn't share the things friends shared. She had her sister, and I had always assumed that was enough for her.

"You must be talking about Gina, because she's the only other person I've see you with. If she's truly your friend, she'll forgive you. You already said you didn't mean to intentionally hurt her."

"That's not all true. In the beginning it wasn't even about her. It started before I even knew who she was."

"Let me guess. It's about a man, right?" Dena smirked.

She took off her shoes and put her tiny feet up on my coffee table. I guess I didn't have to tell her to make herself at home.

"Sort of."

"Shit. Either it is or it isn't."

I said, "I was with him first. She doesn't even know about it."

"Is that the secret? Because if it is, it ain't so bad. I wouldn't get mad at you about something like that. It's a small world."

"That's not the bad part." Suddenly, I was afraid to go on with my story. I could count on three fingers the people who knew the entire story. One of them was dead, and the other two were me and Ronald, and up until now, we weren't talking.

Dena raised a brow. "Oh."

I wanted her to butt in and stop me from confessing, but she didn't. Go figure. Any other time I couldn't stop her from yapping, but tonight she acted as if she were in a library, storing information, instead of in my living room.

"I don't think I should be telling you this. I've never told anyone else, and I promised myself I'd take it to my grave."

This was as close to a warning as I was going to give her. If I ever heard anything back about what I was about to tell her, I would know it came from her.

"I understand. You can trust me. I won't even tell my sister."

It wasn't easy to talk about something I'd spent so much of my life hiding from, but I did it because I believed it was necessary to start the healing process. "When I was younger, I made some very bad choices. I got involved with the wrong guy, got strung out on drugs, and got pregnant."

"Is this the part where I should start throwing stones at you?" Dena laughed, trying to break the somber mood.

"No, I haven't gotten to it yet."

"Tabatha, you are so convinced I'm going to hate you. Will you lighten up? Jeez, you are not the first person in the world to make a mistake."

"Probably not, but it doesn't make it any easier to say it out loud."

"If mistakes were painless, we wouldn't stop trying to make them. God knew what he was doing by bringing the pain."

I was a little taken aback because I'd never heard Dena discuss God on such a personal level before. It wasn't that I thought she was a heathen. I just never would have put her and God in the same sentence or thought. "I guess I never thought about it before. To make a long story short, I got pregnant and my mother forced me to have the children."

"Children, as in more than one?" Dena became animated, and I started to get nervous. She was waving at me, trying to rush my confession along.

"Yeah, I was underage, and the man was old enough to know better. She said she was punishing both of us by making me have them and forcing him to raise them. She threatened to have him arrested for statutory rape if he didn't. I haven't had any parental contact with them."

"Damn, how old are the children?"

"Twenty-seven. Twins. I was fourteen when I had them. The worst time of my life."

"Oh God, you were still a baby. I can't imagine having to make grown-up decisions at that age."

"I didn't make the decision. My mother did. If it were up to me, I would have had an abortion. By the time I found out I was pregnant, I wasn't seeing the guy anymore. I didn't want to be around anything remotely connected to him. She sent me away for the summer to have the kids, and no one knew anything about it when I came home alone."

"What happened to the guy?"

"He's around." I got lost for a moment in the memories, and it made me sad.

"Ah, you miss him."

"Hell, I miss his drugs more than I miss his ass. He knew I was young, and he took advantage of me. He used the drugs to control me, and it worked until my mother found out."

"I'll bet your mother tried to stomp a mud hole in you."

I said, "Actually she didn't. She was young and dumb too when she had me. Besides, her punishment gives me something to think about every day of my life."

"But don't you see that you should be proud of yourself, instead of beating yourself up?"

I frowned. "Proud? For what?"

"You don't do drugs, or at least I've never seen you do drugs. You're a successful, beautiful, and wonderful person."

"True, I might not do drugs, but I haven't stopped thinking about them and how they made me feel, even though it's been years since I've smoked."

"I think you need to give yourself a break. You were young, and the things that happened were not in your control. I don't understand. What's happening now that's got you all crazy?"

Fight or flight? It was another tough decision. I could shut up right now and continue to hold this sickness inside, or I could give it up in hopes of getting better. I tried to speak, but no words came out. Dena patiently waited for me to get myself together. I felt the same way I did when I first came home without my children. Like I'd lost something and I couldn't find it.

I said, "This attorney called, asking a bunch of questions. She knows I'm the mother, and it freaked me out."

"Huh? What's up with that?" She stuffed her mouth with junk food. Then she got up and brought the bottle to us. I was getting a slight buzz. I needed it if I was going to keep on talking.

I sipped my drink, then said, "One of the boys got into trouble, and they were trying to get in touch with their father. I honestly don't know how they got my phone number, because I haven't had any real role in their lives."

"Was your name on their birth certificate?"

"Hell if I know. I was fourteen. I didn't know about any of that stuff. My mom handled everything."

"Well, you know if the attorney was able to find you, the children will be able to find you as well."

"Honey, they ain't looking for me. They had someone in their lives who they called mother, and it wasn't me."

"How does that make you feel?"

"There's no easy answer to this question. At the time, I didn't want to even think about being somebody's mommy. I was still a kid my damn self. My mom made sure I didn't see the guy again, and as much as I hate to admit it, I didn't really think of the boys."

Dena said, "Again, you were a child. Children typically think only of themselves."

She was really trying to make me feel better about a fucked-up situation, but I was still holding on to my pain.

"Yeah, well, it bothers me now. I never wanted kids when I was young, but now that forty has kicked in my door, I'm full of regrets. But you know what? That's a whole other conversation. What I didn't tell you was Gina has been the mother to my kids." I sucked down everything in my glass, ice included, and waited for Dena's reaction.

"Wow. I'm speechless. I did not expect that. Now I can understand why you're such a good friend to her."

"No, you don't understand. She doesn't even know they are mine. I never told her."

Dena almost choked on her drink. "Oh shit. She is going to be hotter than a tick under a cow's armpit when she finds out."

"I know. That's what I'm afraid of."

"Please don't tell me you were fucking around with the same guy she's been living with. I know you didn't do that."

"It was way before she came to town. By the time I found out, they were seriously seeing each other. I had already called her a dumb bitch for raising another woman's children."

"You did not call her a dumb bitch." Dena laughed out loud.

"I sure did. I called her that for months, until she introduced me to the babies' father. If you could have seen his fucking face . . . It was priceless."

"Un-fucking-believable. I would have paid money to see that shit. I can't believe you kept it a secret. Who do the children look like?"

"Thank God they look just like their father. My concern now is that Gina will find out and hate me. Not to mention what might happen if the boys suddenly want to look for their biological mother."

"I know, right? Everybody seems to be looking for their birth parents these days. What are you going to do if they come looking for you?"

"I'm going to be honest and hope they forgive me. The bigger problem is going to be Gina. I don't think she will be as understanding. I saw what she went through because of those kids, and I never offered her any help, just useless advice. She did what I couldn't do, so how can I fault her for that?"

"I think you need to explain it to her the same way you explained it to me. I'm sure she will be okay after she gets over the initial shock."

"Yeah, but you don't know the Gina I know. She's liable to snap and kill my stupid ass before I finish explaining. I don't know what to do, and it's killing me."

I hoped LaDena would offer me some advice on how to handle my situation, but she seemed to be just as clueless as I was. Nothing good ever came of a lie, even a lie of omission, and I was going to have to deal with it and accept the consequences.

"I've got one more question, and I'm going to let this go. What about the children, or adults now, I guess? Are you going to be their mother now?"

"Hell no. I don't have a motherly bone in my body. I proved that when I allowed this secret to go on as long as I did. No, I don't want the role. They know me as a friend of the family. I'm good."

Chapter Twenty-three

GAVIN MILLS

"Well, the errant attorney finally returns. I was beginning to think you'd forgotten all about me," I said when sexy-ass Meredith Bowers stepped into the interview room.

"Unlike you, I don't have a lot of time on my hands. I've been busy. So if you're about to start whining and acting like a little baby, let me know and I'll come back, because I don't have time for those theatrics."

I was surprised by Meredith's response. I'd used the woe approach before on other women, and it had worked miracles. But this chick appeared unfazed by, and uninterested in, my personal pain. Nothing ever came easy for me, so I wasn't surprised by this new development. I was going to have to find another way to deal with her, but I was confident in my abilities. Wooing women had become a specialty of mine. Normally, I enjoyed the challenge, but this time the stakes were higher. I had to get someone on the outside to give a fuck whether I spent the rest of my natural life behind bars.

I could feel each of my brain cells churning as I tried to think of a way around this impossibly stubborn woman who was assigned to defend me. If I had any money, I would have fired her ass on the spot. Since I had no access to the dollars stuffed in the mattress in my apartment, I had to play the hand I was dealt.

"I'm sorry. You don't know how hard it is being locked up in a cage for eighteen hours a day. It's demeaning and demoralizing. The guards treat you like shit, and the cons are full of games. Deadly games. They jacked this guy in the cell next to mine last night, and nobody bothered to help. He was screaming so loud, and nobody gave a fuck." I held my head down, as if I were about to cry and I didn't want her to see. I waited to see if she believed me. In reality, the guy in the next cell was screaming, but it wasn't from pain. As long as they kept that doo-doo dodgeball in another cell, I was good.

"Cut the shit, Gavin. This isn't your first time around the block, so you should be used to this by now."

"What? Just because I've seen the shit before, I'm supposed to like it? Well, fuck you and the monkey shit you're talking. If you ain't here to help me, then I'm out." Feigning anger, I leaped from my chair to call the guard and have him escort me back to my cell. I didn't know what was up with this bitch-ass attorney. Whatever it was, I wasn't about to play the fool.

"Sit your retarded ass down. I told you I don't have time for no games and shit. Now, if you want me to help you get out of here, you've got to stop fucking around and talk straight with me."

Her voice was low, but I heard the threat in her tone. She was going to leave my black ass to rot in jail if I didn't stop playing with her.

"I don't know what you want from me," I answered honestly. *If I can't game her, then what?*

"I want you to stay in your lane. Don't try those mind games with me, 'cause I'm too old for those silly tricks. I don't give a rat's ass if you did what they said you did.

What I do care about is whether I'm fighting a losing battle. I won't stand for you trying to make a mockery of me. So if you want my help, mister, you'd better shoot it to me straight so we can figure out how to fix this. Are you some nut job who needs to be locked up for the rest of your life?"

"No. I told you already. I just want to go home." I wasn't lying, either. I was sick of being treated like the scourge of the earth. I wasn't perfect, but I wasn't the scum of the planet. I was just someone with a few rough patches that needed to be fixed. It was ironic to me the way things had turned out, especially since I had stuff going exactly the way I'd wanted them to until I fucked up.

She said matter-of-factly, "Tell me about your mother."

Stunned, I had to think for a second who she was talking about. She couldn't mean my real mother, because I didn't know her from a can of paint. "You mean Gina? She's is the closest thing to a real mother I had. What do you want to know?"

"I was talking about your birth mother."

"I don't know the bitch. Never met her." I got upset with Meredith for even bringing up this line of questioning, because I failed to see its relevance. The only thing my birth mother did for me was cop a squat and push me out.

"Do you have issues with women because you've never met your mother?"

"I get along just fine with women. Trust me on this. I don't have any problems in that area." I rubbed my dick. If they would let me out of these bars, I would show her ass how well I worked with women.

Meredith sucked her teeth. "I'm not talking about your ability to fuck them. I'm talking about how you

treat them. Do you make it a habit to hit on women?
Do you think you're better than them? Do you value
women in society?"

"Whoa, hold up. You got me all wrong, Ma."

Meredith was making me nervous. I didn't like the
way she looked at me, and I definitely didn't like the
way she was thinking.

"So you say. Would you like to meet your mother?
Aren't you curious to know why she gave you and your
brother up?"

"Not really. The bitch—" I stopped midsentence when
I saw the frown on Meredith's face. "Sorry. I wasn't trying to offend you."

It was apparent she didn't care for the B word, so I
was going to have to curb my lips before they wrote a
check my ass didn't want to cash.

"What would you do if I told you I found your mother?
Would you like me to contact her?" She tapped her pencil on her legal pad. It sounded like she was pounding on
a drum instead of paper.

I felt the beginnings of a headache. "For what? I
don't understand why she is so relevant."

Meredith continued to stare at me, and it made me
uncomfortable and slightly irritable.

I said, "Why are you staring at me?" I got up and
started pacing. If she was trying to push my buttons,
she was doing a damn good job. She was making me
think about things I'd long since given up on. When
I was a child, I often thought my real mother would
come for me and that she'd love me more than Merlin.
It never happened. I felt the muscles around my eye
twitching, and I did my best to conceal it.

She said, "I only wanted to test your reaction. You're
fine. You passed."

"Passed? You giving me some kind of fucking test? What are you? A psychologist or a lawyer?" I was well past irritated and wanted nothing more than to punch the bitch in the face.

"Sort of both, double major. Now, where were we? Hmm . . ." She picked up her briefcase from the floor and opened it, pulling out two files from inside and laying them on the table.

"What's this?"

"Your profile. I believe we can convince a judge you need help rather than confinement. Did you know your stepmother was pregnant?" She threw the last question in as nonchalantly as if she were discussing the weather.

"Are you fucking kidding me? No way." I felt a tingling in the pit of my stomach, then a wild urge to throw up. My mind flashed back to the night not so long ago when I stumbled across my stepmother, half dressed and clearly intoxicated. I was also a little drunk, but that only fueled my desire to fuck her fat pussy.

A shudder starting at the base of my spine crept up my neck. There was no way I'd pissed God off enough that he'd stick me with a child by my own stepmother. Or was it? After all, God did have a sense of humor. I could not help but think how ironic it would be if I fathered a child with her when my own dad refused.

"Tell me how you really feel," she said, laughing.

"The last thing I need is another fucking kid." I had this sinking certainty in the pit of my stomach that it was true.

"Wait. Are you telling me you're the father? Gross. Where they do that at?"

"What can I say? Shit happens."

Suddenly I felt like shit and began to believe I really did belong behind bars.

"Wow. This is actually perfectly good news. There isn't a judge this side of the Mason-Dixon Line who would deny me a petition of insanity based on this information."

"Oh, hell no. If you think I'm going to spend the rest of my life locked up in some loony bin because of this bullshit, you've got another thing coming. I was pullin' your chain. I wouldn't dare sleep with my mother." I was backpedaling, but I didn't even sound convincing to my own ears.

"You don't have a fucking choice in the matter. How I get you out of this mess is up to me. But if it makes you feel any better, my plan is not to have you rot in a nuthouse. Yes, you might have to go in for a little while, but it won't be a permanent thing. How long you stay will be left up to how well you conform to the treatment."

"Fuck you mean, conform? What kind of treatment? You know what? Fuck you. I think I'll take my chances in here." I got out of my chair, ready to go back to my cell. My gut had told me something wasn't right with this chick the first time I laid eyes on her.

"Sit your stupid-ass down! I told you I got this, but if you keep showing your ass, I will fuck you. Believe that."

I wasn't happy as I sat down. I was not liking the way she handled me one bit, and I prayed I'd get the chance to show her—just once—how I rolled.

She said, "There is another option I want to explore."

"I think I'll take what's behind door number two." I prayed it would be better than the first option.

"Ah, a sense of humor. You're going to need it."

"You like keeping a brother's nuts in a knot, don't you? I thought you said you didn't have time for games." Every muscle in my body screamed for me to

smash the smug look off her face. Somehow, I held it
together.

"Boot camp."

"Oh, hell to the no. I ain't doing no damn boot camp.
That shit is for punks and sissies."

"Would your punk ass rather be in there for four
months or prison for twelve years?"

Twelve years? Was she fucking kidding me? I couldn't
do twelve years in jail. I'd go nuts. I hung my head as
the weight of her words settled in.

"I thought so. If you're lucky enough to get boot
camp, it's a one-shot deal. You fuck up, all bets are off,
and there'll be no second chances. You're gonna have
to keep your attitude in check. So it's on you. How do
you want to play it?" She thumped her fingernails on
the table, waiting for my response. It was a no-brainer.

"I'll take boot camp for one hundred dollars."

"Very funny. You don't have a hundred dollars."

She placed her files back in her briefcase, signaling
an end to our meeting. As much as she annoyed me, I
didn't want her to leave, because I'd be alone with myself. Right now I didn't like me very much.

"Boot camp is only another option I wanted you to
think about. You also need to think about your birth
mother, because I may have to use it. On the brighter
side, the other girl, Angie Simpson, she lost the baby. I
haven't had a chance to speak with her yet. It might be
your blessing in the sky."

My head shot up. I was confused. I didn't even know
the girl being pregnant was on the table. I couldn't believe that after years of shooting blanks, all of a sudden
I was hitting bull's-eyes. "Fuck me."

"Keep your chin up. Everything is going to be okay.
Trust me."

She closed her briefcase, as if she no longer needed to talk about the things contained in the files she brought with her. She'd given me a lot of stuff to think about, and to me, none of it was good. I didn't have any other choice but to trust her, especially since she was my only lifeline out of this bitch. It wasn't like anyone else had bothered to visit me while I was being sequestered in this hellhole. It'd been over two months, and I'd ran out of cracks in the walls to count. If I was in here much longer, I would have to find another hobby to pass the time.

Looking at her breasts, I said, "What are you going to do now?"

"I'm going to talk to Gina and Cojo. If this is going to work, I have to get Cojo to drop the charges, and you're going to need Gina's help as well."

"Good luck with that," I said solemnly.

"I'll be back in a few days. If I'm as good as I think I am, you'll be one step closer to getting out of here."

While alone in my cell, I went through a wide range of emotions. It was a good thing I didn't have a cell mate anymore, or we might have ended up in a fight. The one thing I hated more than anything else in the world was the feeling that someone had the upper hand. Meredith's success depended on too many variables for my comfort. It singed my drawers that I wasn't in control of my own destiny, because I felt like no one else had my best interests at heart.

The other thing I didn't particularly care for was when Meredith brought up my birth mother. I was about to turn twenty-seven. What the fuck did I need a mother for? At this stage of the game, I didn't understand why she would be relevant, especially since she'd been absent throughout my entire life. It pissed me off, actually, because I hadn't thought of her in years, and I didn't appreciate having to think about her now, when I didn't have any avenue available to blow off steam.

As I lay across my bunk, I tried not to think about the woman who gave birth to me or the worthless piece of shit my father had turned out to be. I tried not to think about the crappy childhood I had had with Gina, but since I'd learned she was pregnant, she was running rampant in my head. All my life I'd blamed Gina for my troubles. Never once did I consider that she was more of a victim than I was. This thought was so blatantly clear, I was surprised I'd never considered it before.

My father had ruined every single thing he'd touched, and through it all, he'd been the only one left unscathed. The more I thought about my father, the madder I became. I got to thinking maybe I was fucked up in the head. How could I torture the only person in my life who had bothered to stick around? My stomach started to boil again. This time I couldn't stop it from spilling over.

I leaped from my cot as the vomit erupted from my mouth. Sharp pains followed each convulsion, and a montage of my past transgressions played through my mind. I prayed to the porcelain God to make it all stop, the memories and the pain.

My knees were weak when I was finally able to stand upright. My throat burned as I stood over the sink and drank tepid water from my cupped hands. I felt so miserable, I would have bawled were I not locked in with a bunch of men who would use my weakness against me. As I stood up, I felt a calmness and a sense of clarity I'd never felt before. I realized Gina was the only person who had stayed, and I was ashamed about the way I'd treated her. I had never regretted a single thing I had done in my entire life until now. It was a very humbling moment. I didn't want anyone to see me in my time of painful reflection. I stopped short as a new thought took root in my brain.

"Oh fuck, she's pregnant."

I had no doubt the baby Gina carried was mine. My dilemma was what I was going to do about it. The night I fucked her, I was drunk, horny, and angry with the world. The question was, now that I knew better, was I going to accept responsibility or continue to act like my father's child? The thought almost seized my stomach again. Being like him wasn't something I aspired to do. Worried, I couldn't help but wonder whether it was in my genes. This couldn't be true, because if it were, Merlin would have suffered the same fate. There wasn't a sadistic bone in his body, so what was wrong with me? Why were we so different if everything else was the same? I groaned aloud when another wave of pain hit me.

"Motherfucker, shut up all that noise, 'fore I come over there and give you something to moan about."

I heard the bass in my neighbor's voice. I was so angry, I didn't care.

"Fuck off, dude, and mind your damn business." Normally, I would have tempered my words until I knew who I was speaking to. Not this time. I didn't care. I didn't ask for these self-reflective moments, and I was pissed at Meredith for stirring up all those feelings and walking the fuck away. I didn't have that luxury, and unfortunately for me, this was not the place to have a chip on my shoulder. I had to do something to diffuse my feelings, or I'd wind up in even more trouble than I was already in.

I shouldn't have been surprised to find out Gina got pregnant. Her pussy was so tight, I could tell it'd been a minute since she'd gotten broken off. My dick started to get hard as images of her clit flipped like a mini slide show in my head. Drunk or not, if she didn't enjoy it, I couldn't tell. I knew I sure as hell did. And at the time, it was the only thing that mattered. It didn't seem perverted, especially since we both enjoyed it, but now . . . it seemed kinda creepy. Thank God Gina wasn't my real mother, or else my son would also be my brother or some other weird kinda crazy shit.

The hardest part about being behind bars was having to get permission to do even the most basic of functions. The last time I was in, I'd made a promise to myself I would never come back. It was a promise I didn't keep. The other thing I couldn't stand was the lack of information. Not knowing from day to day what was going to happen was a slow torture for me.

I jumped off my bunk as my cell door swung open and pretended like I wasn't slacking moments before. My heart was beating very fast because I didn't like surprises. I had this terrible feeling that I was going to be forced to share my cell again.

Chapter Twenty-four

ANGIE SIMPSON

I was terrified to go to a deposition in the attorney's office. If it wasn't for the cute-looking investigator, I might not have gone. Being a criminal justice major, I had an idea of what went on with depositions. If I wasn't trying to conceal what had actually transpired from my parents, I probably would have refused to attend.

Officially, I was supposed to be in mourning over the death of my baby and my mother. Unofficially, I was ready to have a fucking party. I had got rid of two problems at once. I just needed to get this legal shit behind me so I could get on with my life. I was hoping that by cooperating, it wouldn't be necessary for me to appear in court. If I did have to go, perhaps it would limit direct questioning on how I met Gavin Mills. My mother was no longer a threat. The only thing left to do was get through the trial without unduly disgracing my father.

As it was, I felt like I was being punished by being forced to relive the worst day of my life. It appeared as if I didn't have a choice, so I agreed to go and get it over with. The papers didn't say how long the deposition was supposed to last. I hoped they knew I wouldn't be able to sit still for long. Even though I was no longer pregnant, I was still in a considerable amount of discomfort due to my injuries from the car accident.

My hands were shaking as I was shown into the conference room at Meredith's office and told to have a seat. There was a court reporter there. Other than a nod of acknowledgement, she didn't communicate with me. We waited for another ten minutes before a black woman wearing a suit entered the room and sat down. She carried a yellow legal pad and took a seat right in front of me. I didn't know if I was supposed to stand when I shook her hand. Since I didn't ask to come here, I decided against it.

"Thanks for coming, Ms. Simpson. I heard about your losses, and I am so terribly sorry. I'm Meredith Bowers, and I'm the attorney assigned to this case." She flipped open her pad and began making a few notes. I didn't notice the thick file until she flipped it open as well.

"Should I, um . . . Do I need an attorney with me?" I immediately got nervous. Since I had not committed a crime, it hadn't even dawned on me that I might need one.

"No, not at all. You're fine. If you were on trial, the answer, of course, would be different. This is a formal statement, and your answers will be used in preparation for the trial. Do you understand?"

When I heard her say "Used," I should have asked to have the appointment rescheduled so I could at least consult with an attorney. I knew my father could not afford to hire an attorney for me, especially not after the funerals for my mother and child. But at least I could have known what my options were. "I think so," I said. "Yeah, I think I understand."

"Good. Let's get started. The court reporter will record the entire deposition, and copies will be made available to you at a minimal charge."

"Why should I have to pay?" I could already see where this was going, and I didn't like it one bit.

"Depositions aren't free, sweetie."

Who the fuck is she calling sweetie? I folded my arms across my chest, pissed with her condescending attitude and demeanor.

"I'm going to ask you a series of questions. You are not required to answer any or all of the questions. However, your answers will be used in conjunction with the rape, arson, and attempted murder trial against Gavin Mills."

She patted the file, indicating all the information was in there. I immediately felt uncomfortable; she made it seem like she knew something I didn't. Her first few questions were nice and predictable—my name, address, date of birth, education—and then the bitch took off the gloves.

"For the next few questions, I'm going to take them directly from the information you provided to the police, okay?"

"I guess." I could not help feeling like it was some kind of trick and she was setting me up or something.

"Did you know my client before the night of the alleged incident?"

I took offense at the word *alleged*. *Does she think I made it up?* "No."

"Are you in the habit of getting into cars with strangers?"

I didn't see this one coming, and it contradicted what I had told my parents about Gavin breaking into the house.

"Well, no, but—"

"Just answer the question."

"No."

"Your statement to the police also says the defendant picked you up on Cleveland Avenue. Is that correct?"

"Yeah, I think so. My boyfriend and I went to a party near there, and we got into a fight."

"Is this a yes or a no answer?"

The bitch was starting to get on my nerves. "Yes," I said through gritted teeth.

"That's a pretty rough area," Meredith said.

"Is that supposed to be a question?"

She looked up with a surprised expression on her face. "No, merely a statement. What were you fighting about?"

"Is that relevant?" *Two can play at this shit.*

"No, not really. But I would like to know how things progressed from my client rescuing you from a potentially dangerous situation to sex. Can you explain to me how the conversation took place?"

I could feel my face heat up with embarrassment. I wasn't proud of my behavior that night. I wasn't a cheap whore, and this was exactly how she made me feel. "I don't think I like your attitude." I had had enough of this charade, and I was ready to call it quits and take my chances in court. It was clear she was interested only in protecting her client and I was disposable.

"Point taken, and I will rephrase the question. Did you at any point offer to have sex with my client for money?"

I leaped up from my chair, knocking it over in the process. "What kind of bullshit is this? Why are you attacking me like I did something wrong?"

"Ms. Simpson, please sit down. I'm merely trying to find out the truth of what happened that night."

"Seems to me you already have your own ideas, and they have nothing to do with the truth." I wanted to leave so badly, and if I didn't really need to get this bitch on my side so I didn't have to go through with testifying in court, I would have. Reluctantly, I sat back down.

She said, "Good. Can you please answer the question?"

"No. I did not."

"Did you see my client set fire to your house?"

"Uh, um, no. I think I may have passed out because he was choking me." This didn't even sound good to me, and I was there.

"Isn't it possible that someone else could have come into the home and started the fire? Someone other than my client? Perhaps your boyfriend?"

I stood up again. "I am not on trial, and I didn't do anything wrong," I shouted. I could tell from the writing on the wall that I would get no assistance from this lady. I stomped over to the door, and I couldn't get it open fast enough.

"You might want to get a lawyer, Ms. Simpson, because this is just the beginning."

"Fuck you," I shouted and slammed the door behind me. I was mad at the lawyer and even madder with myself because I should have known better. Too late, I'd realized what she was doing when she brought me into her office. She'd been trying to intimidate me, and the sad part about it was that it had worked. I didn't want to go to court and tell anyone what had happened to me. I wasn't going to do it, and they couldn't make me.

"Yo, Angie, wait up." Young came out of the restroom.

"What?" I didn't feel like talking to Young, and it was my intent to give him a piece of my mind. I faltered when I noticed how good he looked. Self-consciously, I smoothed down my wrinkled skirt.

"Damn, Ma. I did not sleep with you last night."

"Huh?"

"You acting all mad, like I slept with you and never called you again."

"Oh, yeah. Sorry. I didn't know who was calling me." I started walking down the hall again, wanting to get the hell out of the building before I showed my natural black ass.

"Are you coming from your deposition?"

I stopped walking. Young had given me his phone number, so I needed to know whose side he was on before I could even entertain talking to him. "Do you work for that bitch?"

"Wow. Not the B word."

"Answer the question." I stopped in front of the door and waited for Young to open it for me. He took the hint, and I rushed past him and took a deep breath of smog-filled air. It was refreshing, anyway.

"I work with the person you are speaking about. I don't work for her," he said.

"So you know why I had to come down here?" If he said yes, I was going to tear up his number and throw it in the trash.

"I know of the case. If you're asking me if I'm privy to details, no. I'm not. Things must not have gone well."

I was so fucking confused. Ever since the attack, I hadn't been able to talk to anyone, and the stress was getting to me. "No, it didn't. I walked out."

"That's not good."

I said, "Are you speaking on her behalf or your own? Because if you are sweating me to get more information for her, leave me the fuck alone."

He glanced at his watch and smiled. "I'm off the clock."

"What's that supposed to mean?"

"Means whatever you say to me stays with me."

I walked over to a bench and sat down. I had so many things on my mind that I didn't know where to begin. I wasn't sure I could trust Young, but he was about the only person in my life who acted like they cared about me. "I have been through so much over the last four months that you would not believe it. Meeting that dude was the worst thing I've ever had happen to me. I was raped, burned, and left for dead. Plus, a car accident I was lucky to survive. All of this shit is directly related to meeting this guy. I'm tired. I just want it over with."

"Losing your mom and your kid . . . that's tough."

I frowned. "Ugh! I don't want to hear about that baby! I never wanted the kid. Keeping it was my mother's idea."

"Don't you want to see this guy punished? I mean, damn, that's a lot of shit to forget."

"Punishment is not up to me. God handles that, and He can do a much better job at it than I can."

"So why not ask the district attorney to drop the charges?"

"I can do that?"

"Sure you can ask. They might not always agree, but it's certainly within your rights. If you were to ask them to drop the charges, you can also refuse to testify. It's worth a shot if you really want this over with."

I leaned over and gave Young a kiss on his cheek. He'd given me the best news I had heard since this whole mess started. I said, "Thanks. Give me a call in a few days." He just didn't know . . . if he played his cards

right, I might give him some. I jumped up from the
bench and ran back inside, trying to find the DA to tell
them they'd have to find some other bitch to do their
dirty work.

Chapter Twenty-five

COJO MILLS

The bright sun shining in my eyes awakened me. I yawned and stretched my arms out wide. This was the first time in months that I'd slept through the night without having to get up and go to the bathroom. It was a good feeling, and I hoped it was the start of many more restful nights. I glanced at the clock as I put my feet on the floor, and I did a double take. The digital display read 10:00 A.M. For a minute, I thought my clock was broken, because I went to sleep at ten. So this meant I slept for twelve hours.

"Merlin must have slept on the couch," I said aloud. I smiled because he must have known I needed the rest. I went to the bathroom, then into the kitchen to fix myself a cup of coffee. Caffeine was the one vice I wasn't willing to give up, even for my baby. I had expected to see a blanket or sheet on the sofa when I walked through the living room, but there was nothing. "He must have really tied one on."

I rested my hip against the stove as I waited for the water to boil. I was very lucky to have a man who was so considerate, and I wanted to do something nice for him. I opened the refrigerator to see what I could make him for dinner. Merlin loved my chicken and dumplings, and, luckily, I had everything I needed to make them. I pulled some chicken from the freezer and put it in the sink to thaw.

As I was carrying my cup of coffee to my bedroom to get dressed, the doorbell rang. I slipped on my robe and went to the door. From past experiences, I knew not to open the door without checking the peephole, and I was surprised to see Tabatha standing outside.

"Hi, Tabatha. This is a surprise." I stepped back and allowed her to come in. I was self-conscious about not being dressed so late in the day.

"Hey, Cojo. I hope you don't mind my stopping by without calling."

"No, not at all. You have to forgive my casual attire. Normally, I get up when Merlin leaves for work. Today I overslept."

"Child, please. If I could stay at home while my man worked, I would be sleeping late too. Knowing me, I probably wouldn't get up until a half an hour before he came home," she said, laughing.

I was offended. I felt like she was trying to imply I was lazy and didn't want to work. "I can't do that. In fact, staying at home is driving me nuts. I can't wait till this baby is born so I can go back to work. If it were up to me, I'd be working right now. Merlin has other ideas."

"Count your blessings, child. Count your blessings."

We stood silently in the foyer for a few uncomfortable seconds. I was waiting for her to tell me why she'd come over.

"Can I get you something to drink?" I finally asked. "I just made some coffee, so the water should still be hot."

"No, I'm really in a rush to get to the office. I stopped by because the sellers have submitted a counteroffer and I wanted to get it to you as soon as possible."

"Oh, okay."

She handed me a folder, and I took it and placed it on the table.

She said, "Are you feeling okay? You don't look like yourself."

"Uh, I, uh, I'm good."

She held her eyes down, as if she was afraid to look me in the face. She turned and walked the few steps to the door, then turned around before she touched the knob. "Tell Merlin to give me a call. I called him a couple of times, and he didn't answer."

"Really? He always answers his phone. He must be real busy today."

"Actually, I've been trying him since last night. The offer came in a few days ago, and I was late picking it up, so I wanted to get it to him as soon as possible."

"Oh . . . okay. I'll tell him. Thanks for coming by."

"Right, okay. I'll talk to you later."

I didn't remember my dream until I was taking my shower. While I was sleeping, I was visited by a phantom lover who knew exactly what my body needed. As my hand lathered my breasts, I vividly recalled how my lover sucked my nipples. As my hand dipped lower, I fingered my clit, which felt swollen and tender to the touch. My eyes popped open.

"What the fuck? I know he didn't sneak him some while I was sleeping!" As I said it, I knew it was true, because these days Merlin couldn't hit my spot if written instructions said, "Insert dick here."

I quickly washed off the soap and stepped from the shower. I needed to get to the bottom of this sultry seduction. As I was dressing, I realized who my fantasy lover was. Gavin had come to me in my dreams. It was

bad enough that I thought about him all day every day.
Now I was dreaming about him. I wondered how he
was holding up in jail.

I still had five hours before Merlin was due home
from work. I dressed, gathered my things, and was in
the car before I admitted to myself what I was about to
do. I was going to see Gavin. I put in a Fantasia CD and
turned the volume up high, because I didn't want to
think about what I was about to do. For some reason,
it was very important for me to see for myself how he
was doing.

To my knowledge Gavin was still being held at the
DeKalb County Jail pending trial. This was good, since
I didn't have the time or the inclination to travel all
over Georgia just to appease my curiosity. However,
had I known how intimidating the jail was going to be,
I would have kept my happy ass at the house. I sat in
the parking lot across the street from the jail with the
car windows down for a full ten minutes before I had
the nerve to get out of the car. The cool October breeze
caressed my face. The sound of inmates tapping on the
windows beckoned me inside. I felt as if Gavin was the
one sending me a message.

The tapping got louder the closer I got to the jail. I
wasn't so much afraid of seeing Gavin as I was of navi-
gating my way around the other visitors. I felt like I was
being scrutinized and criticized from my hair down to
my shoes. I couldn't help it if I still maintained a sense
of style, even while pregnant. I put my head up in the
air and walked past the other ladies, who appeared to
be held together with plastic and weave.

I felt like I was walking into a clique and everyone
knew each other and I was the odd woman out. I tried
to ignore the shitty looks and rude comments as I
walked past. It wasn't easy, because I knew I could hold

my own on the streets, but I wasn't crazy enough to try some shit at the jail. I took a seat in the corner and waited for my name to be called. When I was told I had already been approved for the visit, I realized Gavin knew me better than I knew myself. After all, he'd had the foresight to place my name on the list. He knew I would come, and it almost freaked me out.

As my group was being called, the noise level rose in the room. Two women were arguing.

"Bitch, what are you doing here? This ain't your visiting day," one lady said.

"The same motherfucking thing you're doing here, boo-boo." The other lady smiled as she sucked her teeth.

"Didn't I tell you to leave my fucking man alone?"

"Get the fuck outta here. I ain't scared of you. He was mine first," the second lady yelled.

They had gotten all close to each other, and it was just a matter of time before this fight escalated. I regretted my rash decision to come to the jail and was about to step out of line when we were ushered forward to be searched. As the line began to move, the beef was quashed. I trained my eyes on the back of the woman in front of me as we were led into a cubicle to be searched.

"I knew you'd come." Gavin was smiling from ear to ear when they brought him into the room.

He came over to the table I was sitting at and sat down. He kept his arms down at his sides even though they'd removed his cuffs. I was surprised when he didn't try to kiss me. My heart felt like it was skipping around in my chest when I glimpsed the hairs peeping up through the V-neck of his orange jumpsuit. He still looked fuckable even though he was badly in need of a shave. My lips felt engorged as I licked them. It felt as if my spit had dried up.

I said, "Don't read too much into it, big boy. I only came to make sure they were treating you right, and I knew your brother wouldn't be making this trip."

"Woman, your words wound me." He grabbed his heart and held down his head. He was joking. I could see the hint of a smile lurking on his lips.

"Cut the crap, Gavin." I was at war with myself. My head said it was angry, while my heart was very happy to see him.

We sat in uncomfortable silence for a few seconds. He was so confident I would come. This made me feel uneasy, because it made me feel like he knew me better than I knew myself.

He said, "I've missed you."

His voice was low, and it felt like he was whispering to my soul. Never before had someone touched me with words. They warmed my heart, as well as my coochie-coo. Perhaps this was the reason he knew me so well: he communicated with me on a deeper level than mere words. I wished we were alone so I could show him how I was feeling.

"Do you have money?" I hadn't intended to offer him any, although I did have a couple hundred I could give him without my husband's knowledge.

"No. I'll be okay. It's enough for me that you're here."

I didn't know whether or not to believe him. All I really heard was his willingness to suffer in silence. "I have some money saved. Merlin wouldn't have to know."

"You'd do that for me?"

I surprised myself when I realized how much I wanted to do for him. There wasn't much I could do about helping with his defense. The least I could do was try to make sure he was comfortable while he waited. After all, he was in this predicament because of me. For a second I thought about how this would look to my husband, and I ignored those negative feelings.

"It's not much—"

"If you don't give a shit about me, Cojo, why are you here?"

I remembered saying that to him, and it hurt. I felt tears burning in the back of my eyes. I was risking everything to be here, but I refused to put it into words. I didn't get what he wanted from me. Wasn't it enough that I was here? "I shouldn't have come," was all I said.

I couldn't understand what was wrong with me. I'd never been attracted to bad boys before, so this wanton behavior was out of character for me. There was something about this man that kept drawing me in, and I had to fight it. It wasn't like I was willing to give up my good husband for him. Or was I? I stood up to leave.

"Cojo, please don't leave. I'm sorry for making you feel uncomfortable."

He knew exactly what to say to make me relax and forget the outside world. But my baby wouldn't let me completely forget my life. The baby kicked, a not so gentle reminder that I was fucking up.

"I'm not uncomfortable. I just realized how badly this would look if anyone ever found out."

"By anyone, you mean my brother, don't you?"

He spit out *brother* like he'd tasted something nasty.

"Well, yeah, and Gina too."

"Why would you give a shit about what Gina thinks? She hates your guts."

I felt his anger rolling off him in waves, and it was hard to sit still as they pounded against me. "Gina and I are in a good place right now. I don't want to do anything to mess that up."

"When the hell did that happen?"

I wished I would have thought about it before I answered him. "We started to become friends after your arrest." Too late, I realized that I'd made it sound like he was the problem.

"Ain't that special." He looked around the room like he couldn't wait to get away from me, and it hurt my feelings. For reasons I was trying to deny, it was very important to me that I remain on Gavin's good side.

"Wait. That didn't come out right. Gina and I started getting close because of the baby. Oh, shit." I slapped my fingers over my mouth, but of course, it was too late. His eyes got round as a small plate.

"Baby? Please tell me this bitch ain't about to have my baby!"

At first I didn't think I'd heard him correctly. I thought he'd said, "A baby." As I replayed the words in my mind, I realized he'd said, "My baby."

"Come again. Did you just say—"

"Um, I—"

"Oh my God! Are you fucking kidding me? You are disgusting!"

I felt sick to my stomach. Here I was, throwing caution to the wind and risking my good, safe life for this low-class piece of shit. I stood up, knocking back my chair in my haste to get away.

"Cojo, please! I can explain."

"How? How the hell can you explain sleeping with your mother?"

"She's not my mother. She's my stepmother."

I didn't care that he was shouting. All I wanted to do was get out of there and forget I'd ever been stupid enough to go there in the first place.

"And that's supposed to make it better? You are a sick man, Gavin Mills. A very sick man." As I turned away, I couldn't believe how stupid I had been. Gavin was a monster and was not worth ruining my marriage for.

"Cojo, wait!"

I could feel all eyes on me as I ran from the room, shoving chairs out of my way. The room felt so much larger as I moved. My hand was down low over my stomach as I retched. I could not stop. I heard loud voices behind me, but I wasn't really paying attention.

"Bitch, have you lost your damn mind?"

That voice belonged to one of the two ladies I'd heard arguing before we were allowed into the visitors' waiting room. I didn't care about her petty comment. I was on a mission. I had half a mind to go over to Gina's house and confront her, but if I did, I'd be giving myself up in the process.

"I done told you 'bout calling me a bitch," yelled the other lady. I heard a loud scraping of chairs, and I almost stumbled trying to see what was happening but regained my footing. I had made it to the door when I was shoved viciously from behind. I had no idea who did it, and it was of little consequence. My head struck the metal door. Instead of falling backward, I felt myself sliding down the door to the floor. For the second time in my life, I saw stars, but it was nothing compared to the pain I felt. I landed on my stomach, on my baby, and I heard a loud pop before I passed out.

Chapter Twenty-six

MERLIN MILLS

Not going to work wasn't an option to me. It didn't matter how bad I felt, I had to show up or risk some armed officers coming to get me. I stumbled around Braxton's apartment, trying to be quiet. To me, I sounded like a bull in a china shop. My head was pounding, and my heart was hurting. I was upset with myself for not going home. Drunk or not, my place was at home, and I knew I was going to have a lot of explaining to do once I got there.

I had three messages on my phone by the time I made it to work, and I imagined Cojo cussing me out on every one of them. I was afraid to listen to them because I knew I'd fucked up.

"Damn, you look like shit."

I looked up when I heard Captain Jamison's voice. I jumped up to salute her, and it only made my head hurt worse. I grabbed the desk to steady myself.

"Private, in my office. Now."

This was not going to be a good day. I knew it the moment I opened my eyes, and this order confirmed it for me. I was not prepared to be on the hot seat with the captain. My head was all fuzzy, and my judgment was impaired.

"Yes, Captain." I followed her into her office and shut the door.

She stared at me for several seconds as I waited for permission to stand at ease.

She said, "Well?"

"Huh?" I was confused. She'd ordered me into her office, so what did she want?

"You look like shit. What do you have to say for yourself?"

I was still standing at attention, so I didn't know if I was speaking to my captain or my friend. "May I speak candidly, Captain?"

"Relax. It's me." She took a seat behind her desk and folded her fingers under her chin.

Once again, her beauty practically blinded me. I relaxed somewhat and took a seat opposite her. "I had a really rough night, hung out with my friend, and quite frankly drank too much."

I could still see the concern in her eyes as she exhaled loudly.

"Is that all? I've seen my share of hangovers."

I didn't know what it was about this woman that made me want to tell her every single thought in my head and in my heart. "It was a rough night."

"Okay, I'm not going to beat you over the head, 'cause I'm sure Cojo got in your ass."

I couldn't even fake the funk when she mentioned Cojo's name. I was so ashamed of the way I'd handled myself. "She hasn't seen me yet. I didn't go home. I crashed at my boy's house."

"Wow. No wonder you look like shit. I'm sure you had your reasons. I wouldn't want to be you right about now. You want to go on home so you can patch this up?"

As tempting as her offer sounded, somewhere in the pit of my stomach, I wasn't ready to face the music, especially since I hadn't listened to my messages. "I'll be okay. I just need to get some more coffee in my system and let the Advil do its thing. Thanks anyway."

"What are you hiding from?"

"You think you know everything." I was so serious when I said it, even though I laughed. She acted like she had a window into my soul.

"I do. Didn't you get the memo?"

It took me a few beats to get the joke, because I was still trying to see past the fog in my head.

"Did you call her at least?"

Damn. Who is this woman? "No, not yet," I admitted in defeat.

"That's not good. Why do I get the feeling there's a lot more to this story than you are telling me?"

"'Cause there is." I felt like a first-class jackass. I cared more about what Captain Jamison thought of me than how my wife must be feeling.

She shook her head and picked up the phone and dialed a number. I was puzzled as to whom she was calling until she passed me the phone. My answering machine greeted me. I left a message.

"Cojo, honey, I am so sorry I didn't come home last night. I got so drunk, Braxton wouldn't give me my keys, and I ended up sleeping at his house. It got too late to call. I hope you're not mad at me. I promise I will make it up to you."

I passed the receiver back, relieved for having made the call without actually speaking to my wife. I wasn't sure if she was at home screening the call because she was pissed or if she was out running errands. With the exception of going to the doctors and hanging out with Gina, I didn't know what she did with her time during the day. I felt myself getting mad all over again; it must have shown on my face.

"What is really going on with you? You don't seem like the type to hang out at all hours of the night."

"Trust me, I'm not. I'm going through a difficult time right now."

"And your wife isn't?"

I could tell she was getting a little pissed off with me by her sharp tone. "There's some things you don't know, and I'm allowing them to fuck with me. I'll be okay."

"You know what, Mills? I've pulled a lot of strings to keep you in town and close to your wife. I've done things for you that I've never done for any other soldier, and I'm beginning to regret it. If you're going to be another fuckup, tell me now and we can start doing this shit by the book."

I was conflicted because part of me wanted to tell her the whole truth. The other part of me was scared she would blow me off. I wasn't ready to throw in my cards, so I had no choice but to come clean. I sighed. "Man, I never wanted to tell you this. I'm really going through it about this thing with my brother."

"Is he out of jail or something?" She edged up on her seat, her anger apparently pushed aside.

"No. It's something else. When I told you he made a move on my wife, it was more serious than that. He actually pretended to be me and slept with her. Sometimes I find myself getting upset with her and the baby. She took a paternity test, and I'm pretty sure it's my kid and all. It's just sometimes I allow it to get to me. Yesterday was one of those days." I was afraid to look up because I didn't want to see censure in Captain Jamison's eyes. I really respected her, and I didn't want anything to ruin our relationship.

"Oh, wow! That's deep. If you told Cojo you forgave her, why is it still coming up? You can't have it both ways."

"In my heart I know it. It's different when you try to apply it. I'm having trust issues all of a sudden. The other day I found out she was keeping a secret from me about my stepmother, and then last night I found out that she had Gavin over to my house while I was locked up."

"Well, before you jump to any conclusions, I think you should find out from Cojo what's really going on. There could be a very good explanation as to why he was there."

"With his shirt off?"

"Fuck." She broke the pencil she was holding in half.

"Exactly. So I tried to drink my ass to death. You feel me?"

"I feel you. I'd have a hard time accepting that my damn self. Although there still could be a good explanation for it. If I were you, I wouldn't make any rash decisions."

"It's easier said than done. I mean, I forgave her for sleeping with him because she didn't know I had a twin. My brother is good at pretending to be me. When he kidnapped her, it didn't cross my mind that anything else could be going on. Now I'm starting to wonder. What if she went with him willingly and I'm Boo-Boo the Fool?"

"I don't think so. I've seen the way she looks at you. She couldn't have fooled me."

"So what are you saying? She fooled me?" I felt myself getting mad all over again, and this was not the time or the place for it.

"Back it down a notch, soldier. I'm not saying that at all. I was trying to say that I'm a good judge of character, and if she were faking it, I would have known it."

I was hurting in more ways than one. I instinctively wanted to lash out at the person closest to me by saying something stupid. I caught myself before I made that mistake. If I said out loud what I was thinking, I was quite sure I would wind up on the first thing smoking out of Atlanta.

"Sorry, Captain. I didn't mean any harm or disrespect. Because if you are such a great judge of character, you should have known I wouldn't intentionally do anything to mess up my marriage."

"None taken. And you're right. I'm sorry. You can't allow these feelings to fester. You are going to have to tell Cojo how you are feeling, or you're going to spend a lot of nights on somebody's couch."

I wouldn't mind sleeping on your couch. The thought stole its way into my head like a thief in the middle of the night. However, I refused to dwell on it. As long as there was a chance to make it work with my wife, I had to try. "She's probably too pissed at me for words. I've got three messages on my phone right now, and I haven't even checked to see what they were." I held up my phone to show her and noticed a fourth message. I had forgotten to take it off silent.

"You should try calling her again."

Nodding my head, I dialed my voice mail first just to see what kind of mood she was in. I was hoping she had listened to my message and had forgiven me for staying out. The first three messages were from Tabatha from the night before, asking me to return her call. I assumed it had something to do with the house we were trying to buy, and I wasn't trying to deal with that right now. I was disappointed because Cojo hadn't called, and it made me feel like she didn't even care that I hadn't come home.

"She didn't even call." I pretended like it didn't bother me. The last message was from just over an hour ago, and I didn't recognize the number. I grabbed a notepad from the captain's desk and copied the name and number.

She said, "Maybe she hung up without leaving a message."

"Nice try, but this is a smartphone, so it shows me that as well."

"Okay, I was trying to help a sista out. Whose number is that?"

"It's unlisted. The message said it was important that I return the call. Give me a second, all right?"

"Yeah, sure. Do you want me to leave?"

I smiled because it would look real crazy if she left her own office so I could make a personal call. "No, of course not. I'll only be a second." I was still smiling as I dialed the number. The smile quickly disappeared when I realized what the number belonged to. I hung up the phone.

"What's wrong?"

I heard the alarm in the captain's voice.

"DeKalb County Jail. Probably my damn brother calling, trying to get some more money from me. The man has some big balls. It's bad enough he slept with my wife. Now I'm supposed to be that sucker who helps him out in a pinch too. Excuse my French, but fuck him and the horse he rode in on."

"Do you think he really cared about Cojo, or was he using her to mess with you?"

"Honestly, I don't know." I had never given it much thought, because either way it went, it still hurt.

"I think you should go on home now and fix things. If you're still in love with your wife, it's worth a try."

I wasn't ready to leave. Captain Jamison was so easy to talk to, and I enjoyed her company. She made me feel like the man I believed I was. Whereas Cojo had had me second-guessing myself a lot lately. "If it's all

the same to you, Captain, I want to clear my head before I go home."

"Suit yourself. And if you ever need to talk, give me
a call. I hope you know I consider you more of a friend
than an enlisted person."

"Thanks. I feel the same way about you. I get tired of
feeling like a human dump truck, unloading my shit off
on you."

"There is a difference between dumping and sharing.
Friends don't dump. They share."

"Do you think I should take Cojo flowers?"

"Flowers shouldn't be given when you've fucked up.
When you give a girl flowers just because, they will appreciate it more. If you only do it when you've screwed
up, they start to hate flowers."

"Gotcha. Thanks."

I closed the door to her office, feeling a little better,
but I still had a lot of stuff on my mind. I knew things
couldn't go on as they had been. I was going to go home
and have a long talk with Cojo to see if we could get
back to the happy place we'd been in before my brother
ever came into our lives.

Chapter Twenty-seven

GINA MEADOWS

I took my time getting dressed to go to the meeting because I wanted to look perfect, but in the end, I felt like a dressed-up piece of shit. I changed my mind several times about going and lay back down on the sofa. Each time I did, the same commercial came on, prompting me to do something. When I was finally finished getting ready, I grabbed my purse, but I couldn't find my keys. Frustrated almost to the point of tears, I flipped my apartment upside down trying to find them. It seemed like some cosmic force was trying to keep me sick and miserable. I was bound and determined I was going to this meeting, even if I had to walk.

"They aren't here. I must have left them in the car." I didn't really think they were in the car. I simply didn't know of any other place they could be. I had to go to the bathroom before I took my search outside, so I used the guest bathroom and was pissed to see my keys sitting on the vanity. I never thought to look in this bathroom because I rarely used it.

"Whatever."

I was not a happy camper, because I had a big mess on my hands in the living room and kitchen. I'd tossed all the cushions off the sofa and chairs, emptied out several purses in the middle of the floor, opened every damn cabinet, and gone through the trash while searching for those keys, which were sitting in plain fucking view. I was tired and ready for a nap. I kept going, because I knew it was the devil trying to keep me stuck. I yanked open the front door, and my heart practically stopped. Ronald was here. It took me a few seconds to recover.

I said, "What the hell are you doing here?"

God had a serious sense of humor bringing Ronald here today. I didn't want to see him now, especially since I was trying to come to terms with having his son's baby. I placed my arms over my stomach. That did nothing more than make the bulge more obvious.

"Hello to you too," he said.

He looked good, and I hated it. For once, I wanted to see a big-ass pimple or wart hanging off his nose. A huge green snot ball or anything else that would repulse me would have been nice. If he had any flaws, I couldn't see them. He pushed past me and came into my apartment. I cringed, because every time he graced me with his presence, my house was a wreck. Ronald hated clutter, and I'd become a master at it. I still had the boxes I'd packed to move into his house sitting in the corner as a shrine to my most embarrassing moment.

"What do you want, Ronald? I was on my way out."

He looked over at the sofa, as if he was about to sit down, and realized he would either have to pick up the cushions himself or wait for me to do it. "So it's true. You really are going to have a baby." He swiped at his shoulders as if he were dusting off something dirty.

I had always known Ronald was an arrogant son of a bitch. Funnily, I had never seen it as a negative until today. I was pissed. How dare he march into my house unannounced and pass judgment on me after all the

shit he'd done to me? This motherfucker had some
brass fucking balls.

"I don't see how it's any of your business." I was still
trying to figure out how in the hell he found out. It
wasn't like we traveled in the same circles or anything
like that. I hadn't seen him since the last time he came
over to return my stuff and I stabbed him in the neck
with a fork! I edged my way to the kitchen counter,
because if he didn't believe fat meat was greasy, I was
about to show him.

"Who's the daddy?"

"Did I ask you who you're fucking? Last I checked,
you married someone else." I was so mad, I was shaking, and this time it wasn't because I was excited to see
him. I felt pure unadulterated anger.

"Hey, I was just checking, 'cause I didn't believe it."
He kicked a cushion out of his way as he walked into
the kitchen, then opened my refrigerator with his back
toward me like he lived here. His sense of entitlement
drove me nuts.

I heard something click inside my head and felt a
soothing calm come over me. I imagined I could hear
the second hand moving on the clock in the kitchen,
near his head. "Do you remember what happened the
last time you came over here?" He'd have to be a fool if
he didn't notice the menace in my voice. I had a knife
within my reach, and I was about to use it.

He shut the refrigerator door. "Yeah, I remember. I
still wear the scar." He touched the side of his neck.

"Then, I repeat, what do you want?" I was done being nice. He took my kindness and my love and used it
against me. I didn't need this motherfucker in my life,
and as far as I was concerned, the world would be a
better place if he wasn't in it. I grabbed the knife with
both hands.

"The last time I didn't press charges. I won't make the same mistake again, so don't get cute. A little birdie told me you were going to try to pin this baby on me. So I came over here to talk some sense into you. You know how you get when you get pregnant."

I never believed it was possible, but I actually saw red. Ronald looked like a mean-ass devil standing in my kitchen, complete with horns, a tail, and a pitch-fork. I put down the knife; he wasn't worth the trouble.

"You scum-sucking, low-life bottom feeder. If I acted crazy when I was pregnant, it was because you made me that way. I gave you everything I had, and it still wasn't enough. You're like a damn tick. You latch on to someone and keep on sucking them dry, and when you're done, you move on to your next victim."

"See what I mean?" He twirled his finger near his temple, suggesting I was acting crazy.

It took everything I had not to pick up the knife and stick it where the sun didn't shine. I wanted to cut his dick off, filet it, fry it in a skillet, and then make a dumpling soup with his hairy balls. It was like an in-fomercial in my head. I would take the soup out to the woods and toss it on the trees for the birds to feast on. With a strength I didn't know I possessed, I ripped the sleeve off my shirt.

His brows resembled the McDonald's arches. "What are you doing?"

"I want you out of my house now." I didn't raise my voice. I pushed the glasses drying on the counter to the floor, breaking them.

"Gina, stop it. I only came over here to talk some sense into you. You're too damn old to be having a kid."

My vision had cleared, and I saw Ronald for who he was, and if he wasn't trying to destroy me, I might have felt sorry for him. I almost pushed over the canister sets in the kitchen, until I realized who was going to have to clean that shit up. "Obviously not old enough, since my plumbing still works. Now, I suggest you get your ass out of my apartment before I call the police and tell them about this mess you made." I proudly held my belly, no longer feeling ashamed. I was doing this for me, and if he didn't like it, he could kiss my black ass.

"You'd better not try to pin this shit on me, Gina."

"Why the fuck would I want to do that? You ain't the only man in the world with a damn dick." It was becoming real clear that although he didn't want me, he didn't want anyone else to have me, either.

He said, "So you're out there fucking random people? How pathetic is that? Do you even know who the father is?"

"Why do you even fucking care? Get out of my house, Ronald, or I swear to God you're going to regret it."

"No, you're the one that is going to regret it if I ever hear one word about a paternity suit. I'm not going to let you fuck up my life like you did my boys. And don't think I don't know you put Merlin up to coming to see me a couple of weeks ago." He started walking to the door like his shit didn't stink, and I backed up to get out of his way. I didn't know about Merlin's visit, and I couldn't think of any reason why he would do that.

"Merlin doesn't even know about my baby, so you're wrong, as usual." I'd told only two people about my pregnancy—Cojo and Tabatha. Although it was possible Cojo had mentioned it to Merlin, I doubted it, and Tabatha couldn't stand Ronald.

"I'm going. Don't forget what I said. You're a bitter old woman, and I feel sorry for the bastard you're carrying. I just hope you do a better damn job raising it than you did those other two." He pulled a small plastic bag out of his pocket and threw it on the floor. "Give this to your girl. I know she wants it. She knows where to find me when she needs some more." He slammed the door behind him.

I was too stunned to move, because I knew what was inside the Baggie. But what did it all mean? To the best of my knowledge, Tabatha didn't do drugs. Crushed, I sank to the floor, careful not to harm my baby.

Ronald had said some hurtful things, and I tried not to dwell on them, but they kept replaying in my mind. I'd already apologized to Merlin for being a lousy mother. The only other person I'd yet to come clean with was Gavin. Now, more than ever, it was important I do so. I didn't want to continue repeating this vicious cycle.

I didn't move from the floor for what felt like an hour, until I couldn't stand it anymore. I had to go to the bathroom. My eyes were red and swollen. I had a plan, and I felt much better now that I knew what I needed to do. I swept up the broken glass from the kitchen floor and replaced the cushions on the sofa and chairs. All thoughts of going to the meeting were temporarily put on hold. I had more important matters to attend to.

"Wow! You sure you're not having twins? How many months are you?"

Tabatha stood nervously outside my door. My stomach had popped since the last time she'd seen me, so I understood what she meant. I stood aside to let her come in, my heart hammering against my chest.

"Can I get you something to drink? Coffee, tea, or something stronger?"

She said, "I'll have whatever you're having."

"Milk?"

"Yuck. I hate milk. Show me the booze, and I'll fix my own."

I chuckled. Milk wasn't my favorite, either, but I had to do what I had to do. "It took some getting used to, but it's okay now."

I watched her as she fixed her drink, while I was trying to think of the best way to approach the situation. I made up my mind I wasn't going to fight with her. We'd been friends for a very long time, and I hoped we'd still be friends by the time this night was over with. She finished making her drink and came back into the living room.

She said, "How are you feeling?"

"I'm good, but I stay hungry all the damn time."

"I guess so. Did you say whether it was twins or not?" She seemed preoccupied.

"No, last I checked, it's only one. But he's a big one."

"Ah, a boy. Congratulations. You look absolutely beautiful." She kept fidgeting with the hem of her shirt and the ends of her hair.

The silence that filled the room was thick as each of us tried to figure out what was safe to say. The thing about being friends for so long was we were both hot-headed and tended to say whatever was on our mind and would apologize later, if necessary.

"Thanks," I said finally, breaking the silence.

"Gina, I'm so glad you called me back. I was getting ready to start stalking your ass if you hadn't. I really owe you an apology, and it was killing me not being able to say it to you. I'm sorry for not being a better friend when you needed me."

"You have your reasons. I'm over it." I didn't mean for it to come off sounding like I couldn't have cared less, but it did. We had too much history for me to try to start sugarcoating my responses to her now.

She said, "So what have you been doing with yourself?"

"I've been working from home since the job didn't like my idea of taking a leave of absence from work. I didn't feel like explaining to my coworkers about the baby, so it works out better for all of us. If things go as I've planned them, I will continue to work from home so I can spend more time with the baby."

"That's fantastic. Think about all the money you will save on gas and stuff, not to mention babysitters."

"Yeah." I nodded.

"Hey, I didn't get a chance to tell you I saw Merlin and I finally got to meet Cojo. Thanks for referring them to me. We found a nice house, and they've put in an offer on it."

"That's nice. I hope it works out for them."

I was never good at small talk, especially when I had something else on my mind. I pitched the plastic Baggie on the table in front of Tabatha. She flinched, as if I had tried to strike her with a two-by-four.

"What the fu—" Tabatha's eyes narrowed, and I noticed a small sheen of perspiration on her forehead. She scratched her left arm, and it was the confirmation I needed.

"Ronald left it for you." I couldn't hide the hurt I felt. I'd known Tabatha for over twenty years, and I never knew anything about her addiction to drugs.

"For me? Why would he?" She did not take her eyes off the Baggie, and it tore me up inside.

"I don't know. Why don't you tell me?" I folded my arms underneath my ample breasts, pushing them up in the process.

"Gina, I, uh—"

"Don't get to stuttering now, bitch."

"Would you please put that way?"

She tore her eyes away from the table. I might've felt sorry for her if I didn't feel so betrayed. How could she judge me all these years and still hide this dirty secret from me? I'd lost all respect for her, something I thought I would never do.

I said, "I'm sorry. Did I break your fucking concentration?"

"Fine. Leave it there, because I have a feeling I'm going to need it by the time I leave here tonight."

I snatched the Baggie off the table and stuffed it down my bra. I wasn't feeling that generous. If she was going to get high tonight, the bitch would have to go out and buy it, since she obviously knew where to get it.

Chapter Twenty-eight

ANGIE SIMPSON

"So did you tell your boss that I dropped the charges against her client?"

"I told you she isn't my boss. She's a coworker. And second, I haven't talked to her in a couple of days. She'll find out eventually."

I was satisfied with Young's answer. If he had said yes, I would have walked out of the sporty little bar/restaurant he'd taken me to, which was called Spondivits. I'd been skeptical about going out with him, especially because of how we met. He was so cute, I couldn't help myself.

"I have been dying to ask you this. Why would your mother name you Young?"

He laughed. "She didn't. Young is my last name."

"Oh. I thought she was trying to chase her past or something like that."

"Nah, nothing like that. I never liked my first name, so folks started calling me by my last name. It stuck with me."

"Am I ever going to get to know what your first name is?" I said, batting my lashes.

"Maybe, if you stick around long enough."

I liked the mystery surrounding him. He was different from the other guys I'd gone out with in the past. "Would you tell me if I guessed?"

"Trust me, you will never guess."

"Don't tell me your mother gave you one of those ghettofied names that uses damn near every letter of the alphabet, or, wait, I know, she combined two names together."

"No, I'm telling you, Mom Dukes is normal. Besides, she didn't name me. My dad did."

"Oh." I picked up the menu to see what I wanted to eat. Young had said they had crazy seafood, and I loved to eat.

"If you like crab legs, this place has the best. I also recommend the fried lobster and the steamed shrimp."

"I've never had fried lobster before, and I don't think I'm ready to start now. I love me some shrimp and crab legs."

He said, "We can get a bucket of both and share them."

"Sounds good. I'd also like a drink."

"No can do, baby girl. You're too young, and they card everyone here."

"Come on! It's my birthday. I'm almost legal." I pulled out my driver's license and laid it on the table, smiling.

"Wow. Happy birthday. How come you didn't tell me? I would have gotten you some flowers or something."

"Aw, aren't you sweet? You don't have to make a big deal of it."

"Are you kidding me? It's your birthday. It *is* a big deal. What would you like to drink?"

"I don't know . . . something fruity."

"Leave it to me. I know exactly what to get you. A virgin daiquiri."

"Ballbuster."

He didn't give me what I wanted, I liked that. I sat back in my chair and admired him as he placed our orders and conversed with the waiter. I loved the confident way he handled himself. His charm was making it very difficult to remember my resolve to go slow with him.

"What do you do when you're not chasing down folks and serving up bad news?" I asked after the waiter had left our table.

"Hey, don't knock the paycheck, baby. I'm glad to have this good government job. It's rough out there."

"Tell me about it. I took off a couple of semesters from school to get my mind right, and I haven't been able to find a job yet. Thank God my dad is still able to help me out until I can get on my feet."

"I know that's right. It must be hard on him losing his wife."

"Humph. Truth be told, I think he's glad the old battle-ax is gone. My mom was something else, and the fact that the accident was her fault, we had to fight the insurance company to pay the bills. I had to sue my mother's estate to get my medical bills paid too."

"That's tough."

"Yeah, my dad told me to sue for pain and suffering too. So maybe when I get my settlement, I can get a place of my own. But I need to find me a job so I can pay the bills."

"What were you going to school for?"

"Criminal justice. Can you believe it? After the shit with your coworker, I almost quit. Good thing I'm not a quitter."

"Shut up. I was a criminal justice major myself. How much longer do you have to go?"

"I started school early. This is my last year. I needed a break to get my head on straight."

..t's understandable. Don't sit out too long. The ..ger you put it off, the harder it is to get back in the swing of things."

"I know. I know."

Our food arrived and halted our conversation. I detested guys who liked to talk with food hanging out of their mouth. We started popping crab legs, peeling shrimp, dipping them in butter, and stuffing our faces. He washed his down with a beer, and I had my Blue Lagoon, which was superb. This was one of the best meals I'd had in my life.

He said matter-of-factly, "You know, I might be able to help you out on the job front. The lady you so graciously called my boss is going to be leaving the public defender's office at the end of the month. I happen to know she's going to need a good personal assistant. If you want, I could put in a good word for you."

"That would be so cool, if you could make it happen. I was not the nicest person when I was last in her office."

"Don't worry about it. If you want me to put in a word, I will. She owes me, so I doubt it will be a problem."

"What's she like to work for? I'm not trying to sign up for no dragon master."

"She is nothing like the person you've been dealing with. And she's not one of those people who wants you to do everything for them. She's real passionate about her work. Aside from that, she's good peeps. I think you'll like her."

"Okay. I'm willing to give it a try. I'm not afraid to check the bitch if she gets out of hand."

Chapter Twenty-nine

MERLIN MILLS

Problems seemed to fall out of the sky every time I attempted to shut off the computer and go home. Despite my best efforts, I was unable to get out of there early. My head felt heavier than normal, and I was still nursing a slight headache. At least my appetite had returned. I was starving. I couldn't wait to sit down to eat another one of Cojo's home-cooked meals. However, Cojo's car was not parked in the parking lot. To my knowledge, she didn't have any doctor's appointments, so I was mildly concerned about her absence.

I sure hope she left dinner on the stove, 'cause my stomach's about to eat through my back. I placed my keys on the counter and searched for the mail. It wasn't on the counter. This meant one of two things: either we didn't get any mail or Cojo left before the mail arrived. This was not making any sense to me and made me feel a little nervous. I noticed a large brown envelope on the sofa and picked it up. It was from Tabatha.

"Damn. I forgot to call her." I opened the envelope, and it contained a counteroffer on the house we were trying to get. I threw the envelope back on the sofa. I wasn't ready to think about the house yet. First, I had to find out what was going on with Cojo.

The kitchen didn't hold any lingering smells, not even from the night before. The bedroom was disheveled, as if Cojo had left in a hurry. I started to get worried as I walked back into the kitchen and noticed the flashing light on our answering machine. My hands shook as I picked up the receiver, because I had a feeling it was not going to be good news. Before I listened to the messages, I scrolled through the numbers, none of which would cause my wife to run out of the house. I played the messages.

"This call is for Merlin Mills. I am Detris Hamm from Emory Hospital. Your wife, Cojo Mills, has been in an accident and has been admitted to the hospital. Please call—"

I didn't wait to get the number. Feeling numb, I grabbed my keys off the counter to go to the hospital. As I was running, I dialed the first person who came to mind. "Captain Jamison, sorry to bother you. I just received word my wife was involved in an accident."

"Oh God, no. Is she okay?"

"I don't know. I'm on the way to the hospital now."

"Which hospital? I'll meet you there."

"Emory. Thanks. I don't want to be there alone."

"On my way."

As I drove, I tried not to think bad thoughts. I was a firm believer that it was possible to speak things into existence. So I prayed. *Father, please hold my wife and child in your loving arms and keep them protected. Tell her that I'm so sorry for doubting her and that everything will be all right. Father God, I ask this in the name of the Lord Jesus Christ. Amen.*

When I got to the hospital, I tried to act like I had a modicum of sense. I approached the information desk with Cojo's insurance card and my identification in hand. On the outside I was as cool as a cucumber. I was a hot-ass mess on the inside.

"Good evening. I received a phone call that my wife was involved in an accident."

"What's your wife's name?"

"Cojo Mills."

I handed her the information I assumed she'd need to find Cojo. She typed something into her computer, photocopied the insurance card and my identification, and passed them back. The seconds it took for her to enter the information seemed like hours to me. I didn't act a fool, because it would not help the situation.

"Your wife is in surgery. I have made a note on her chart that you are here, and the doctors will come and speak with you as soon as they are available."

"Surgery? What happened to her?" I heard my voice rising. I couldn't help myself. How was I supposed to act when all I was being told was she was in surgery?

"I'm sorry, sir. This is all the information I have. You can take a seat in the waiting room."

I opened my mouth to protest and stopped. What could I have said to change anything? Showing my ass would have done absolutely nothing but piss off a few folks, so I took a seat and waited. It wasn't long before Captain Jamison came through the double doors. She was dressed in civilian clothes, which put her military wear to shame.

"Merlin, I got here as soon as I could."

"Thanks, Captain."

"My friends call me Candace. Have you heard anything?" She took my hand and held it.

Tonight we weren't officer and soldier, we were friends, and I appreciated her being here with me. I could have called Gina or Braxton had I not been operating on pure adrenaline. As it was, Candace was the closest to me and my situation.

"No. The only thing they told me was that she was in surgery. I don't know what's going on."

"They didn't say what type of accident?"

"No. It has to be a car accident, because her car wasn't at home."

"Dear God, I didn't even think about a car accident. I was thinking more of her falling or something like that."

"I just want to know where she was going, because as far as I know, she didn't have anything to do today."

"Merlin, don't do this. You haven't talked to her since yesterday, so you don't really know."

Damn. She was right. A lot could have happened. Surely she would have phoned me if something important had happened. "I feel like such a fuckup. This shit is all my fault. If I'd just taken my black ass home, none of this would have happened."

"You don't know that, Merlin, so don't beat yourself up. Until we know something concrete, all we can do is pray. Have you eaten yet?"

"No. I thought I was going to eat when I got home."

Candace was still holding my hand, and she gripped it tighter. "I'm sure they have a cafeteria in this place. I'm going to go grab us a couple of sandwiches."

"No thanks. I don't think I'm going to be able to swallow anything right now."

"You have to eat. I'll be right back."

I followed the gentle sway of her hips as she walked away. She might not have been trying to entice me, but she did, and I had to force myself to look away. It was only natural for me to have some kind of feelings toward the captain, especially since we'd shared so much in a short period of time. I wasn't trying to mess up our friendship. She was vulnerable, and so was I—a good recipe for disaster.

I thought about calling Gina, because I knew she would get mad if I didn't. However, I was still a little upset with her for not confiding in me about her pregnancy. I decided to hold off calling her until I knew what was going on.

"Are you Mr. Mills?"

I looked up into the eyes of a young woman wearing a white coat. I was so lost in thought, I didn't hear her approach. I stood up.

"Yes, I am." I was scared.

"Please sit down." The woman took the seat once occupied by Candace.

Still scared, I sat back down.

"My name is Dr. Floyd, and I am the surgeon assigned to your wife."

"How is she? Can I see her?" The whole conversation felt surreal to me. Our voices sounded muffled, and I felt as if I were talking in slow motion.

"She is resting now. Mr. Mills, are you here alone?"

What the fuck does that have to do with anything?
"Uh, no. I have a friend of the family with me. She's down in the cafeteria, getting something to eat. Why?"

"You're not going to be able to see your wife tonight, and I wanted to make sure someone was with you to drive you home if necessary."

"I don't mean no harm, Doctor, but you're not making any sense." I was at the end of my patience and knew it was only a matter of time before I exploded.

Dr. Floyd said, "I know and I'm sorry. I'm not very good in situations like this."

"Situations like what?" I wanted to tell the bitch to go get someone who knew what the fuck was going on, because she was making a bad situation worse.

"Mr. Mills, can you please lower your voice?"

I wiped my hand across my face, trying to get a grip. I had promised myself I wasn't going to act like a fool, but that was before I'd met this doctor. "Sorry. It's been a long day. Can you please tell me what happened to my wife? The only thing I know is she wasn't home when I got in from work. When I checked the answering machine, I was told she was here." I was speaking very slowly, like I was talking to a three-year-old child instead of a fucking MD.

"I understand."

Is she fucking kidding me! I was about two seconds away from snatching this bitch up by her collar and shaking the shit out of her. Fortunately, Candace walked over to us and sat down beside me.

"Your wife had a very bad fall. I'm sorry to be the one to inform you that she lost the baby." Obviously, the doctor had been waiting until she had backup before she gave me the bad news.

I might have had an outer body experience, because I felt removed from the conversation. I saw both the doctor's and Candace's lips moving. For a second or two, they carried on the conversation without me. I couldn't understand what they were saying. The only thing I heard was that Cojo had fallen. Stuff like this didn't happen to me, so I was ill equipped to handle it.

I shook my head to rattle my brain. "How?"

"It is my understanding she was involved in an altercation."

"With who? My wife doesn't have many friends."

"Oh, I doubt these ladies were friends of hers. At least I don't think so," Dr. Floyd said.

What the fuck is this bitch saying to me? I looked at Candace to see if she was as clueless as I was, and she nodded her head.

Candace said, "Dr., uh—"

"Floyd."

"Okay, Dr. Floyd. Can you please start at the beginning, because I'm lost? We were under the impression that Mrs. Mills was in a car accident."

The doctor flipped through the papers she'd been holding in her hand while shaking her head. "No, that's incorrect. His wife was brought here by ambulance from DeKalb County Jail. There is nothing in here to suggest a car accident."

I said, "Cojo was arrested? What the hell?"

"No, no. I am so sorry. I must have been absent the day we were taught how to deal with family situations, because I suck at this," the doctor said, laughing.

To me, there wasn't a damn thing funny.

Candace said, "You ain't lying. Maybe you should get someone else to speak with us, because this shit here ain't working."

I didn't know which one of us wanted to beat the bitch up more, me or Candace.

"Right. I'm sorry." Dr. Floyd got up and quickly left. A good thing, because I was about to lose it.

Candace said, "I'm sorry about the baby."

Candace had placed her arm back around my shoulders. I must have been in shock, because I didn't feel connected to what was going on around me. I had just lost a child, and the only thing I felt was relief.

I pulled away from Candace, ashamed of my feelings. "This shit isn't making any sense. What was Cojo doing at the jail?" And then it hit me. The phone call from the jail and now this. "Let's go." I stood up and grabbed Candace's hand.

Candace frowned. "What do you mean? We can't go yet—"

"I said, let's go." I knew everything I needed to know, and I wanted to get out of there as fast as I could, before I did something I knew I would regret. For the second time in my life, I felt an overwhelming rage, only this time I refused to give in to it.

Candace tried to grab the sandwiches as we walked away. I waved her off. I didn't want anything to eat, and I damn sure didn't want anything from this hospital.

I turned to her once we were outside, pausing to take a couple of deep breaths. "Thank you so much for coming, and I'm sorry to have bothered you again. Where did you park?"

She didn't answer me right away, and I was growing impatient. I started walking to the deck, assuming she'd point out her car when we got close enough to it.

"What are you doing, Merlin?"

"What does it look like?" I wasn't mad at Candace; I was mad at myself. Two times in less than twenty-four hours I'd backed my truck up on her front porch and poured my shit on it. She might be a glutton for punishment, but I was done.

"Why? You still don't know what's going on."

"Just drop it, Candace. It's not worth it."

"So you're going to give up? Are you kidding me?" She sounded surprised.

I stopped walking. "What do you want me to do? I can't fight this battle by myself." I felt like screaming because that was exactly how I felt. No matter how hard I tried, something or someone seemed determined to fuck up my marriage.

"Fine."

We had arrived at her Jeep, and I held her door while she got in. She was moving way too slowly for me. Every time I looked up at the hospital, I wanted to puke.

She said, "Get in. I'm hungry, and you're going to sit with me while I eat." It was not a request; it was an order.

I walked around to the driver's side on autopilot and got in. "What about my car?"

"It ain't going nowhere. I'll bring you back when we're finished."

I stared out the window and tried not to feel. It was still early, so the roads were empty, much like my heart. She switched on the radio and drove. I didn't ask her where we were going. I didn't care.

"You're scaring me, Merlin."

"I'm okay. I just needed to get out of there."

Fifteen minutes later, she said, "We're here."

She'd taken me to her house. I'd assumed we were going to go to a restaurant, but this was even better because I didn't have to put on a front for a bunch of strangers.

"You got something to drink in there?" I hadn't opened the car door and wouldn't until she answered my question.

"Yeah."

"Good." That was all I needed to know, because I planned on drinking every bit of it.

Chapter Thirty

MEREDITH BOWERS

"You still packing?" Young poked his head in my office after a soft rap on the door.

"Yeah, I'm doing a little bit each day. I don't know how I accumulated so much stuff." The entire left wall of the office was stacked tall with boxes, and I would need to go get more boxes to finish the job.

"I feel ya. So when's your last day?"

"It's still kind of up in the air. I don't want to leave any open cases. I also want to take a short vacation before I become my own slave master. You know what I mean?"

"Must be nice. Just don't forget about us slaves still stuck on the plantation."

"Hey, trust me, I won't. I might even want to use your services from time to time."

"Word? That's what's up. You know they don't pay no overtime in this joint, and they still got the freeze on raises."

"I know. It's one of the reasons why I'm leaving. I don't understand how they expect folks to live when everything around us is going up except our salaries."

"Right, right. I'm still the new kid on the block, and this no raise shit still sucks."

"Well, once I get on my feet, I'm sure I can help fill your pockets. I like the way you work." It wasn't the only thing I liked about Young. He didn't need to know about the rest of it. I liked the kid a lot, and I was still trying to maintain a professional relationship with him.

He said, "I have a good assistant lined up for you when you open up shop."

"Oh yeah? I haven't even thought that far. Good looking out. I'm sure I will need one."

"You already know her. You scared the shit out of her in her deposition, so I think you owe her."

"What girl? Oh, I know who you mean. Angie Simpson, right?"

"Yeah, got her so scared, she asked the DA to drop the charges."

"I heard. That was a trip. I would have never expected it. Shocked me."

"Well, I did kinda help a sista out. After she lost the baby, we had a conversation."

"I should have known you had something to do with it. I was beginning to think my guy was capable of shitting horseshoes."

"Excuse me?"

"My bad, I was talking about my client. I thought the man had a horseshoe stuck up his ass."

"Are you going to fill in the blanks or leave me hanging?"

"Sorry, Young. It's an old habit of mine I'm trying to break. Angie was going to be the nail in my client's coffin. If her mother had anything to do with it, she was going to see his ass rot in jail. Now she's dead, and the child is too."

"Kinda sucks if you ask me."

"Yeah, it does. This whole case was crazy. I don't believe all of old girl's testimony, either. Something happened, more than she was admitting to. I'm not saying she deserved to be set on fire or raped, if that actually happened. It wasn't as innocent as she proclaimed it to be. So if you're getting involved with this one, be careful."

"So, are you saying you won't give the girl a chance and give her a job?"

"No. I don't really care what went on that night. If she's good, I'm good. She certainly made my job easier."

He said, "What if the guy is really nuts and tried to kill her?"

"That's not my problem, Young. My job is to provide reasonable doubt in the minds of the potential jurors. If I do it and he gets acquitted, I did my job."

"I know. You've told me this before. I just don't want to open the paper up one day and see his mug looking back at me."

"I honestly don't believe you will. I think this last dance with the law scared him straight. If I get him off, he may well become a model citizen."

"You really believe that?"

I nodded. "Yeah, I do."

"So what do you want me to tell Angie?"

"You seeing her?" I shook off a twinge of jealousy. I could have given birth to a child his age.

He looked me right in the eyes, his face expressionless. "Does it matter?"

"Nope. Tell her to give me a call."

"Cool. Let me know if you need any help moving these boxes."

"No doubt I will. And, Young, thanks again."

I was making a big move by going out on my own and opening up my own practice. I was ready for the challenge. I was a very hard worker and was confident in my abilities as a lawyer. The problem with the public defender's office was that no matter how long or hard I worked, my paycheck stayed the same. It was safe, but safe was also boring.

There was only one more obstacle standing in the way of Gavin Mills being released from jail, Cojo Mills. I pulled his file from my desk and began reading over my notes. I hadn't spoken to Cojo yet, because I was trying to figure out the best way to handle her. Since she was older, intimidation wouldn't work. In his interview, Gavin claimed they had consensual sex. If it was true, I might be able to get the DA to drop those charges as well. Especially if Cojo wanted to keep their relationship a secret from her husband. The DA was in the same boat I was in. It didn't matter if he had ten cases or twenty, he'd still get the same amount of money on his check, and I was banking on this to work in my favor.

I placed the file in my briefcase, because I wanted to speak to Gavin one more time before I approached Cojo. First impressions were everything. If I blew it on approach, I'd never get her to cooperate with me.

"It's about time you showed up," Gavin said as he was led into the interview room at the jail.

I'd requested a private meeting with him. I waited until the guard had removed his cuffs and left before I responded. I didn't appreciate the attitude one bit. "I thought I told you before that you're not my only client, so I suggest you chill." I didn't know what type of women he was used to dealing with, but he'd met his match in me. I wasn't going to allow him to talk to me any kind of way, and he'd best recognize it.

"Damn, man. Fuck. I'm sorry." He ran his fingers over the stubble on his head. He appeared to be worried, almost frantic.

"What's wrong?" I was on heightened alert. I knew enough about what went on inside of our jails to know situations could change overnight. Altercations between prisoners were common daily occurrences, and if I were Gavin's paid attorney, I would have taken precautions to ensure I'd get notification of anything involving my client. However, since this was not the case, I hadn't gone the extra mile.

"I've been calling your office for two damn days." He was pouting, and it wasn't a good look for a grown-ass man.

I shook my head because that was one thing I didn't do, whining-ass men. "I came when I had something to tell you. Now, unless you have something to say that is relevant to your case, I suggest you zip your lips."

I could tell Gavin wasn't used to a woman like me, and it was funny watching him squirm in his seat. Under normal circumstances, he probably would've smacked the shit out of me. Under normal circumstances he might have, and now he had to take it. It felt good to watch him suffer in silence.

"Great. I have a little bit of good news for you," I revealed. "The DA has decided to drop the charges against you in the case of Angie Simpson."

Gavin didn't say a word; not even a smile crossed his lips. While I didn't expect him to do backflips, I expected at least a thank-you, but I got nada.

"Aren't you going to say anything?" I was livid.

"You told me to zip it."

This motherfucker was trying my patience big-time. His behavior reminded me of a child's, and part of me wanted to walk away and leave his carcass to rot in his cell with his stinky-ass attitude.

"I told you to stop whining like a big-ass baby."

"I wasn't whining. I had something important to tell you."

"Is it pertinent to your charges?"

"Yeah."

"Then what is it?" If he expected me to sit there all day and pull the information from him one word at a time, he was barking up the wrong tree.

"Cojo came to see me the other day."

"Is she going to help, or is this another problem that I have to deal with?" My pen was poised over my pad, ready to take notes. We were so close to the end, and I hoped he wasn't going to open up a whole new can of problems that would delay his release.

"She wasn't happy with me when she left. Cojo practically ran out of here, and she walked in between two ladies who were fighting. It was fucked up. This one lady pushed this other bitch, and she fell into Cojo. The guards put us on lockdown and moved us out of the room, so I don't know what happened next. It looked bad."

"Fuck. How bad is bad?"

"She was on the floor when I last saw her, and she didn't get up."

I looked through my notes and found a phone number for Cojo and dialed her house. The phone rang at least five times before the answering machine picked up. I didn't leave a message.

"What was she doing here? She violated her own protective order. That doesn't make any sense to me."

"She said she wanted to make sure I was okay."

"Ain't that special." I rolled my eyes. Either this man had a magic stick in his pants that made women lose their damn minds or he was the luckiest man alive. I couldn't figure out which one it was.

"Whatever. I told you she has a soft spot for me."

"But you said she was mad at you when she left."

"Yeah, well, that was because I messed up and told her I might be the father of Gina's baby."

"I already told you that was nasty, anyway, and you should have kept that information to yourself." I put my pad back in my briefcase. I had to find out what was going on with Cojo, and I needed to do it quickly.

I leaned in close to Gavin, my face inches from his. "When this shit is over, you're going to have to make some serious changes in your life, because if you don't, you're going to bust a hole in hell when you get there. I'm sure they are holding a spot for you." I snapped my briefcase closed. I had never been so serious about something in my life.

"I know. Will you let me know what you find out?"

Chapter Thirty-one

TABATHA FLETCHER

The sight of the familiar plastic Baggie seemed to burn a hole in my brain. I could almost see it nestled in between Gina's breasts. I couldn't stand it. I gulped down my drink and poured another. I refused to look at Gina because my eyes wouldn't rise above her chest.

"Gina, it isn't what you think. The drugs . . . It was a very long time ago. Way before I met you."

"Oh yeah? Well, it must have been a serious addiction for you to have kept it a secret for so long."

"It was. You don't know the half of it." I didn't mean to say that. The words just slipped out.

"Obviously. But it wasn't *such* a damn secret, considering that Ronald knew. What's up with that?"

I exhaled, because there was no way I was going to be able to dress this shit up. It was going to hurt us both. These were secrets I'd intended to take with me to the grave. "It's a long story."

She pitched the Baggie back on the table. "I've got time."

I turned my head and prayed for the strength we'd both need to get through this.

"I met Ronald when I was about thirteen or fourteen. We lived in the same neighborhood. He was older than me, and my mother wouldn't let me hang around him. Even though he didn't go to my school, he was always there."

"Humph. Sounds familiar."

"I didn't know he was dealing until I started spending time with him. He got me hooked, and when my mom found out, she moved us to another apartment. I kept sneaking out to be with him. I thought I was in love."

"So why didn't you tell me, especially since it was before I met him?"

"There's more." I finished my drink and poured another one. I had a feeling I could drink the entire bottle of booze and it wouldn't be enough to dull my pain. "I got pregnant at fourteen, and my mother refused to let me get an abortion." I stole a look at Gina, but either she'd missed what I said or she hadn't made the connection.

"I had a three-hundred-dollar-a-day heroin addiction I couldn't afford to feed. My mom sent me to live with my aunt Theresa in Virginia. She stayed out in the country, so I couldn't get the drugs I needed. I got clean there and have been ever since."

"What about the baby? Did you leave it there too?"

I shook my head no as I started to cry. "My mom was going to have Ronald arrested for statutory rape and for what he did to me. She made him raise the babies in exchange for his freedom. She said I shouldn't have to pay for the rest of my life, and I was forbidden to see him again. Once the drugs were out of my system, I didn't want to see him. I hated him."

Gina just stared at her hands, which were on her lap, and I waited for her to connect the dots. I didn't know what else to say. It was so quiet in her apartment, I could hear her neighbors walking on the carpet. If I hadn't already bitten my nails down to nubs, I would have gnawed on them then.

"Gavin and Merlin are yours?" She was rocking in her chair from side to side. It was eerie. There was no malice in her voice, but I knew she had to be hurting.

"Yes. When Ronald tired of me, he gave me to his friends. I was so high all the time, I didn't care as long as the drugs kept coming. When I got pregnant, my mother made all the guys take a paternity test. Ronald was the father."

"Figures. All this time I thought I was fighting devils I didn't know, and it turned out I had invited them into my living room and didn't even know it. I could kill you for this, but you're not worth going to jail over."

"Gina, I'm sorry. That's why Ronald didn't want us to be friends. He was afraid I would tell you." Being honest with her wasn't helping my case.

"He didn't have to worry about that, now did he? I'll bet you two got a real chuckle out of this big-ass sham y'all pulled on me. I ought to kill both of you."

I moved farther away from her icy stare. "You had the kids for two years before I realized who they were. I begged you to give them back, and you wouldn't listen."

"You called them little bastards almost every chance you got!"

"What was I supposed to do? I couldn't love them. I didn't even love myself! Why do you think Ronald was so hell-bent on keeping us apart? He didn't want to ruin a good thing."

"They made my life hell, and so did you."

"I can't tell you how sorry I am. I wanted to tell you."

"I don't believe a motherfucking word of it. You were so fucking perfect. All the time telling me what I should do with my life. At least I wasn't a motherfucking druggie who gave up her own children!"

"Damn, I was a child, Gina. I couldn't take care of no babies."

"I couldn't either! I struggled, and you know it. You were there!"

"I swear, Gina, on everything, I never meant to hurt you. I love you."

"You have a fucked-up way of showing it."

I wanted to go to her and hold her, even though I knew I was the last person in the world she wanted to touch her.

She said, "You were never there when I really needed you. And the whole time you were, you had an ulterior motive."

"That's not true. I tried to get you away from Ronald, and you wouldn't listen."

"That's because you probably still wanted him for yourself. For all I know, you're still fucking him. Looks like he did the same thing to you that he did to me."

"The only time I saw Ronald was a couple of weeks ago. I went looking for him when you told me about the lawyer wanting to speak with you. I told Ronald he needed to tell you because I wouldn't lie for him anymore."

"Oh, so you developed a heart after twenty fucking years? Gee, thanks."

"It wasn't like that. When I realized how attached you were to my kids, I tried to help you with them."

She flinched when I called them my kids. It was the first time I'd called them that out loud, and I didn't know how to feel about it. I wasn't like other women I knew, who yearned to have children and seemed to blossom at the mere thought of kids. I didn't want them. I'd never wanted them.

"You could've helped me with the truth. Don't you think if you'd have been honest with me about your relationship with Ronald, it would have given me the strength to pull away, instead of wasting all those years on a jackass?"

"Well, when you put it that way, yeah. Hindsight is a motherfucker. I wasn't thinking like that."

"Apparently not." She got up from the sofa and opened the door. "Get the fuck out, and take your dope with you. The sight of you is making me sick."

"Gina, wait—"

"No, you don't understand. I want to kick your ass so bad, it's hurting me, and the only reason why I haven't broken my foot off in your ass is that I don't want to hurt my baby."

"Please tell me you are not going to raise another one of Ronald's children."

Her face turned bright red, and her eyes bulged slightly. Her lips turned down on the sides as she glared at me.

"What I do and who I do it with are none of your motherfucking business. Now, I suggest you get the hell out of my house before I change my mind about pissing on your grave tomorrow. And don't you dare contact *my* children! You and that fucker Ronald can both kiss my ass."

She stomped over to the table with her shoulders pulled back and picked up the drugs. She tossed them outside, and like a true addict, I followed them. She might not have wanted to scrap with me, but it didn't stop her from flinging a book at me as I walked out the door. It bumped me in the back of the head as I bent over to pick up the drugs.

Chapter Thirty-two

GINA MEADOWS

Getting to sleep last night was next to impossible. I tossed and turned for so long, I finally got up and went to the living room to watch television. Every time I closed my eyes, I heard Tabatha say she was really the twins' mother. She was such a hypocrite, and it made me question everything I thought I knew about her. She used to call me dick whipped and criticize me for drinking too much. At least I didn't stick a needle in my arm and fuck random guys for drugs.

Tabatha and I had done our share of fighting, and I had never doubted her love for me, even when we were cussing each other out. This time it was totally different, because now I no longer trusted her or what we shared together. How could she do that to me and still be my friend? I didn't give a fuck about the drugs, because we've all been enslaved by one thing or another during the course of our lives. I cared that she'd lied to me for over twenty damn years! And if this shit with Gavin hadn't come up, I might not have ever found out.

God didn't like ugly, or else I would have told Tabatha she was about to become a grandmother and rub her face in it. Karma was a bitch, and I was trying to do a better job with the second half of my life than I did with the first.

When Gavin and Merlin were younger, Ronald was adamant about them not calling me Mom. At the time it didn't bother me, because I thought it would only be a matter of time before I had a child to call my own. Ronald's sperm was so potent, he could fuck a rock and make a baby. Every time I asked him about starting a family, he claimed the timing was wrong. This was obviously a lie; the fucker didn't want any children with me.

The truth hurt, especially because I had never bashed his trifling ass in front of his children. I had always put on a good front, until I could no longer hide what they could see for themselves. So when they started calling me Mom, it wasn't so much out of respect for what I'd done for them. Rather, it was because I was the only constant in their lives. Ronald was a part-time father at best during their early years and an absentee parent when they needed him most.

Whether I liked it or not, I had to tell Gavin and Merlin about their mother. If I kept Ronald and Tabatha's dirty little secret, I'd be just as guilty as they were, and I refused to be a willing party in their lies. I finished off the glass of milk I'd been drinking and got dressed.

I had never visited anyone in jail before, and I was nervous. Even when Ronald had his brushes with the law, I never came to visit. He had the money to hire a lawyer, and they handled everything. While I should have been behind bars for some of the shit I'd done, I felt like God had punished me in other ways. And one of those ways was Gavin. Gavin was a difficult child to love. He'd been a needy, manipulative, spoiled brat screaming for attention that I didn't have to give. I'd been too busy trying to keep a roof over our heads and food in our mouths to notice his cry for help.

His brother, Merlin, was the exact opposite: smart, self-sufficient, and an absolute target for his brother's repressed anger. I had done them both a terrible injustice, because I had never loved them for them. I had tolerated them as a means to hold on to their father. How could I not have seen it at the time, when it was crystal clear to me now? It was a damn shame I'd waited so long to have twenty-twenty clarity.

When Gavin was led into the room, I thought about all the times I'd failed him, and I felt ashamed. I hung my head, unable to meet his gaze.

He said, "Damn. You must have been reading my mind."

Stunned, I looked up and met his eyes. I had no idea what he was talking about, and I braced myself for the worst. "Hello, Gavin." I cleared my throat because my throat felt abnormally dry and hoarse.

"I was hoping you would come to see me. I feel so horrible about all the things I've done to you. Being here"—he held up his arms and spread them wide about his head—"a brother got a lot of time to think."

I wasn't expecting him to apologize to me, and I honestly didn't feel he owed me an apology, because I'd failed him too. "Are they treating you okay?"

He laughed. "It's not the Ritz-Carlton. I'm doing okay."

No barbs or verbal jabs. I kept feeling like Gavin was setting me up for a punch to the stomach. "Gavin, I have something very difficult I need to tell you, and I really don't know how to say it."

"Please tell me you are not going to give my baby up, like my father did my brother and me. Please don't say that to me."

Although Gavin had put his head down, I could tell he was getting emotional, and it damn near broke my heart. Ronald had caused so much pain for all of us. "No, that's not what I was going to say at all. I'm keeping my baby, and I promise to be a better mother to him than I was to you and your brother."

"Thank you. I am not proud of the way our child was conceived. If you would let me, I would like the chance to make things right for both of you."

I could not believe my ears. This was not what I'd expected from him. I'd been prepared to fight with him over my decision to keep his child. "I'm not proud, either. At first, I thought I was losing my damn mind. It was such a horrible time in my life. I feel like God is giving me a do over, and I plan to do it right."

His eyes lowered to my stomach, and I protectively placed my arms over it.

"When's the baby due?"

I must have flinched or had some other visible reaction, because I saw something like concern or compassion in his eyes. The look was so foreign to the Gavin I knew, I didn't understand it. I kept waiting for him to call me a fucking fool, much like his daddy did.

I said, "Three months."

"Do you know what it is yet?"

Once again his expression was foreign to me. On someone else I would have labeled it as expectant. "It's a boy." I couldn't help but smile, because I'd always wanted a boy.

"Oh, wow. I'm about to have a son."

He actually appeared to be happy. I was overwhelmed with emotions. Before I got too carried away, I had to tell him the reason for my visit.

"Gavin, I found out who your mother is yesterday, and I thought you needed to know."

"For all intents and purposes, Gina, you are my mother. However, in light of the current circumstances, we're going to have to clean it up a bit before our child starts asking questions. I intend to be in his life, if you'll let me."

I leaned forward and lowered my voice. "Who are you?"

He laughed out loud. "I know. I'm scaring myself. I had a long talk with my attorney yesterday, and she kinda put things perspective for me. If I get out of this mess, I'm going to do things differently."

"Wow. I'm speechless. For your sake, I hope you're telling the truth. You don't get many chances in life to make things right. I should know. It's happening to me now. We'll figure out how to explain it to our child, without telling a lie. Nothing good ever comes of a lie."

"So, I guess that means I need to know who our real mother is. Go ahead. If it makes you feel any better, tell me. It won't make a difference now, anyway."

"I'm not telling you out of spite or anything like that. I just feel you deserve to know. When you were little, you used to ask me all the time, and I didn't know."

"Yeah. You said if you ever found her, you'd send me back."

"Ouch. That hurt. I'm sorry. I wish I could take back every mean and hurtful thing I did to you and your brother, but I can't."

"Gina, chill out. I didn't say it to be mean. Lord knows I said and did some nasty shit to you too."

"Yeah, like when you threw my toothbrush in the toilet."

"You should be glad I threw it in the toilet. I used it to clean up the bathroom."

"Ew! You were a mess, and then you blamed your brother for it. You keep trying to change the subject, and I understand why."

"My lawyer tried to tell me who she was. I told her it didn't matter." His eyes did not meet mine.

"Well, now that you mention it, I think she's the reason why I found out too. How we found out is irrelevant. Your mother was a part of your lives. You just didn't know it."

"Say what?"

"I found out last night that my ex-friend Tabatha is your birth mother. What you decide to do with this information is strictly up to you. I think what they've done is wrong, but the blood will not be on my hands. That's between your father and Tabatha. I had nothing to do with it."

"Wow. I wasn't expecting that one. Bummer. All this time you thought she was your friend."

"It is what it is."

"Time," a guard yelled.

I looked around, confused. I didn't know why I thought I could go up to the jail and stay as long as I liked. Gavin and I had only scratched the surface of our issues, and I wanted more time.

He stood up and put his arms behind his back. "You coming back?"

"If you want me to."

"I'd like that."

I waited until he was led from the room before I left the building. Our visit was much more pleasant than I'd envisioned, except we ran out of time. I still had a lot of unanswered questions. We didn't talk about the night I got pregnant. Those details were still more dreamlike and very fuzzy to me. As I walked to my car, I decided the less I knew about the circumstances, the better off I might be. The last thing I wanted to do was find out some shit that would piss me off or be another source of embarrassment. As it was, explaining our situation would be complicated enough.

In a way, it helped me to understand how Tabatha must have felt keeping a secret from me for all those years. But it did not excuse her behavior. She should have trusted me enough to understand, and she should have loved her children enough to make them understand what it was like for her. Instead, she messed up a bunch of lives for nothing. She and Ronald could both kiss my ass. I might have grown up a little over the past few months, but I wasn't all the way there yet.

I had one more stop before I could go home and get some rest. I needed to talk to Merlin and let him know what was going on with me. I was afraid of his reaction the most, especially since he was also having a child. I hoped I could get him to understand how much my child meant to me. Right now things were going pretty well, but I was afraid of fairy-tale endings. For me, when things appeared to be going good, something always happened to fuck them up, and I was waiting for that to happen.

Chapter Thirty-three

MERLIN MILLS

I was operating on autopilot without much thought. When Candace opened the car door for me, I got out of the car and followed her into her house. She steered me toward the sofa, and I sat down. When she poured me a drink, I accepted it. And when she placed the bottle on the table, I made sure my glass was always full.

Candace was in the kitchen, I assumed, to fix us something to eat. She was wasting her time trying to feed me, because I wasn't hungry. My stomach was so tight, I barely had room for the booze I was pouring down my throat. But where there was a will, there was a way . . . and I had the will. I needed to numb my brain and my heart.

She said, "Are you all right in there?"

I didn't want to answer her question, so I ignored it. I wasn't ready to tell her or anyone else how I was feel-ing. I was numb.

"I'm heating up some Chinese food I picked up on the way home from work. I hope you like shrimp fried rice."

Silence. She had a digital picture frame on an end table I'd never noticed before. I picked up the frame, intrigued by the story it told. Pictures of a small child with pigtails and buck teeth morphed into one of a stunning woman who took my breath away. The woman in the picture was smiling so hard, I couldn't help smiling back at her. Candace caught me smiling at her pictures, and I quickly put the frame back on the table.

"Sorry. I never saw those before."

"No problem. I just put it out. I got the frame as a Christmas present a couple of years ago and never did anything with it. As you can see, I don't have many recent pictures."

I detected the loneliness in her eyes, and I sympathized with her. In all her pictures, even as a child, she was alone. Obviously, someone took the pictures, and whoever they were, she didn't chose to include them in her pictorial life. She placed the food on the table, and it smelled good. It didn't matter how good it smelled, though. I wasn't interested in trying any of it.

I said, "You looked happy."

"In those pictures I was."

She didn't have to qualify her statement, because I understood the words she'd left out. It made me think about the pictures of my life and made me wonder how many of them I could find of me when I was smiling. The thought wiped the remnants of the smile from my face.

"Life sucks, and everyone is stupid." I drained my glass and poured myself another drink.

"Merlin, I know you're hurting. Maybe you should slow down on the drinking. You're going to feel like shit in the morning."

"It won't be the first time. It's the story of my life."

"You don't have a monopoly on pain, boo. Trust and believe that."

She poured herself a drink after she fixed a small plate of food for herself. I should have followed her lead, but I didn't. I wasn't thinking about tomorrow. I was only trying to medicate the right now.

I said, "It's not too late to take me home, because I promise you, I won't be the best company tonight."

"Are you going to explain why we ran out of the hospital like we stole something?"

"We didn't run."

"Well, we left before the doctor came back. We still don't know what happened."

"I know enough. Our child is dead, if it was my baby."

"Come again. Why would you say that?"

I looked up sharply because she sounded like she was mad at me.

"Did you forget me telling you my wife slept with my brother? Cojo said the baby was mine, but Gavin and I are identical twins, so there was still a chance the baby could have been his. I don't give a shit what the doctors said or what she told me they said." I was angry now, because in my heart of hearts, I still believed the child could have been Gavin's. Perhaps that was one of the reasons why I didn't feel as bad as I should have upon learning my child had died.

"I didn't forget anything. You told me you were going to make your marriage work, and I understood it meant caring for the child as your own. Shit, Merlin. You said yourself that Cojo didn't know about you having a twin!"

"So why the fuck was Cojo at the jail? Riddle me that ole bright one! Wait! Don't answer, because I already know. She was visiting her lover and the father of her child." I was so hurt, I couldn't move.

"You can't know that for sure." Candace moved closer and placed her arm around my shoulders. I didn't have it in me to push her away.

"Oh, I know. Nothing else makes any sense to me. She had a fucking restraining order against him, for Christ's sake. She violated her own order by going to the jail to see him."

"She might have gone there for some other reason."

"Like what? If you know something, please tell me."

Once again, an eerie silence filled the room. The only sound was the air recycling in the room. My iPhone vibrated in my pocket. I didn't want to talk to anyone, so I ignored it. Candace removed her arm and went to the kitchen and returned with a tissue box. She placed the box in front of me and left me alone for a few minutes. I threw the box on the floor. I was beyond tears. I had done enough crying to last a lifetime. I heard a toilet flushing somewhere in the house. When she came back in the room, she had taken off her heels and had replaced them with a pair of fuzzy pink slippers.

"Nice shoes." I smiled.

"Thanks. You can take off your shoes too, as long as your feet don't stink. I'm afraid I don't have any slippers that will fit you." She picked up her plate and started eating.

"I'm good." I fixed myself another drink. The fiery liquid burnt its way to the pit of my empty stomach. My phone buzzed again.

"You can't keep ignoring the world."

"I'm not trying to ignore the world, because the only person I care to talk to is right here with me."

"Gee, thanks. Don't act like you don't know what I mean. Cojo might be trying to reach you or maybe even the doctor."

"I don't have shit to say to Cojo."

"What about the doctor? If you're not going to answer it, at least let me look at it to see who's trying to reach you."

I thought about it for a few seconds and pulled the phone free of my pants and gave it to her. She'd made a valid point.

"How do you use this phone? I'm not up on all these gadgets."

I took the phone back from her and opened the screen to my missed calls and gave it back to her. I was feeling the effects of the alcohol, so I rested my head on the sofa.

"Gina Meadows called you twice. Isn't that your step-mother?"

"Yeah, and I'm mad at her too. She got knocked up and obviously thought I didn't need to know about it, so she told my stinkin' wife instead of me."

"Ouch. Cojo told you?"

"Yeah, I had to damn near drag it out of her too. I swear, Candace, I don't know what's going on right now. Ever since my brother came back into my life, it's turned to shit, and that's no lie. Everything I thought I knew has come into question, including my damn wife."

"I feel you. But you need to address these problems head-on. You can't drown them, because they will still be there when you wake up. Your stepmother probably had a good reason for not telling you about her preg-nancy, and I'm sure it has nothing to do with whatever you might think it could be. The only way you're going to find out is to ask her."

"You don't know my stepmother. If she doesn't want to answer me, she'll blow me off. And to be honest, I don't think I can handle it right now. We're just getting back to a place where we communicate, and I don't want to mess it up."

"Then put the shoe on the other foot. What if her rea-sons for not telling you were the same, and she didn't want to mess it up?"

"And you might be right, Candace, but goddamn, how am I supposed to deal with her shit right now when my own shit is so fucked up?"

"Maybe you should deal with her shit right now. At the very least, it would take your mind off your own problems."

"Nah, I'm good. Besides, I'm drunk now. I think I need to take a nap." Candace was sitting a little too close for comfort right now. Her perfume wafted through the air, enticing me.

"Maybe you should try to sleep it off. You can sleep in the guest bedroom." She got up and started putting away the food.

I followed her with my eyes, completely aware of every move she made, my thoughts dangerously bordering on sexual excitement. "I probably should go home." I was just talking shit, because I really didn't want to go home alone. Home would be the safest place for me to be given my current state of mind.

"Wrong answer, buddy. Let me make up the bed, and I'll be back. I'm gonna keep my eye on you for tonight."

I closed my eyes against the visual forming in my head. I wanted her to keep more than an eye on me. More than anything I wanted Candace to touch me, and I realized it had nothing to do with my current situation. I'd always been attracted to her; however, the desire to save my marriage had kept me from acting on those impulses. On the surface, Candace was everything I wanted in a woman. I wished for an opportunity to find out if she really was what she appeared to be.

I realized it could never happen for a number of reasons. Number one, she was my superior officer and was off-limits to me. Candace was putting her own career on the line by having me over to her house. Second, the desire I was feeling probably wasn't mutual, and I was setting myself up for yet another heartbreak. She didn't need a married man with a fucked-up track record of keeping his wife satisfied. So a relationship with me was out of the question.

"Oh, you, you got what I need, and you say he's just a friend," I sang loudly while snapping my fingers.

"Shut up, Merlin. You can't carry a tune in a bucket."

She grabbed my arms and pulled me from the sofa. My body affixed to hers like an article of clothing. The physical contact sobered me instantly. I wanted to pull away, and I couldn't. More importantly, she had an opportunity to push me back, and she didn't. Our eyes locked.

She said, "Oh shit."

There was no denying the chemistry between us. The temperature in the room had risen several degrees; I felt sweat trickle down my back. My arms felt like they were on fire. I didn't want to run away from the flame, even though I knew I should.

"We can't do this," she mumbled.

"I know."

My lips were so close to hers, we shared the same breath. I breathed deeply, savoring the smell. Our noses touched, and the resulting jolt was much like an electrical current running through my body. Common fucking sense was telling me to back away, but who the hell listened to common sense? I sure wasn't, and neither was she.

"I can't be your mistake, Merlin."

"Who said anything about a mistake?"

"You haven't yet—"

"Shush," I said to quiet her fears. Nothing I'd ever done in my life felt so right. I brushed her lips with mine and stifled a moan. She felt so good, and I hadn't even tasted her yet.

"But you may regret it."

She was determined to talk some sense into my hard head, although she'd yet to back away. I wasn't holding her; she was holding me. I tasted her, sucking on her full lips, drawing them into mine. She swayed, and I grabbed her to me. I wasn't ready to let her go. Her eyes were like liquid pools of fire, and I wanted to feel their burn.

I said, "Which way?"

I was taking a big risk. She could have slapped the hell out of me and told me to get the fuck out of her house. Instead, she bumped me with her body, directed me with her hips, and lured me with her thighs to her bedroom. It was a seductive two-step, and I learned the contours of her body as she nudged me backward to her bed. I didn't take my eyes off hers until my legs touched her mattress. A make-or-break moment, and I was all fucking in.

I said, "Are you sure?"

I didn't know what I would've done if she had said no. Thank God I didn't have to find out, because she nodded her head yes. I smiled as I began unbuttoning her blouse. I wanted to undress her, and I thought she knew it, or she was too afraid to help me.

The faint light spilling in from the living room allowed me to see as I pulled the blouse from her shoulders and planted kisses on her neck. I took my time, wanting to savor every minute of it. My fingers tingled as I unsnapped her bra and dropped it to the floor.

"Sorry."

I reached down to get it, and she pulled me back to her lips, slipped her tongue deep in my mouth. My heart was racing as my dick pressed urgently against my pants. I undid the button of her pants and eased down the zipper. I slid my hands inside and coaxed the pants down her legs.

Her skin was soft as satin. I grabbed her hands, and she stepped out of her pants and turned around so she could lie on the bed. She scooted backward on her floral comforter, a complete contradiction to the manly attire she wore to work. Damn, she looked good in her skimpy thong, good enough to eat. She pushed the comforter down with her feet, exposing satin sheets. I'd never fucked on satin sheets.

I was still wearing my uniform and never realized how many fucking buttons where on my shirt until I tried to get out of it in a hurry. If I didn't need something to wear home, I would have ripped them off. So I carefully undressed, folded each item of clothing, and put them on the dresser. Her eyes followed my every movement as I crawled to her. She reached over in her nightstand and pulled out a condom. Relieved, I took it from her since I hadn't thought far enough ahead. I didn't use one with my wife, so I didn't even carry them. I hoped she had enough, because I had a feeling one wouldn't be enough.

I removed her thong and tossed it aside. It was cute and unnecessary. My dick lengthened as I spread her legs wide.

"Down, boy," I whispered to my unruly friend, who was bobbing up and down in anticipation.

She smiled at me seductively, and the shit was on like catfish and collard greens. I ease up to her, sliding my naked body over hers. I wanted to make love to her in the worst way. I paused to make sure she was still on board.

"Can I hold you?" It was a rhetorical question, since she was pinned underneath me. I asked it anyway. I was loving the way her body fit mine.

"Um, you feel good."

Four simple words, and I was ready to bust. "Damn, Ma. If you only knew what you were doing to me. I knew you'd feel like this."

She pushed against my chest. "You've thought about this before?"

"I'm not proud of it, but yeah. I thought about it. I never believed it would happen, if you know what I mean."

"I thought about you too," she whispered.

My dick pulsed in response. If it could've said something, I imagined it would say, "Oh hell, yeah." I squeezed her tighter, drowning in her honeysuckle scent.

"You smell so good. I just want to eat you up."

She said, "Well, what is stopping you?"

I never, ever, ever imagined she would be a talker, and it turned me on even more. I wanted her to act like the captain she was and give me sexual orders.

"Ma'am, yes, ma'am."

I greedily attached myself to her taunt nipple as I massaged her clit with my other hand. She moaned deeply. As she exhaled, I felt her tremble. I couldn't stand it any longer. I needed to taste her sticky softness. My head dipped lower, sucking each spare inch in between. She tasted like caramel popcorn, a mixture of salt and sugar, which had me licking my lips, wanting more.

I poised my lips over her lower lip, practically drooling with anticipation. Her eyes had closed to tiny slits, yet I could tell she was still watching me watch her. She squirmed, lifting her ass off the bed, almost touching my face. She wanted me as much as I wanted her. Her pussy had been recently shaved, a soft stubble greeting my hands as I caressed it.

I said, "I like my pussy bald."

She moaned again, bucking against the bed, as if her lower half was attached to a string. "Suck it," she hissed in a commanding fashion.

Her pussy was so plump, I couldn't get it all in my mouth. My tongue was in a feeding frenzy, trying to be everywhere at once. I couldn't make up my mind whether I wanted to suck on her clit or make love to her honey hole until she came all over my face.

"Damn. You taste good," I growled. If God chose that moment to strike me dead, I would die a happy man.

She screamed and pushed me off her. Her legs were trembling so hard, she frightened me.

"Did I hurt you?"

She shook her head no. My non-talking dick wanted to know what seemed to be the problem so we could fix it and get back to what we were doing. It hadn't even touched her, and it was still as happy as a fat girl in a bakery. She turned upside down and slid down between my legs and put me in her mouth.

"Oh shit."

My knees were weak as I tried to hold on to something. I gripped her thighs for support. I was about to start screaming like a little bitch. I stuffed my mouth with her pussy to keep from yelling as I gently pumped her face. Her mouth felt like a warm mitten on a cold winter day. Her cum exploded in my mouth, sending small shock waves down my spine. I couldn't take it anymore and gently pulled my dick from her mouth. She opened her mouth to say something, and I shook my head. She looked so sexy to me, if she said one syllable, I was sure to nut all over her.

I grabbed the condom and ripped the wrapper with my teeth. I rolled it down tight over my dick and slid it inside of her. She screamed against my mouth, her pussy speaking a language that needed no translation. She held me so tight, I couldn't have cum if I'd wanted to. We moved together like a fine tooled machine, and this time when she came, I came with her. We held each other while shaking in the aftermath of sexual bliss. As I rolled off her, I pulled her into my arms, her head resting on my chest.

I said, "Honey, that was fantastic."

"Sure was." She tried to pull away from me. I wouldn't let her go.

"Where are you going?" I wanted to snuggle and maybe catch a nap before round two.

"Gonna take a shower."

I felt the wetness on my arm before I noticed the tears on Candace's face. I allowed her to sit up as I held on to her hand. "Why are you crying, baby?"

"Don't call me that, Merlin."

I knew instantly what the problem was. Candace was having a taste of regret, and it was a major blow to my manhood. I wanted to lash out at her and make her feel my pain.

"So I guess I'm your mistake. I get it." I rolled over and grabbed my clothes off the dresser. I wasn't going to let her know I was hurt.

"I never said it was a mistake. I'm only being realistic. This can't go anywhere. You're married, and I promised myself I'd never be the other woman."

"It's a little late for that, ain't it?"

She rocked back, as if I'd slapped her, and I regretted it immediately. However, I couldn't take back what I said. She went in the bathroom and slammed the door. As much as I wanted to go in the bathroom to apologize, my pride wouldn't let me. I was done begging for love and affection.

I put on my clothes and went into the living room and called a cab. I could have waited until she came out of the bathroom, but I didn't need to see her face. I didn't want her to see the pain I was feeling. I slipped out the door, locking the bottom lock behind me.

Chapter Thirty-four

MEREDITH BOWERS

I was finally able to speak with someone who could shed some light on what had happened the day Cojo visited Gavin. The guard who was on duty at the time had taken a couple of sick days, and I had to wait for him to return to work before I could question him. He was very cooperative and gave me a lot more information than I needed to know.

"It's a damn shame how they did that woman," the older guard stated.

He was in his late forties or early fifties and was a tad bit fat to be a guard, in my opinion.

"By woman, I assume you're referring to Cojo Mills, right?"

"Yeah, I think that's her name. She wasn't one of the regular visitors. First time I ever saw her. She was with your client."

"So what happened? When did the altercation start?"

"I don't know about all that. Alls I know is she got in between two of my regulars."

"Regulars?" I was confused.

"Yeah, dem two women who was fighting come here regularly. So I call them my regulars. Only difference is they normally don't come on the same day. Both of dem got kids by this inmate named Darwin. And he ain't got the good sense the Lord gave him to keep dem she devils apart! They busted up the visitors' room pretty bad."

"So the argument was between the two women, and my client's wife walked in between them?"

"Yeah, they got to pushing each other, and one of dem slipped and fell on your guy's wife. She fell pretty hard too."

"So what happened next?"

"We locked dem she devils up and called an ambulance to take the other lady to the hospital. She was bleeding, and with her being pregnant, I don't know."

"Do you know where she was bleeding from?" I felt a huge knot form in my stomach. If Cojo was bleeding when they took her away, it wasn't a good sign.

"Down there, you know."

"Thanks. Do you know where they took her?"

"Yeah, they took her to Emory. Other than that, I don't know anything else."

"I'll find out. Thanks again." I rushed off without seeing Gavin. I would come back to see him once I found out what was going on.

Getting information from the hospital staff was like finding shade in the desert. Because I had no family ties or legal precedence, I wasn't allowed to see her and could learn only the most basic of information, which was that she was listed in fair condition. No mention was made of the baby. It was frustrating, to say the least. I needed to find out what was going on with Cojo, because she was the final thread holding the case against Gavin together. I pulled out my phone and called Young.

"Inspector Young."

"Young, it's Meredith, and I need a favor."

"Shoot."

"Remember that case I asked you to work on for me?"

"Yeah. What's up?"

"I need you to check your notes and give me the contact numbers of Merlin Mills. I'll need his addresses too. I'm not in the office, and I need to get in touch with him as quickly as possible."

"I'm not in the office, either. Lucky for you, I have my Sony Tablet with me and I backed up the report. Bear with me for a second. I need to pull over."

"Good, man. Thanks," I said after I had jotted down the information.

I didn't relish a physical confrontation with Merlin. I was beginning to believe the only way I was going to get him to talk to me was to get in his face. Based on the information I knew, I decided Gina was the most approachable person at this point, so I went to see her first. She had a vested interest in the disposition of Gavin's case. I was banking on this as I rang her doorbell a short time later. She answered the door immediately.

"Oh, it's you," she said.

I thought it was a good sign that she didn't immediately slam the door in my face. This meant she was at least willing to hear me out. I wondered what had happened to make her have a change of heart.

"I am sorry to bother you this morning—"

"Then why are you here?"

"Right. Well, as I told you before, my name is Meredith Bowers, and I represent your stepson Gavin in his criminal matters. And I have reason to believe that something may have happened to your daughter-in-law, Cojo, and I'm trying to get some information."

"What?" She opened the door wider and allowed me to come in.

"Yes. Thank you. I went to see Gavin, and he mentioned a visit from Cojo. From what I gathered, she was injured in an altercation at the jail and was taken to the hospital. Since I'm not family, I've been unable to get any additional information, so I stopped by to see if you could be of some assistance."

"I have no idea what you are talking about. Why would Cojo go to the jail? I was just there myself, and Gavin didn't mention anything about it to me."

I was surprised by her revelation and leery of it. It also made me wonder what else Gavin had been keeping from me. I remained quiet when she picked up the telephone and made a call. I assumed she was calling Cojo. She was unsuccessful in reaching her.

"Did you say you went to visit Gavin?" I asked.

"Yes, I went to see him yesterday. We had some things we needed to discuss."

I felt better knowing she'd seen him after my visit and that he wasn't purposely withholding information from me. "Mrs. Meadows, I'm not trying to alarm you unnecessarily. I think Cojo's accident is serious. I went to the hospital, and they would only tell me she was in fair condition. Have you spoken with Merlin?"

"Actually, I've been trying to reach Merlin for a few days now, and he hasn't returned my call."

"Oh, dear."

"What are you not telling me?"

Her voice was raised, and I felt like our conversation was about to take a turn for the worst.

"As I said, the hospital hasn't told me anything. One of the guards at the jail mentioned blood."

She clutched her stomach, and I took it to mean she knew what I was referring to. She picked up the phone and dialed again, clearly distraught. "He's not answering the phone, either. I'm going to that hospital, and they are going to tell me something."

She was, in my opinion, in no condition to drive.

"Mrs. Meadows, if you'd like, I'd be happy to take you there myself. Since you cannot reach Mr. Mills, either, do you think he might be on some type of military assignment and unable to answer a call? If that's the case, he might not be aware of his wife's condition."

She stopped in her tracks, as if she hadn't considered that possibility at all. She appeared to have lost her train of thought.

"Mrs. Meadows?"

"Oh yeah. I'm sorry. Let me get my purse so we can go. I hope everything is okay."

The ride over to the hospital was quiet. I wasn't sure how much I should tell her about Gavin's case, especially since she was so adamant about not helping him the first time I tried to speak with her. She sat in the seat, looking straight ahead, like I was a damn taxi driver. It could have been worse; she could have gotten into the backseat. I pulled up to the front of the hospital and let her out at the curb.

"I'll park the car and meet you inside."

If she heard what I said, she didn't acknowledge it. The bitch didn't know I'd leave her ornery ass right at the hospital if she wasn't careful. I hurried up and parked, just in case Gina was able to get further with the front desk than I did. And apparently, she did, since she was standing by the elevator, insistently waving me over, when I walked inside the lobby.

"She's on the third floor. I told them I was her mother. I guess you can be her sister if anyone asks you."

I was somewhat surprised that Gina would willingly allow me to be present when she saw Cojo, although I tried not to let it show. I would have been satisfied with getting thirdhand information about her condition. As we approached her room, I fell back and let Gina enter first. I'd never met Cojo, so I didn't want her to get alarmed by a strange face.

Cojo was sitting up in bed with a meal tray within easy reach. She obviously wasn't interested in the food, as it appeared untouched. Even though the television was on, she was looking out the window when we came in. She turned her head slightly, and tears spilled from her eyes when she looked at Gina. She glanced at me without paying me any attention. Gina went to Cojo and gathered her in her arms. They silently cried as they rocked together. It was such a touching moment. My heart went out to Cojo. Words weren't necessary, we knew.

Gina said, "Honey, it's going to be all right."

"But it's gone. My baby is gone," Cojo cried.

Gina never let her go. "Honey, why didn't you call me? How long have you been here?"

I felt so out of place and was about to slip out of the room when Cojo locked eyes with me. This was such a private moment. I didn't know what to else to say, so I told her, "I gave your mother a ride." It wasn't the real reason I was there. However, it was a legitimate excuse. Later, if I had an opportunity to speak with Cojo alone, I would ask her what she planned to do about Gavin.

"A couple of days, I guess," Cojo said. "I haven't felt like talking much. They're going to let me go home tomorrow if my fever doesn't come back."

"Where's Merlin, baby? I thought for sure he'd be here with you."

"I, uh—"

Cojo's eyes sought mine again as she pushed Gina away. They told me I didn't belong, and I completely understood. I was also curious about her husband's whereabouts. What I came for could wait. I knew it wasn't the right time for me to be asking any questions. I turned to leave, even though I wanted to hear what she had to say about her husband. Normally, when someone started a sentence with "I, uh . . . ," a lie or something akin to it was about to be told.

Gina said, "Oh my God, I don't like the sound of that."

Gina turned around, as if she had suddenly remembered I was with her. Her eyes were hard like steel balls, and I stood there waiting for her to nut up on me. She'd given me this look before, so I was expecting it.

"I'll wait in the hall." My comment was for both of them.

Cojo said, "Wait. It doesn't matter, anyway. She can stay."

"What don't matter, boo? You ain't making no sense." Gina frowned and rubbed her hands on Cojo's arms, as if she were trying to warm her bones or something.

"I know who she is, and it doesn't matter if she hears what I have to say," Cojo explained.

"Who? Me?" I eased closer to the bed. I was curious to know how she knew who I was when I'd never laid eyes on her before.

"Gavin mentioned I'd probably hear from you. You're his lawyer, right?"

I was so surprised, the only thing I could do was nod my head in agreement. I'd never told Gavin when I would be coming to see her, so it surprised me he'd even mentioned it to Cojo. "Yes, I am. I'm sorry for your loss," I said finally. *What in the hell is really going on? This whole family is bat-shit crazy if you ask me.*

Cojo nodded her head. "Yeah. Thanks."

Instead of looking sorry about the loss of her child, she appeared as nonchalant as if I'd just told her that her slip was hanging. Although I had never been pregnant before, I seriously doubted if I would act anything close to the way she was behaving.

"Where is Merlin, honey?" Gina sounded on the verge of hysterics.

Cojo shrugged her shoulders. "He won't answer the phone."

Gina's head bobbled. "Oh no, sweetheart. What do you mean, he won't answer the phone? When's the last time you talked to him?"

Cojo seemed confused, as if she had to think about it before she answered. "Monday, or it may have been Tuesday."

"But it's Friday." Gina looked at me.

I couldn't help her out with this one. She was on her own. I didn't know anything about these people, except the common denominator that was my client. The irony of both of them having slept with the same guy did not escape me. Sounded like a case of dick making folks stupid to me, but who was I to judge. It had been so long since I'd had me some dick, I might lose my mind, too, if I had some.

"I was told he came to the hospital after I was admitted, but left before the doctor finished talking with him," Cojo revealed. "I've been calling the house and his cell phone, and he's not talking. I guess he don't want anything else to do with me."

"Child, Merlin loves you."

Gina's words were not convincing, not even to me. I couldn't have been happier. I knew I was about to piss off some folks, and I didn't care. I had a job to do.

"Cojo, why did you go to the jail? Didn't you know it was a violation of your restraining order?" I asked.

She hung her head. For a moment, I felt bad for whipping her when she was down. I couldn't allow her the time to ponder what the rest of her life might be like, or else she might decide to flip the script on Gavin. Gina had to know that if Cojo did that, she could kiss her chances of having a father for her child good-bye, assuming Gavin agreed to be in the child's life.

"I had a dream about him. I had to make sure he was okay," Cojo replied.

"You know I'm going to have to tell the district attorney's office about your visit, and that they will probably dismiss the charges against Mr. Mills, right?"

"I understand." Cojo lowered the bed and pulled the covers up tight to her neck.

I had got the information that I had come to get, so I stepped out in the hallway, just in case Gina wanted to say something else to her in private. However, she was right behind me.

She turned at the door and said, "Honey, call me when you're ready to go, and I'll come get you. You can stay with me while we sort this mess out."

Cojo didn't answer.

I felt like doing a dance. Even with the odds stacked against me, it looked like I was about to pull a rabbit out of a hat. I was eager to drop Gina off so I could go back to the office and prepare a motion to dismiss the case against Gavin.

Gina said, "Could I trouble you one more time?"

"Uh, I guess so."

"I want to stop by Merlin's house. He's still not answering the phone, and I just want to reassure myself he's okay. After all this foolishness, I don't know anymore."

Chapter Thirty-five

GINA MEADOWS

As we pulled into the parking lot of Merlin's apartment complex, I was relieved to see his car was not in front of his apartment. It would have hurt me to my heart if it was and I knew he was ignoring my calls.

"Good. His car's not here. We can go," I said.

"Just because his car isn't here doesn't mean he isn't."

"Fine. I'll check. Come on." I pushed open the door and pulled myself out of her tiny car, which sat low to the ground. This might not have been so difficult if I wasn't carrying so much extra weight. "What the hell kind of car is this? I feel like I'm riding around in a tin can."

"It's a Mini," Meredith said, laughing.

"Least they got the name right. This is some bullshit right here." I pushed the door closed, perhaps a little harder than necessary, as I made a mental note never to get in that contraption again after today.

I was nervous as we walked up to the door. No one answered when I rang the bell. Merlin could still be inside, so I decided to use the key he'd given me a long time ago. I could hear the television playing inside when I stuck my head in. I was taking a big risk by entering their apartment, especially since I knew Merlin was licensed to carry a gun.

"Merlin, are you in here?" I shouted.

After a few seconds we came all the way inside and shut the door. I looked at Meredith to see if she had any suggestions. She shrugged her shoulders. We edged our way deeper into the apartment. Merlin was lying on the couch, an almost empty bottle of Patrón at his feet. He appeared to be fast asleep.

"Looks like someone had a party," Meredith whispered.

"Shut up."

Still dressed in his uniform, Merlin was snoring loudly. If he hadn't scared me so badly, I might have punched him in the face.

"Merlin, sweetie, wake up," I said.

He still didn't answer, and I was beginning to get annoyed.

I turned to Meredith. "Can you go do something useful, like make some coffee?" I was irritated, and it was showing. First, the hospital visit with Cojo, and now this shit. I wanted to go home and sleep. All this stress couldn't be good for my baby.

Meredith raised her eyebrow at me, like she was about to give me a piece of her mind, but changed her mind. She went and did as I asked. I didn't even know if Merlin liked coffee. I just didn't want her gawking at me while I figured out what to do.

Common sense told me to turn around and get my ass out of there now that I knew he was still alive. The other motherly part of me wanted to make sure he was okay.

"Merlin, honey, wake up now. I need to talk to you." I patted his cheeks and shook him. He only grunted and rolled over. If the bottle next to him was full when he started drinking, he could very well sleep till next week.

Kind and gentle weren't working. "Merlin, get your ass up right now!"

He sat straight up, like he were being pulled by some invisible puppet strings. His eyes were cloudy and unsteady. "Huh?"

"Boy, what are you doing?" I was deliberately talking to him like I did when he was a child. It apparently penetrated his fog.

"Ma, what's wrong?"

My heart softened. He might be damn near thirty, but he was still my little boy. I took a seat next to him on the sofa. I'd been in his shoes before, and drinking never solved the problem. I placed my arm around his shoulders. "It's going to be okay, son."

He put his head down on what was left of my lap and sat back up immediately, almost at the same time that Meredith came out of the kitchen.

"Who the fuck is she, and what are y'all doing in my house?" He looked around, as if he was trying to be sure he was actually in his own home. With a satisfied nod, he stood up.

I could have told him it wasn't such a good idea to make sudden movements, if he had asked me.

"Aw, damn, my head." He sank back down onto the sofa.

"How do you take your coffee?" Meredith was carrying a tray with several cups and a carafe. She handed him a cup of steamy liquid. When he didn't take it, she put it on the coffee table and sat down. Tactfulness wasn't one of Meredith's best attributes.

I said, "Why haven't you been answering any of my calls? I've been worried sick about you."

"Been busy." He reached for the cup and attempted to drink it straight. I could tell he burned his tongue by the way he was wagging it, and it served him right.

"So have I."

He looked at my stomach for the first time, and I felt ashamed, because we had never had the conversation about my being pregnant.

"I can fucking see that," he said.

I hit him on the side of his head. Hurt or not, I wasn't going to tolerate his being disrespectful to me. "If you'd answered the phone, I would have explained it to you. You've been ducking me for days."

"Come on, Ma. You're more than a few days pregnant. I may be dumb. I ain't fucking stupid."

I raised my hand to strike him again and stopped myself, because he was right. He had every right to be upset with me. "Honey, I wanted to tell you. I was afraid. At first, I kept it a secret because I didn't know what I was going to do. Then I kept trying to figure out how to tell you without making you hate me."

"You're a grown-ass woman, Gina. If you want to keep being a fool, chasing behind my daddy's black ass, trying to make him love you, that's on you. You already know how to raise a kid alone, don't you?"

His words stung, as he'd intended them to. It was hard to listen to, even though it wasn't the first time I'd heard those words.

"I'm not having this baby for him. He doesn't have anything to do with it."

"You mean, he doesn't want anything to do with it. I went to see his sorry ass, and trust me when I say that he's done. He's not paying your child support, so if you're thinking about it, forget it."

"Your dad is not the father, and even if he was, I wouldn't ask him for anything. I gave that man the best part of me, and he threw it away. As far as I'm concerned, he can kiss my ass. I told him that when he came to see me the other day."

I saw Meredith fixing herself a cup of coffee from the corner of my eye. I'd forgotten she was there with us. She was like a damn tick, made herself at home without waiting for an invitation. Then again, I did tell her to come with me. I was exposing a lot of information about myself in front of a virtual stranger. I decided it was those secrets that were keeping me from getting over it.

"He told me you came to his house, even accused me of sending you. And that's not all he said." I wanted to get it all out, but the timing was all wrong. Merlin was already hurting.

"Did you stab him again? If you did, I hope you didn't miss."

Meredith gasped, and I laughed. It was funny to me.

"Believe me, I thought about it," I said. "I wasn't trying to go to jail, though. He finally told me who your real mother is."

He pushed away the coffee and poured a generous amount of Patrón in his mouth. If I wasn't pregnant, I would have snatched the bottle from him and drunk some too.

Merlin said, "'Bout time his punk ass said something. I already know. Suspected it for years."

I was stunned. "You knew Tabatha was your mother?"

"Yeah, we look just like her."

"But why didn't you say something?"

"For what? She obviously didn't want us. You might have been mean as hell, but at least you were there. Which is a lot more than I can say for my real parents."

I didn't know what to say. I had agonized about telling Merlin the truth because he had always been the more sensitive of the two boys. I couldn't believe he already knew and did nothing about it. I didn't know how to feel about it. Regardless of how fucked up the situation was, I still felt the need to defend Tabatha.

"Merlin, she was young, dumb, and scared."

"Don't make excuses for her, Mother. She did what she did, and it's over. She had her chance to make it right, and she didn't. I honestly don't hate her for it, and neither should you."

I was outraged. "She lied to me for over twenty years."

"And what's your point? Do you think being mad at her is going to change a motherfucking thing?"

He was angry again, and I wondered how much of it was directed at me.

"The point is, you kids needed to know who your mother was. They kept that information away from you, and it ain't right. She was my friend, sat up in my house day in and day out, and never said a damn thing to me. How do you think that makes me feel?"

"Get over it, Mother. Now, I know it may seem harsh to you right now, but you can't change it. Shit, my wife's been fucking my brother, and the kid she was carrying probably wasn't mine. And you know what is so fucked up about it? I'll never know the truth, because it's gone. How's that for fucking problems?"

I pried the bottle from his fingers and hugged my son. "I know. I went to see Cojo before I came." He stiffened in my arms.

"I—I hate her." He choked out the words as his body shook.

"Honey, I told Cojo I would pick her up tomorrow, when they release her from the hospital. She can stay with me until she gets herself together."

He didn't have to tell me their marriage was over. I knew it in my heart, and I wasn't going to try to talk

him out of it. Once Merlin said he was done with something, he was done.

"I don't want to see the bitch."

"Don't worry. You won't have to. It will only be a
temporary stay." I had one more thing I needed to tell
Merlin, and it might cause the end of our relationship
as well. I braced myself as best I could. "This is your
brother's child, and I intend to raise him by myself."

I held fast to Merlin as he tried to pull away.

"If he wants to be a part of my child's life, I won't
stop him. However, it's not a requirement. This lady is
his attorney, and they are probably going to dismiss the
charges against him."

I waited for the fireworks I felt sure were coming.
Merlin didn't say a word. When he attempted to lift his
head this time, I let him go. The secrets were exposed
and couldn't hurt us anymore. What he chose to do
with the information was on him. I sat quietly, hoping
for the best.

Merlin got up and walked into the bedroom. He
came back a few minutes later with a manila envelope
and tossed it on the table. "Can you call your friend and
tell her we changed our mind about the house? She can
send the deposit to you. Consider it a gift for the baby.
I'm going to request a transfer. I'll be in touch when I
know where I'll be stationed."

He walked back in the bedroom and shut the door.
Meredith and I continued to sit in the living room for
about fifteen minutes, until I realized he wasn't coming
back out.

I said, "I guess that's it."

She nodded, and I picked up the envelope and locked
the door behind me.

Chapter Thirty-six

TABATHA FLETCHER

I awoke again to incessant knocking on my door. This shit was getting old quick. Ever since my encounter with Gina, I'd been hiding out in my house, feeling sorry for myself. Deep down inside I knew I needed to get some help. A part of me decided I didn't deserve it. The knocking continued. Whoever it was, they were determined to get in. I shuffled to the door after throwing on a robe to cover my nakedness.

"What is it?" I screamed as I yanked open the door. I knew I looked like shit, and I couldn't care less.

"Bitch, if you would answer the phone, I wouldn't have to bring my ass over to your house." LaDena barged in like she owned the place.

"If I didn't answer the phone, it usually means I don't want to talk to nobody." I shut the door, touched to know someone still cared.

"Well, I don't know about you, but we still have a business to run, and you are fucking up. You had three walk-ins this week, and I don't have time to do your work and mines too."

"I'm sure your greedy ass don't mind making the commission if you get them to buy something."

"You damn right, and I ain't sharing it, either. Should have brought your ass to work."

She walked around my apartment, throwing away the evidence of the feeding frenzy I'd been having. I didn't ask her to clean up my place.

"Put that shit down. I can do it myself," I barked.

"If you were going to do it, heifer, you would've already done it. What is wrong with you, girl? I thought you were going to handle your situation." She sat down when she cleared a place for her to sit.

"I did handle it. I told Gina the truth, and she hates me. Are you fucking satisfied?"

"Bitch, please. You didn't do me no favors. That shit was for you."

"What do you want, Dena?"

"I want your ass to come to work and handle your business." She threw some mail at me, hitting me in the chest and face with it.

"You'd better be glad I don't feel like kicking your ass right now, because if I did, it would be on and popping."

She said, "I ain't scared of you. You must have me confused with some other bitch."

Ignoring LaDena, I sorted through the mail. Most of it was junk, except for a handwritten letter in Gina's handwriting. My heart started beating real fast as I opened it. It was short and to the point.

Per my son's instructions, please withdraw his offer on the property you showed him and return his deposit via U.S. mail to my address. And just so you know, you didn't fool him. He knew it all along.

Also enclosed in the envelope was the voided counteroffer I had delivered to Merlin's house. Gina's instructions were clear. She didn't want to see me, and apparently, neither did Merlin. I felt cheated, because I wanted the opportunity to explain it to him myself. I guessed it wouldn't happen now. There was no telling what Gina might have said to him, and it made me very angry.

I stuffed the contract back into the envelope with the note. "Thanks for bringing the mail, Dena. I've got some things I need to attend to. I'll give you a call later." She might not have been ready to go, but I didn't give her much choice as I stood by the door, holding it open for her.

"Yeah, okay. Make sure you do. Don't make me have to come back over here. Next time I'll bring my sister." She laughed. I didn't see the humor in her joke.

"Bye, Dena." I closed and locked the door. I didn't want to start crying again. I had cried enough, and my tears hadn't changed a thing. I went back in the living room and called Gina. I didn't have a problem with sending her the check. I needed to know who to make it out to.

"Hello?"

I didn't recognize the voice, and I thought I'd dialed the wrong number. "Who is this?"

"Who do you wish to speak to?"

"Gina." I felt like she was having her calls screened, and it irritated me.

"She's not here right now. May I take a message?"

"Oh, okay. My name is Tabatha Fletcher. My num—"

"Hey, Tabatha. It's Cojo."

I was taken by surprise. Even though I knew Cojo and Gina had mended their fences, I still wasn't expecting them to be down like two flat tires. It only reminded me how far removed I was from Gina's life.

"Oh, hey, Cojo. It's good you answered the phone, because this call concerns you. I got a letter from Gina directing me to return the good-faith deposit Merlin made on the house. She said to send it to her, but since he's the one who signed the check—"

"Merlin and I have split up, so if Gina said to send the check to her, you may as well do it. I'm staying with her for a few weeks, until I get myself together."

"Are you serious? What is wrong with that boy, leaving you with the baby coming? I've got half a mind to go on over to his house and put him over my knee!"

She sobbed. "It's not his fault, Tabatha. I messed up, and I lost the baby too. I'll tell Gina you called."

My heart went out to her, even though I didn't know her well, but my biggest concern was Merlin. He hadn't been returning any of my calls, and now I understood why. It was a terrible feeling knowing your child might be hurting and there wasn't a damn thing you could do about it. I didn't know what surprised me more, the fact that I was referring to Merlin as my child or the fact that I wanted to get involved and do something.

It wasn't like he'd asked for or wanted my help. It was more so the thought of doing something that motivated me to call him one last time. If all else failed, I could use the money as a reason for my call. Instead of calling him on his cell, I dialed the number he'd listed on his application, under employment. He answered on the first ring, and the sound of his voice made me want to cry. Merlin sounded like he had the weight of the world on his shoulders.

"Specialist Mills."

"Uh, hi, Merlin. It's me, Tabatha. How are you?"

"Didn't you get my message?" He sounded angry.

How rude. I'd been calling him for days with no response, and when I finally managed to get ahold of him, he bit my head off. "Well, yeah, but I have a problem. Since you wrote the check, the law says I have to return the check to you and not to a third party."

"For Christ's sakes, can you give me a break and just issue the check to my mother? I'm leaving town soon, and I don't have time to be running around, messing with this shit."

There was no mistaking the animosity in his voice, which only made me hurt more for him. He was such a good kid; he didn't deserve this heartbreak. "Merlin, what's going on?"

"My brother apparently has the same dick appeal as my dad. He's got my wife's nose wide open, much like my dad had Gina's and yours. Now, if you'll excuse me, I've got work to do. Bye."

I held on to the phone for several seconds, reeling from his verbal assault. If I hadn't heard it myself, I never would have believed Merlin was capable of it. Merlin had dogged me and Gina out because we'd loved a worthless man, while Ronald got off scot-free. Where was the justice in that? I was sick and tired of being sick and tired. I went in the bedroom and re-trieved the emergency kit I'd kept hidden in my closet for over twenty years. The only thing missing from the kit was dope, and Gina had provided that a few days ago. Having the shit was dangerous enough for a dope fiend like me. Digging up my old kit doubled the stakes.

I carried the kit to the kitchen and sat down at the counter. My hands shook as I pulled down the zip-per, revealing two hypodermic needles, a spoon, some matches, and a strap to tie off a vein. I hadn't seen a book of matches since my getting-high days. They were a trigger for me, so I avoided them. I got the dope out of the cookie jar and set it on the table, next to the kit. I prayed for the strength to throw all of it in the trash, but I didn't have it in me.

I cooked the drug as if I were brewing a cup of tea instead of a deadly cocktail. My mouth watered as I prepared it. My favorite vein in my left arm seemed to twitch in anticipation. "Soon, boo. Real soon." I filled the first syringe and tested it. Satisfied it would do the trick, I put it aside in a plastic Baggie.

I poured the last of the heroin on the counter and chopped it with a razor. Next, I sliced a d-Con Bait Block into a fine powder and mixed it with the heroin. I smiled as I prepared the final cocktail. After I filled the syringe, I put it back inside my kit, along with the one I'd put in the Baggie, and zipped it closed. I was almost finished.

As requested, I wrote an escrow check to Gina and put it in my purse. I grabbed my keys and locked my apartment for the last time. I felt at peace as I drove to Ronald's favorite spot. I'd timed it just right. He was there, as I knew he would be. I pulled my car up to the curb and left the motor running. He sauntered up to the car with his shit-eating grin in place. I hated this motherfucker.

He said, "Back so soon? What chu need?"

His eyes appeared to be dancing on his face. I hated that he knew I wouldn't be able to resist the temptation. He sickened me with his smugness.

"I can't do it, Ronald. I need your help," I pleaded.

"My help? To do what? Get away from here with your foolishness. Can't you see I'm running a business?"

"Please, Ronald. I haven't self-injected in years, and I'm scared." I was an old dopehead, so I could find a vein on a mosquito. I was banking on Ronald's arrogance to get him into my car.

He opened the passenger side door and climbed into the car. "Pull around the corner, and you'd better make this quick. I don't do this shit for everyone."

He acted like he was doing me a fucking favor, much like he did when he first gave me the drugs. If I remembered it, I was sure he remembered it too.

"I will. It's all ready."

I drove to the Piggly Wiggly, a supermarket prominent in the hood. They were quick to close its doors when it got dark. I parked the car away from the streetlights to avoid immediate detection. Ronald was gloating at my apparent nervousness.

"I was beginning to wonder what you did with my shit. I was beginning to think you'd actually gotten the monkey off your back." He smiled.

I could tell he was counting dollar signs as I pulled my kit from my purse. I handed him the strap and the syringe that was in the Baggie. "It's been a long time." I felt a mixture of emotions as I watched him pluck the tip of the needle and tie me off.

"You'll be happy in a minute. I saved the best shit for you, you'll see." He bent his head close to my arm, trying to find my vein in less than stellar lighting conditions.

I retrieved the other syringe from my kit and drove the needle in his neck at the same time he injected the drug into my arm.

"Argh! What the fuck did you do?"

"Payback is a bitch, Ronald."

"I'm gonna kill your stupid ass. Just let me—"

He grabbed at my arm, twisting and turning, trying to get a better hold on it. He lifted his leg, kicking it against the dashboard. No matter how hard he thrashed, I refused to let him go. I injected the cocktail. It was my turn to smile as his eyes bucked out from his face.

He grunted, spit pooling out the sides of his mouth. "You got to get a doctor. You have to help me!"

"I am helping you, Ronald. I fucked you like you fucked me. See you in hell, Ronald."

His body grew stiff. Seconds later he began to convulse, his arms swinging wildly in the air as he fought for air. He tried to open the car door. I'd locked all the doors. I watched his eyes roll in the back of his head as I felt the effects of the drug take hold of me. Watching him suffer like he'd made me so many times before was worth the risk I'd taken. Fucker could burn in hell, for all I cared.

"I saved the good shit for you, Ronald," I whispered as I nodded off, closing my eyes. My head felt so heavy, I could no longer hold it up. It might have been a long time since I'd gotten high, but it still felt the same, an incredible rush of euphoria followed by an "I don't give a fuck, give me some more" feeling. I fell into the steering wheel. The horn was loud. I couldn't do anything to stop it.

Chapter Thirty-seven

MERLIN MILLS

Candace hadn't been to work in a couple of days, and I was beginning to get worried. At first, I assumed it was because she was so angry with me for leaving and didn't want to see me. She didn't appear to be the type of woman to hide from her problems, so I was concerned. Several times I picked up the phone to call her. Each time I hung up before the call went through. I assumed she'd arrange to have me transferred before she came back to work. So each day I waited to receive my new orders. Thus far I hadn't received them. I'd made up my mind that if I didn't received them by the end of the week, I would go over her head and put in the transfer request myself.

Since Cojo was staying at Gina's house, going over there wasn't an option. Cojo had called me several times since her release from the hospital. I didn't have anything I wanted to say to her. She'd made her bed, and she was going to have to lie in it. If she chose to lie in it with Gavin, I'd say good riddance to both of them. She'd find out soon enough the kind of man she'd chosen over me.

I pushed back from my desk, tired of the bullshit running rampant in my life. I snatched up my keys and marched out to my car before I changed my mind. As I drove to Candace's house, several different scenarios

played in my head. Most of them weren't good. Whatever was going to happen, I needed to know. I got but-
terflies in my stomach when I saw her car in the drive-
way. I killed the engine and waited for a few seconds,
trying to get up the nerve to ring the bell.

"Nigga, please. The worst thing she can do is kick
you in the nuts and slam the door in your face. You'll
get over it." I opened the car door and grabbed the
transfer request I'd filled out for her signature. I saw
the curtains move, and she opened the door before
I had a chance to ring the bell. Even with the circles
under her eyes and her disheveled hair, she was still
beautiful to me. I lowered my head, unable to stand the
sadness in her eyes.

"What are you doing here, Specialist?"

"I, uh . . ." I cleared my throat. I rolled the pages in
my hand nervously. I didn't want to do this on her front
porch. But I would if I had to.

"You brought me papers from work?"

She wasn't making this shit any easier on me. If the
situation were reversed, I'd probably play it the same
way.

"Yes, Captain."

She took the papers from me and walked inside, with
me following behind her. I closed the door as she read
them.

"You don't have to do this, Merlin." She tore up the
pages and threw them on the floor. "It was a mistake,
and we both know it. I think we can be responsible
adults and deal with it."

"And I suppose you're dealing with it by not coming
to work?"

She might regret sleeping with me, but I didn't, and
it hurt my feelings.

She frowned before she answered. "I was due some time off."

"How convenient for you. If it's all the same to you, I'd prefer to leave. So if you're not going to sign my orders, I'll run it up the chain of command and see what happens."

"That's ridiculous, and you know it. First thing they are gonna want to know is why I didn't sign it. And then the shit is really going to hit the fan."

I was having a difficult time keeping my emotions off my face as I stared her down. I wanted her to know how serious this was to me without being insubordinate. It was unfortunate that things couldn't have ended better.

Candace appeared to be on the verge of a panic attack as she thought about the harm an affair with an enlisted man would do to her career.

"I don't want to hurt you. I just think it's better if I leave and get a new start somewhere else."

"You mean you and Cojo, I suppose." She spat out the words like she'd eaten something nasty. Her venom surprised me. For someone who didn't care, she sure was fired up.

I said, "I said I wasn't going to be the only one trying to save my marriage, and I meant it."

She shrugged her shoulders, dismissing what I'd said. "You were also drinking heavily that night."

"I was there. I remember. It doesn't change a thing. It took me a minute to get there, but once my mind's made up about something, I rarely change it."

"What if I told you that I was thinking about resigning my position? Would it change your mind then?"

"Why in the hell would you do that? That's dumb, and you know it."

She glared at me with her hands on her hips. "Why is it dumb for me to quit but okay for you to volunteer for combat?"

"What difference does it make where I am? If something is going to happen to me, it will find me."

She said, "Well, I'd prefer it find you in the States."

"That's not your decision to make."

Her shoulders slumped, and we were at a standoff. I didn't want to argue anymore.

"How are you going to make things work with Cojo if you're traipsing around God knows where?"

"I wish you would let that go. I have. I put my heart and soul into my marriage, and it didn't work. I won't keep banging my head against that door. I would've never started with you if I wasn't finished with her."

"I thought—"

I said, "You thought what? If memory serves me, and it does, you said we couldn't go anywhere."

She shook her head. "I didn't mean it like that."

"Oh yeah? Then how did you mean it?"

"Never mind. It's water under the bridge now."

I said, "Hell, don't punk out now. If that's how you felt, own it."

"Stop it, Merlin. I only meant to give you a way out. I didn't want for you to throw it in my face the next morning, when—"

I took a step closer to her. "When what?"

"Fine! When you sobered up! I wouldn't have been able to handle that if you did." She turned away from me.

"So you blow me off so you can feel better? What kind of fucked-up shit is that? I thought you were better than that!" I was hurting, and I wanted her to feel as badly as I did.

 She sank to her knees, as if I'd punched her. "I didn't mean it that way. You've got to believe me."

I pulled her from the floor into my arms. We rocked together silently for several minutes. I nudged her neck with my nose. "If we're going to do this thing, you're going to have to do a better job at communicating with me. You feel me?"

"Yes, baby, I really do." Her lips sought mine, and I greedily accepted them.

My phone ringing stopped us from taking it to another level. I pulled it out of my pocket and frowned when I saw Gina's number on the display. I braced myself for bad news as I answered the call.

"Hello?"

"Merlin, thank goodness you answered." She didn't sound good, and I assumed it had something to do with her child.

"Gina, what's wrong?"

"Can you come over right away?"

My grip tightened on the phone. I wasn't ready to see Cojo, despite all the talking I'd been doing. "Is Cojo still there?"

"Uh, yeah. But—"

"Whatever it is, you can tell me over the phone."

She wailed, "It's Tabatha. She's dead, and so is your father."

I felt the phone slipping from my fingers, and I caught it. This was the last thing I'd expected to hear. The sad part about it was I felt nothing. "I don't know what to say. I'm sorry."

"It's on the news, baby. She killed him, and then she killed herself. I feel so bad."

I could hear Cojo in the background comforting Gina, and I was glad she were there with her. "Gina, I know I'm wrong for this, and I will apologize to God later. I don't know that man. I'm not saying I'm glad he's dead, but he didn't care about me when he was living, so why should I care about him now that he's dead? I'm real sorry about Tabatha. She was a nice lady, and she might have done both of us a favor."

"Merlin, how could you say something like that?"

I said, "It is what it is."

I heard Cojo in the background say, "What did he say?"

"I got to go, Mother. I'll be in touch." I turned off my phone and slipped it in my pocket. I pulled Candace into her bedroom to finish what we'd started.

Chapter Thirty-eight

GAVIN MILLS

"We did it, Gavin. You're a free man. Do me a favor and stay out of trouble."

I turned to Meredith with a big smile on my face. I was so excited to be on the outside of the jail, I didn't know what to do with myself. The air almost smelled fresher. "Meredith, I told you before, this time I'm going to do things differently. I got a lot of making up to do, and I damn sure don't want to go back inside that place anymore. I don't even want to see the shit on television."

I refused to turn around for another look. I was so determined not to see the place again, I'd made a promise never to drive down Memorial Drive again.

"I hope so. You definitely lucked up, because things could've gone a whole different way."

"I know. I can't thank you enough for all you've done."

"Is someone coming to get you?" She looked around, and I followed her eyes.

"Yeah, Gina said she would be here."

Meredith's brow furrowed. "Oh yeah? What's up with that?"

"It's not what you think. We're not hooking up or anything like that. We have a common interest, our child. I'm going to be there for him."

"What about Cojo?"

"She's gone. Moved back home, to wherever she's from. I couldn't get down with her, not if I ever expect to have a relationship with my brother."

"How's that going for you?"

"He's being stubborn. I hope he'll come around in time. Gina said he didn't attend the funerals for my real mother and father. I don't blame him. If I were on the outside when it happened, I don't think I would have gone, either."

Meredith reached in her purse and handed me her card. "Here's my new card. I'm hoping you won't ever need it. Stay in touch."

Meredith stepped forward and gave me a hug. I'd fantasized about this moment for a long time. Now that she was so close, it was like hugging my sister. I smiled, because it meant God was still working with me.

"Thanks, Meredith. I'll drop you a line now and then."

"You do that, Gavin Mills. You do that."

THE END

Notes

Notes

ORDER FORM
URBAN BOOKS, LLC
78 E. Industry Ct
Deer Park, NY 11729

Name:(please print):_____

Address: _____

City/State: _____

Zip: _____

QTY	TITLES	PRICE

Shipping and handling-add $3.50 for 1st book, then $1.75 for each additional book.

Please send a check payable to:

Urban Books, LLC

Please allow 4-6 weeks for delivery

ORDER FORM
URBAN BOOKS, LLC
78 E. Industry Ct
Deer Park, NY 11729

Name: (please print):_____

Address: _____

City/State: _____

Zip: _____

QTY	TITLES	PRICE
	16 On The Block	$14.95
	A Girl From Flint	$14.95
	A Pimp's Life	$14.95
	Baltimore Chronicles	$14.95
	Baltimore Chronicles 2	$14.95
	Betrayal	$14.95
	Black Diamond	$14.95
	Black Diamond 2	$14.95
	Black Friday	$14.95
	Both Sides Of The Fence	$14.95
	Both Sides Of The Fence 2	$14.95
	California Connection	$14.95

Shipping and handling-add $3.50 for 1st book, then $1.75 for each additional book.

Please send a check payable to:

Urban Books, LLC

Please allow 4-6 weeks for delivery

ORDER FORM
URBAN BOOKS, LLC
78 E. Industry Ct
Deer Park, NY 11729

Name: (please print): _____

Address: _____

City/State: _____

Zip: _____

QTY	TITLES	PRICE
	California Connection 2	$14.95
	Cheesecake And Teardrops	$14.95
	Congratulations	$14.95
	Crazy In Love	$14.95
	Cyber Case	$14.95
	Denim Diaries	$14.95
	Diary Of A Mad First Lady	$14.95
	Diary Of A Stalker	$14.95
	Diary Of A Street Diva	$14.95
	Diary Of A Young Girl	$14.95
	Dirty Money	$14.95
	Dirty To The Grave	$14.95

Shipping and handling-add $3.50 for 1st book, then $1.75 for each additional book.
Please send a check payable to:
Urban Books, LLC
Please allow 4-6 weeks for delivery

ORDER FORM
URBAN BOOKS, LLC
78 E. Industry Ct
Deer Park, NY 11729

Name: (please print): _____

Address: _____

City/State: _____

Zip: _____

QTY	TITLES	PRICE
	Gunz And Roses	$14.95
	Happily Ever Now	$14.95
	Hell Has No Fury	$14.95
	Hush	$14.95
	If It Isn't love	$14.95
	Kiss Kiss Bang Bang	$14.95
	Last Breath	$14.95
	Little Black Girl Lost	$14.95
	Little Black Girl Lost 2	$14.95
	Little Black Girl Lost 3	$14.95
	Little Black Girl Lost 4	$14.95
	Little Black Girl Lost 5	$14.95

Shipping and handling-add $3.50 for 1st book, then $1.75 for each additional book.

Please send a check payable to:

Urban Books, LLC

Please allow 4-6 weeks for delivery

ORDER FORM
URBAN BOOKS, LLC
78 E. Industry Ct
Deer Park, NY 11729

Name: (please print):_____

Address: _____

City/State: _____

Zip: _____

QTY	TITLES	PRICE
	Loving Dasia	$14.95
	Material Girl	$14.95
	Moth To A Flame	$14.95
	Mr. High Maintenance	$14.95
	My Little Secret	$14.95
	Naughty	$14.95
	Naughty 2	$14.95
	Naughty 3	$14.95
	Queen Bee	$14.95
	Say It Ain't So	$14.95
	Snapped	$14.95
	Snow White	$14.95

Shipping and handling-add $3.50 for 1st book, then $1.75 for each additional book.
Please send a check payable to:
Urban Books, LLC
Please allow 4-6 weeks for delivery

ORDER FORM
URBAN BOOKS, LLC
78 E. Industry Ct
Deer Park, NY 11729

Name: (please print):_____

Address: _____

City/State: _____

Zip: _____

QTY	TITLES	PRICE
	Spoil Rotten	$14.95
	Supreme Clientele	$14.95
	The Cartel	$14.95
	The Cartel 2	$14.95
	The Cartel 3	$14.95
	The Dopefiend	$14.95
	The Dopeman Wife	$14.95
	The Prada Plan	$14.95
	The Prada Plan 2	$14.95
	Where There Is Smoke	$14.95
	Where There Is Smoke 2	$14.95

Shipping and handling-add $3.50 for 1st book, then $1.75 for each additional book.

Please send a check payable to:

Urban Books, LLC

Please allow 4-6 weeks for delivery